Will

Of the Valley

Also by Jane Shoup

Wright and Wrong in the Valley
Hidden in the Valley
The Restoration
Zan, Birth of a Legend
The Key
A Choice of Captors
Ammey McKeaf, Book 1~ The Chronicles of Azulland
Heirs to the Throne, Book 2 ~ Chronicles of Azulland
Into Shadow, Book 3 ~ The Chronicles of Azulland
Charity Cases
Santa:2020 The Final Ride
The Time Tunnel of August Kaplan
An American Baroness, Book 1~ Sons of Barons
Nearly a Marquess, Book 2 ~ Sons of Barons
London's Adonis, Book 3 ~ Sons of Barons
Christmas at Manoria, Book 4 ~ Sons of Barons
The Stewart Women, Book 5 ~ Sons of Barons
Ruan3
Manley Georgine
The Barretts of Crimson Hall
The Uncounted

Copyright © 2016 by Jane Shoup
ISBN 978-0692831199

.

To my sweet, spunky Maggie with love.

Prologue

Friday, February 3, 1888
Green Valley, VA

Briar Lindley squinted through the smoky haze at the mayor's son, Lonnie Hastings, who sauntered into Jackals, clumsy in his drunkenness. Hastings was at least twenty. He was an asshole and a peacock, but old enough to know better than to come into a place like this.

He was rumored to be good to have around if you needed to get away with something, which was the only reason he was safe. Still, he reminded Briar of a mouse strutting around a teeming snake pit seemingly unaware that any of them could strike him dead and eat him whole at any given moment and never think twice about it.

Briar, an uncommonly good-looking man with long black hair, sat slumped in his chair while one of the girls fondled him under the table. She was trying to get him enthused enough to take her to a room but the liquor he'd consumed had him drunk enough to be disinclined. Matter of fact, it had him occasionally seeing double.

Briar threw back the rest of his drink, waited for the burn to subside, and watched Lonnie Hastings pull up a chair at the table where cousins Andre and Salvador Pettijean were playing a dice game. The Pettijeans, natives of Louisiana, weren't just any ole' snakes, they were fanged water moccasins, slippery, cool and venomous.

They had come to Green Valley a few years back, claimed this bit of land with a bunch of derelict shacks. The structures had been restored as much as necessary, and the place named Jackals. It specialized in rotgut moonshine, backwoods whores, and fights of every sort, bare-knuckle, dog, and cock fighting.

There was a schedule of fights at least four nights a week with no-holds barred betting, so the pots got sweet. There were few rules, but one of them was that a fight continued until it was called by a Pettijean, which usually meant a man was out cold or a dog was dead. On occasion, a man would be dead and an animal out cold, fit only to be put down.

The second largest shack was a whorehouse they called Honey Creek, supposedly named after the place the Pettijeans had come from. There were few rules there, as well. Pay for what you got, and never leave a mark on one of the women where it was visible. Not unless you wanted to bear a similar mark.

It was rumored that the Pettijeans had fled Louisiana with the law hot on their heels for the assault of a man that led to his death. "Coulda' kilt him outright and fed him to the gators," Sal often recounted. He was a beefy, dark-haired man with thick features, and his speech was lazy sounding with that strange almost musical accent the Louisianans all had. "But a point needed to be made. Eh?"

Given the expression of enjoyment on his face, it was a memory he relished. When pressed, and not very hard, Sal would share the gruesome story, which involved skinning a man alive. Unfortunately for them, that man had a brother who happened to be sheriff of the parish which had required their fleeing the jurisdiction.

Andre didn't resemble his cousin. He had a look women liked, but beyond the comely face were eyes with a gaze as cold as Sal's. Not that they intimidated Briar. Until the Pettijeans had shown up, no one had been as feared as a Lindley. Matter of fact, any of the upstanding citizens of Green Valley would still swear they were a close match.

Hastings was getting louder now as he ranted about some cheater and getting even.

"Why would we care?" Andre asked in a disinterested tone as he slowly rolled the dice back and forth in his hand, his full attention on Hastings.

"Because he's got *hundreds* on him," the mayor's kid said, although the word hundreds had been almost unrecognizable in his inebriation. "Help teach him a lesson ... and it's yours."

A heavy-breasted prostitute shoved in and refilled Briar's drink, but the girl who'd been working on him hissed and said, 'He's mine!'

He looked at the one who'd spoken scoffingly. As if any woman could make that claim. Only one woman ever could have and she'd rejected him. His own father had helped see to it; something Briar had never forgiven the old man for and never would. As the big whore took heed of the warning and moved away, Briar noticed the Pettijeans following Hastings toward the door. Apparently, they'd been tempted into action, although they didn't move with urgency.

Briar's attention shifted to the middle-aged woman in the corner who read cards and told fortunes, supposedly a relation of the Pettijeans. Her graying black hair was worn loose and she usually had an expression of half-amused contempt on her face.

She had an idiot son they called Johnny, a grown man with the mind of a ten-year-old. At the moment, Johnny was throwing knives at a badly scarred wooden target and hitting near the center almost every time from a distance of at least ten yards away. He was an idiot, but he could throw a knife.

Briar made it a practice to avoid the gypsy woman, if that's what she was, and she made it a practice to let him be, but now she was staring hard enough to give him pause. His expression hardened because he didn't care for being stared at, especially by card reading gypsies.

"Tower, Judgment, Death," she said in a deep voice.

He squinted harder to see if she was looking at him, but his vision was too fuzzy to tell for sure.

"Something is set in motion!"

He sneered and pointedly looked away, shaking off the whore who was half laying on him now. He didn't like being pressed on or stared at. "Get off."

"It will change everything," the gypsy woman warned. He looked back at her, but she wasn't looking at him, nor did she look amused. She looked disturbed, maybe even frightened. She gathered up her cards and dealt some of them out in a row, studying them intently.

Briar had had enough. It was cold outside, but it was time he got started home to his own bed. He rose to his feet, ignoring the whore's whining protest, and made his way to the door. He'd just reached it when the gypsy's final utterance was made.

"The beginning of the end!"

She hadn't hollered it or anything, so it was strange how clearly he'd heard it. How clearly everyone must have heard it because the room suddenly went quiet.

He didn't mind the cold one bit when he stepped outside.

Chapter One

Green Valley, VA
Monday, February 6, 1888

J oin you?"

T. Emmett Rice looked up from his paper at Sheriff Louis Swanson who'd just spoken. Emmett was sitting at his usual table by the window, having finished his breakfast. "Sure thing." Emmett signaled a waitress and pointed to his coffee cup, getting a nod in return.

It seemed apparent something was troubling the sheriff this morning. At forty-six, Louis Swanson was still a fine figure of a man, other than some scarring on the right side of his face, and the fact he was missing part of his right ear. It had been shot off in the war. A son of Green Valley, he'd joined the war as an eager nineteen-year-old.

Wounded at the battle of Rivers Bridge, he'd been nursed back to health by the woman he fell in love with. He'd married her and lived the next few decades of his life in Bamberg County in South Carolina until her passing. He'd moved back to Green Valley and taken the role of sheriff thinking it would help ease his grief. Now, he sat across from Emmett, still wearing his coat. He set his hat in the chair beside him.

"Coffee, Sheriff?" Callie Jo, one of the waitresses, asked. She already had a cup in hand for him.

"Yes, please," Swan replied. "Miss Callie Jo."

"Anything else for you this morning?" she asked after filling his cup and refilling Emmett's.

"No, this'll do," Swan replied. "Thanks."

"So what's happened that's gotten your face looking like a thundercloud this morning?" Emmett asked when she'd walked on.

"Did'ja hear about the man found in the alley beside DeWitt's late Friday?"

Emmett frowned. "No."

"He was hit from behind and then beaten. Hands smashed, fingers broken."

Emmett grimaced. "Good Lord."

"His left hand may have to go," Swan continued. "Doc's watching for signs of blood poisoning."

Emmett's attention was complete. At sixty-three, he was the most well-known and seasoned attorney in town. Physically, he was in good health. Admittedly, he was too robust, although he had lost a bit of girth over the course of the last few years. That was due to the good impression he wanted to make on Miss Cessie Blue, one of the loveliest ladies in town or in all the whole wide world, for that matter.

He hadn't heard about the incident because he'd spent the weekend at the Blue farm, which had become his habit of late. Although the Blue's place wasn't far from town, it seemed a world away when he was fortunate enough to be there. "Who is it?"

"One of Wayman Brock's journeyman. Garrett Trentwell. You know him?"

"Sure. We've passed the time of day. Nice young man. What, about twenty-five, I'd say?"

Swan nodded. "About that. Talented blacksmith, right on the brink of becoming a master at his craft. Now he may never work at it again. I've never seen hands that smashed up." He shook his head. "Sickening to look at."

The thought caused Emmett a twinge of actual pain. "Makes no sense. He's not a hell raiser. You know who did it?"

Swan took a moment to reply. "Do I know or can I prove it?"

Emmett waited, knowing more was coming.

"Garrett played cards at DeWitt's on Friday."

DeWitt's was a fancy, new establishment in town catering to high-stakes poker, blackjack, and craps. Emmett had visited a time or two, but it was too ritzy for his taste.

6

"He won a few hands," Swan continued. "Course, it all disappeared by the time he was found."

"The attack was about robbery, then."

"If it was just about getting the money, why not knock him out, grab it and run? Why beat him once he's down? Why smash his hands to pulp?"

It was a nauseating description but a good point.

"Care to guess who he was playing with?"

Emmett suddenly knew who he was talking about. A man named Lawrence Hastings had come to town some seven or eight years ago and started Hastings' Mercantile, a highly successful business. Three or four years back, he'd become mayor.

He was a sharp looking, smooth-talking man and a decent enough mayor, but his sons, twenty-two-year-old Lonnie and eighteen-year-old Timothy drank too much, argued too easily and got away with everything. They'd gotten themselves into several scrapes, which their father had promptly gotten them out of. "One or both of the Hastings boys?"

Swan nodded. "Lonnie lost a game of poker to Garrett and then accused him of cheating. He was belligerent enough about it that he was asked to leave."

"So, you think they left and then waited around."

"I sure as hell do."

"Garrett didn't see who attacked him?"

"Naw. He was hit from behind. Hard. Hard enough that he can't even remember earlier that night. Of course, I *must* be dead wrong about the Hastings," he added sarcastically, "because they vouch for one another, and daddy backs them up. Oh yes," he said mockingly. "They were home only minutes after they left the saloon. It couldn't have been *them* that attacked that poor lad."

Swan shook his head slowly. "Swear to God, Emmett, if I could prove otherwise, I'd arrest those boys faster than you can slap a tick. And I would enjoy doing it."

"They are a menace," Emmett agreed. "Especially Lonnie. There's pure spite in that one. I haven't heard anything about Timothy being violent though."

7

"Maybe not, but they both think they're above the law. And damned if they haven't been." He took a sip of the coffee and set it back down. "Feels to me like they're rubbing my nose in it. Yeah, I did it, but you can't prove it. In fact, everybody knows I did it, but you still can't prove it." He huffed. "Like it's all a game."

Outside, the snow began falling harder. Emmett looked at his office across the street. He'd started a fire in the woodstove before coming for breakfast and his gaze followed the smoke rising from the chimney. "Maybe the town council could take a position," he said thoughtfully.

"A position?"

Emmett looked back at Swan who'd cocked his head. "Let Lawrence know we're not fools. We know what his son or sons have done. Our position could be that we feel it's high time for the young men to move on. Make their way in the world somewhere besides here."

"We can't force them out or I'd have done it already."

"True, but with reelection around the corner, the mayor might just listen."

"I don't know. He backs those boys up at every turn and I don't think this time will be any different."

"Well, we can have a say in who the next mayor is. I get the feeling he wants to keep the job, don't you?"

"Sure, I do, but he's as used to getting his way as he's made his sons. Betcha' he thinks he's got it all sewn up."

"He does right now because who else is running? But that can be changed." He pushed his plate to the edge of the table. "The council meets on Thursday. I'll get word out to the members to meet a bit earlier than usual. See if the others are of accord."

"You don't know how much I wish a witness would come forward that could put those boys behind bars."

"Garrett have any family?"

"No. His ma passed before he started with Wayman. I don't know anything about his pa. No siblings."

"Does he live at the smithy?"

"No. Only the apprentices have rooms there. Journeymen make a wage and get out on their own. He boards at Mrs.

8

Bullock's place. I'm headed there to see him now. See if he remembers anything more. You want to go?"

Emmett nodded. "I'll go. Let him know we care."

Chapter Two

It took a long time for Garrett to rouse himself and sit up in bed. He had no idea what day or time it was. Not that it mattered. The morphine he'd been given dulled the pain, but it also dulled his senses.

He looked down at his splinted hands and felt lightheaded and nauseous. Each finger was splinted separately, and a brace encircled his right wrist and encased the rest of the hand. He saw the ominously darkening skin on the fingers of his left hand. Doc Simmons hadn't pulled any punches. It meant the blood was poisoned.

Garrett squeezed his eyes shut and held his breath, trying to stave off the urge to vomit again. He collapsed onto his side, his skin cold and clammy with perspiration. Why had this happened? How would he make out without use of his hands? The anguish he felt was heavy enough to crush him. It *was* crushing him. It was hard to draw breath.

He heard muffled voices coming closer, two men conversing in hushed tones. Wayman and the doctor. But when the door opened, the doctor entered alone. The older man looked grave as he made his way across the room and sat on the chair next to the bed and leaned close to examine Garrett's hands. When Doc sighed, his breath smelled of pipe tobacco. Garrett held his breath and tried not to retch. He felt so sick these days.

"I'm sorry, son," Doc said with a shake of his head. "But we don't have a choice with the fingers of that hand."

Garrett squeezed his eyes shut, ashamed of the tears just below the surface. He had no say in anything. No control. None. It was either cut off the hand or die. He wanted to live, but how in hell would be make it without use of both hands?

"The longer we wait, the bigger the risk."

Garrett didn't open his eyes. Despite that, hot tears slid out.

"I am sorry as hell," the doctor said again.

The chair creaked as Doc rose. Garrett heard him getting prepared. Was he going to operate then and there? He opened his eyes and wiped his face.

"Lay on back," the doctor said tenderly.

What choice did he have? He laid back and shut his eyes again, trying to think of anything except what was about to happen. He smelled a strong odor and felt something hovering just above his mouth and nose, and he knew that soon he'd be out cold, and his hand would be cut off. When he woke, he would not have a hand.

No hand.

What kind of a man would he be then? It was his final thought before he lost consciousness.

Chapter Three

Wheeling, WV
Thursday, March 22

Susanna's face was cold and her stomach was in a knot as she closed in on Wiley's Restaurant, glancing around for anyone who might know her. Seeing no one that would cause a problem, she sniffed, swiped beneath her nose with the back of her hand, and stepped through the front door.

Inside, the savory scent of bacon, pastries and rich coffee lingered, although the breakfast crowd had cleared out.

There were at least a dozen other young women seated at various tables while listening to a professional looking lady in front of the room. A man stood beside her, equally as professional looking in his suit, nice clean shirt, vest and string tie.

The lady was thanking them for their time and interest, although almost all the girls had glanced over at the sound of the door and taken a few moments to size her up. One dark-haired young woman gave her a particularly disdainful once over before looking back at the lady who was speaking.

Feeling embarrassed and conspicuous, Susanna moved to the closest table and carefully pulled out a chair so it wouldn't scrape the floor. She sat and set the burlap bag she'd brought on the chair next to her and then eased out of her coat. It was ugly and moth eaten because it was old as the hills, not that the dress underneath was much better to look at. But so be it. She didn't have a better one.

Surreptitiously looking around at the other young women, Susanna fought the urge to get right back up and leave again. She'd fixed her unruly strawberry blonde hair as usual, which was to say she'd pulled it back in an unflattering, no-nonsense bun, but it suddenly felt even more unflattering than before. The other young women looked better. Their clothes were finer, of course. She had no doubt that their manners would be nicer, and they'd be better spoken, and the list could go on and on.

Not that there was any point to making such a list. She was here and she would do what she came to do. If they didn't want her, she'd live. As long as someone hadn't spotted her and reported back to Cheever that she was somewhere she wasn't supposed to be.

"I am Mrs. Gaines," the lady said. "And this is Mr. Dennis." She was an attractive, well-coiffed woman in her late forties. The bodice of her dress was a pleasing shade of bluish green and she wore an eye-catching pendant of silver with a dark blue center. *What would it be like to own such a fine thing? I'd wear it every day,* Susanna thought.

"First, we shall give an overview of the position," she continued. "Explain what would be expected of you, the remuneration and so forth. Then we'll meet with you individually should you wish to pursue a position."

It was spoken as if she'd delivered the exact same speech a hundred times before. *Just get on with it, lady. Not like I got all day to be here.* The others probably did, but not her.

"The requirements were clearly stated in the advertisement, but I shall repeat them. We require young women between the ages of eighteen and twenty-five, unmarried, of good moral character and in excellent health. You must be able to both read and write proficiently and be of pleasant temperament. If selected, you will be sent to a location where there is a need. You will be trained and supplied with room, board, uniforms, including shoes, and a salary of seventeen dollars and fifty cents a month."

The sum practically robbed Susanna of breath, although she noticed that the others in attendance merely nodded agreeably. To her, it was a fortune.

"There is also a signing bonus," the man spoke up. He was a plain, balding man, but both his face and his voice were pleasant. "Five dollars will be paid after successful completion of your training and a probationary period. For most girls, that's only a few weeks. *And,*" he added significantly, "—there is a bonus paid at the end of the first year, provided you are in good standing, of course."

A hand was raised, and he gestured to the girl it belonged to, inviting her to speak.

"Is that if you agree to stay another year? That second bonus, I mean?"

"That is an excellent question," Mr. Dennis replied. "If your choice is to move on at the end of the first year's employment, we will pay a bonus of three dollars and fifty cents, providing, as I said, you are in good standing."

Susanna wondered if any of the others were thinking what she was. *In good standing* sounded like a sneaky way to keep from paying anything. Not that it mattered. She wasn't about to nit-pick over something happening a year down the road if she was lucky enough to get the job.

"However, if you elect to stay another year, the bonus is five dollars," he concluded.

Counting on her fingers under the table, she calculated that would amount to twenty-seven dollars and fifty cents. Almost thirty dollars. *Thirty dollars.* For someone who had never had any money of her own, it seemed like a fortune, especially since they had room and board and even clothes paid for.

"We provide everything," Mrs. Gaines said, giving a sweeping gesture. "From a comfortable room in a safe dormitory with fellow workmates, to medical care, to a good wage. Our girls work six days a week, although one of those is a half day. They agree to maintain a strong work ethic, a positive outlook and good behavior. They abide by the store managers and the housemother's rules. Contractually, they are not allowed to marry for the duration of their employment. Any questions so far?"

A hand was raised in the front of the room.

"Yes?" the woman asked.

"Do we have any say about where we get stationed?"

"If you are chosen," the woman replied coolly, "—you may request a location, although we would want to know the reason for the request. Naturally, we are hiring based on company need. Not every store has openings."

14

"As Mrs. Gaines said," Mr. Dennis spoke up again. "Today we'll conduct an interview and ascertain whether you're a good fit for Wiley's. Mrs. Gaines, Miss Heller," he said gesturing to a dour looking lady who'd appeared from the kitchen, "—who is our store manager here in Wheeling, and I will speak with you one on one."

Several girls nodded.

"Feel free to line up at any of our tables. You will need to speak to at least two of us. Afterwards, if you'll wait a short while, we will confer and then announce those whom we wish to remain behind for further instructions. If your name is not called, please know that we may call you back at a later point in time, so be sure you leave your name and address where we can contact you." He paused and looked around the room. "Any other questions before we begin?"

There were a few seconds of silence before the interviewers exchanged glances and then moved to different tables to sit. One young woman stood, quickly followed by all the rest. Most gravitated toward the ladies, so Susanna went to the man's table, walking with a brisk step to arrive first. She'd had no better luck with women than men in her life so who interviewed her first made no difference.

The man gestured to the seat across the table. "Please."

She sat. "I'm Susanna Jones."

"Susannah with a z?"

"No, sir. S-u-s-a-n-n-a. And I go by Susanna."

"Pleased to meet you, Susanna. Your age?"

"Eighteen," she said. "And in good health. Strong as an ox."

"What makes you interested in being a Wiley's girl?"

"I'm ready for something new. I'm sure I can do a fine job. I learn real good."

He considered her a moment before leaning slightly forward. "You may want to say you learn easily when you speak to the ladies. You pick up instructions easily."

She frowned, not exactly sure why he was telling her that.

"How do you get along with others?" he asked.

"Fine." *As long as they aren't stuck up and think they're too good for me.*

15

"What do you do now?"

She blinked. "Uh—"

"Help at home?"

"You could say that."

"And who is at home? Parents? Siblings?"

"My parents died a long time ago. I guess you could say I have, uh, brothers and a sister."

He looked at her curiously. "Can they manage without you?"

"They're moving off, too."

"Oh?"

"Well, my brothers are. Same time as me. My sister ... she's way prettier and sweeter than me. A little younger than what you said, but do you ever have younger girls that can fill up glasses and such? Or maybe wash and dry dishes?"

"I'm afraid not. Our age requirements are firm."

The disappointment Susanna experienced was like a stab.

"How quickly would you be able to start, if selected?"

"Probably as soon as you'd want me." She was getting the feeling she amused him, although she didn't see anything amusing.

"As soon as the day after tomorrow?"

"That'd be just fine. What time?"

His smile broadened. "It wasn't an invitation just yet. I was just trying to pinpoint your availability."

She became aware that a line had formed behind her to speak to him, and she suspected he was the nicest of the bunch. If he didn't like her, she was done for. "Nobody will work harder," she stated earnestly. "I'm not the prettiest girl here or the smartest, but nobody will work harder."

The mild amusement on his face was replaced by a flicker of regret and confusion. "Your appearance is fine, Miss Jones."

She felt her face prickle with heat because, of course, that was a lie.

"And I believe that you work hard. You seem most eager."

"I am. I bet I want the job more than anyone else here."

His expression was one of intense interest. "Why is that?"

He looked like he cared, which made her feel all kinds of strange, both defensive and like spilling her guts. "I was taken

16

from an orphanage a long time ago for one reason, to be used for labor on a no-account farm. Now I'm eighteen and it's time to move on. I don't plan to be a slave all my life," she added with a note of bitterness.

He nodded slowly. "Thank you for your honesty. Why don't you go and speak to either Mrs. Gaines or Miss Heller and, if you meet with their approval, we'll see that you get set up."

She sat up a little straighter. "Are you saying … I got your vote?"

He smiled. "I am."

She was shocked but didn't want him to know it. "Where would I go?"

He turned a printed list on the table and slid it toward her. "We concentrate on a six-state radius, so it might be anywhere in Ohio, Kentucky, Virginia, Pennsylvania—"

The paper in front of her listed a lot of cities. Louisville. Virginia City, Pittsburg. She didn't know diddly squat about any of them, so she shrugged. "One place is as good as another, long as it's away from here." He looked at her with a mixture of curiosity and sympathy, which made her uncomfortable. She didn't like people trying to figure her out. As if they ever could. "Thank you for your time, Mr. Dennis," she said as she rose.

"Susanna?"

"Yes, sir?"

"Our customers expect a friendly waitress with a ready smile. Is that something you can do?"

The response *Well, why couldn't I?* almost popped out. Instead, she forced a smile, which felt foolish as all hell.

"Maybe you can work on that," he suggested quietly, his eyes twinkling with humor.

Her smile vanished and she turned and moved on. The next girl in line stepped by her with a bright smile already on her face. Smiling came a whole lot more naturally for some than others.

"How did you hear about the position?" Mrs. Gaines asked about twenty-five minutes later when Susanna finally got to sit across from her.

17

"I saw it in the newspaper." *After I snatched it from the bench in front of the barber shop.* Mrs. Gaines didn't approve of her; she could tell already. The lady had a pinched, closed off expression that suggested maybe Susanna had some potent underarm odor or she'd eaten a big, fat onion just before she'd opened her mouth and every word spoken was an affront to the woman's senses. All because she didn't look as good as the others.

That's right, I don't. I don't have two cents of my own to rub together, you hateful ole' sow, so how could I?

"What is your education?"

"I learned at home mostly."

The lady handed her a small pad of paper and a pencil. "Please write down what I say."

Susanna felt her face grow hot as she picked up the pencil. She hadn't seen any of the others having to do this. What? Did she look stupid as well as ugly?

"I shall have roast beef and mashed potatoes with gravy," the woman said. "A side of collard greens. Peach pie for dessert. And my friend will have—"

Susanna wrote as quickly as she could, her letters a sloppy mix of block and cursive letters. She couldn't write as fast as the woman was talking.

"French onion soup," the woman continued. "Yeast rolls. Cake for dessert and … coffee for both of us." She paused. "Read it back, please."

Susanna knew she'd failed the test. She hadn't gotten all the words down. *But guess what, you old biddy?* "You'll have roast beef and mashed potatoes with gravy and a side of collard greens," she said as pleasantly as she could without even looking at the pad of paper. "Peach pie for dessert and coffee. And you, sir," she said, addressing an invisible companion. "You would like the French onion soup with rolls. Cake and coffee for dessert. Is that right?" She looked back at the lady whose eyes had narrowed slightly.

"Would you like gravy on both your taters and meat?" Susanna added.

"We do not say taters," the lady commented. "The word is potatoes," she said, enunciating crisply. She paused before adding, "You have a good memory."

"Yes, ma'am. I also learn easy and I don't forget."

"Thank you, for coming today, Miss Jones," Mrs. Gaines said dismissively. "I believe that will be all."

"Thank *you*, Mrs. Gaines." Susanna returned. She rose with all the grace and pride she could muster after such a thorough cold shouldering. She walked out of the restaurant, stopping only to retrieve her coat and bag. She felt stung as she headed to the general store for the supplies she'd been sent to fetch. If she'd been the type to cry, she probably would have been blubbering right about now. Luckily for her, she wasn't the type. She never cried. She hadn't cried since she was eight.

~~~

At the store, Susanna glumly filled her bag with the items on her list, flour, baking powder, chicory, tobacco and dried pinto beans, and left again resentful of the time she'd wasted and the walloping she'd endure because of it … unless she came up with a really good excuse. She stepped outside and began the long walk back to the farm.

"Miss Jones!"

Susanna turned and saw Mr. Dennis coming toward her.

"You didn't stay," he said when he reached her.

"She didn't like me," she stated without a flicker of feeling. "I didn't need to stay and hear the list to know that." She noticed that he seemed uncomfortable, because he knew it was true. "She looked at me like I was dirt," she added to drive the point home. "I may not be much, but I ain't dirt."

"Isn't it possible you're making a wrong assumption?" he asked kindly. "Jumping to a conclusion based on … well, possibly your own insecurities?"

Susanna lowered the bag to the ground because it was heavy. "No, sir. I know people. When they're good, when they're bad, when they think they're better than me. And she probably is, but

19

what does that have to do with me being a waitress in your restaurant when I'm willing to work hard and do a good job?"

He pursed his lips before speaking again. "Day after tomorrow. The train depot. Nine a.m. sharp."

Her breath caught. "What about it?" she asked warily.

"I believe you'll work hard and do well, Miss Jones, and I'm willing to give you a try."

He wasn't kidding, was he? "I'll be there," she said with all the voice she could muster.

"Good. Now, if you'll excuse me, I have to get back to it." He started back to the restaurant and all she could do was gawk. Unless he was fooling, and he didn't seem the type for a mean joke, he'd just given her a chance.

Astonishment and excitement coursed through her, and those feelings alone, much less a chance at a new beginning would be worth whatever punishment Cheever dished out since she'd taken so long.

She hefted the bag over her shoulder and started on her way feeling strangely light. She felt struck dumb from the shock of the last two minutes, but there was a *feeling* ... a pure excitement she'd never known before.

But what about Lily? She couldn't leave her, but how could she take her? She couldn't *exactly* take her, but she sure as hell wouldn't leave her behind. As the saying went, where there is a will, there is a way. And she had one strong will, so there had to be a way. There just had to.

Ruth Cheever usually took kids from Reverend Jones Home for Unwanted Children at age ten or so, but she'd plucked up Susanna at eight because of her sturdy build and unflinching gaze. Boys were for plowing, building, repairing, planting, wood chopping and reaping. Girls were for hoeing, weeding, planting, milking, cooking and housekeeping.

Around about age ten, certain children had strength enough to be worth their keep, albeit a meager keep. They shared rooms, beds and were clothed and fed enough to sustain them for the work they performed.

They were up at four if they milked, otherwise at five. They worked all day long and were in bed by eight. There was no laughter or joy. Ruth Cheever was a taskmaster known to fly into rages and beat her wards with whatever she could get her hands on with little provocation.

Susanna, Cheever called her Sue, was tough, so she could take it. Levi was tough, too. At almost seventeen, he was six feet tall and well-muscled. He could have picked up Cheever and snapped her in two and, many a time, Susanna wished for it more than anything, especially when Cheever hurt Lily or Nate.

Nate was a twelve-year-old with too much dusk in his skin. Either his father or mother had been a negro, so he was doomed to be an outcast, not accepted by either race. Not accepted by anyone except the other inmates of Cheever farm. He was a fine-looking boy. Personally, Susanna liked the color of his skin. Besides, there was goodness to him.

Why Cheever had picked Lily was a mystery, a cruel one at that. Lily was a beautiful girl with fair hair. She was sweet and soft spoken – everything Cheever despised. Typically, Ruth Cheever chose the strong in body and mind, hardened by the harsh circumstances of their lives. She liked them toughened and resentful, but smart enough to obey. Lily wasn't hardened or tough, nor would she ever be. Susanna sometimes suspected Cheever, the old witch, had chosen Lily in order to punish her for no other reason than she was so gentle and pretty. It made Susanna detest Cheever even more than before.

There had been others adopted from the home, but they had all run away when an opportunity presented itself. Martin had run off at sixteen and was never heard from again. Cheever stayed in a rage over it for a solid week, and they all paid a price for his escape.

Axel had made a run for it when he was fourteen, but he got caught and brought back. He was beaten so badly, his arm ended up broken and he stayed wobbly and staggered for days. Cheever fixed his arm that day; Susanna had been made to help but was a week before he could walk straight again. Not even a month later, he up and ran again. Fortunately for him, that time, he got away.

Tanya was fifteen when she ran. She turned up later, married and pregnant, glaring at Cheever like she'd like nothing more than to cut her throat. Of course, she'd only shown back up to gloat, and she'd only gotten away with it since she was with her new husband whom she seemed to have wrapped around her little finger. Unfortunately, the rest of them had paid for her insolence.

Matthew was the most recent one to get away and, for that, Levi had been beaten black and blue since Cheever felt sure he knew something about either Matthew's escape plan or his whereabouts. Susanna had wondered, too, but if Levi knew anything, he never admitted it.

A few days after Matthew's escape, it was discovered that Cheever's stash of money was also missing, causing the most violent rage of all. They'd all borne the brunt of it, especially Lily, which made no sense at all, except Cheever knew it would get to all of them.

When Cheever turned the buckle of the belt on Lily cutting a deep gash beneath the girl's bony shoulder and causing blood to fly, Levi went at Cheever with his fist reared back. For a few seconds, Susanna thought he might just lose his grip and kill her.

He didn't deliver the blow he'd wanted to, but he was shaking and close to the breaking point, and Cheever knew it. She stopped the beating after that, but Lily was scarred from the blow. Susanna wanted it to be the girl's last scar. She could not leave Lily behind. She wouldn't. But how would she take her? Except *where there's a will, there's a way.* It became a silent chant in her mind as she walked. Hadn't everyone always called her willful?

Susanna limped once she was in sight of the house. Cheever was sitting on the side porch, cracking pecans as she smoked her pipe. Her eyes narrowed. "Why you limpin'?" she called without removing the pipe from her clenched teeth.

"Twisted my ankle on a dern hole in the road." Susanna reached the porch and made a good show of the pain it caused as she stepped up. "On the way to town. I kept going anyway. I need to get off it."

"Get your chores done and we'll see about you puttin' it up." Susanna huffed.

22

"Tell the girl to start peeling taters," Cheever snapped.

Susanna kept a sour expression on her face until she stepped inside, but once the door was shut, a surge of triumph filled her, and a smile appeared. A rare occurrence.

~~~

As the sun set, Nate stood at the barn door, keeping an eye out for Cheever while Levi and Susanna conferred in hushed voices. The three of them had mucked the stalls in record time to afford the few precious minutes needed to make a plan. Inside, Lily worked on dinner.

"I guess I could take Lily with us," Levi said quietly.

Susanna rolled her eyes at the ridiculous notion. "You know that she needs to stay with me."

He huffed in frustration. "You just said you couldn't take her."

"I said they *said* I couldn't take her. Obviously, somehow, I got to take her. Or we got to get her there."

"Where?"

"To wherever they're sending me!"

"You're not making a lick of sense. You don't even know where you're going."

"Yeah, but I'll know the day after tomorrow. Right before I get on the train. If we can just get her to the new town, wherever the hell it is, I'll find a way to keep her. Once I get there."

Levi rubbed the back of his skull thoughtfully. He had thick, dark hair and dark eyes. In Susanna's opinion, his features were too masculine to ever be considered handsome, but some girl would fall head over heels one day, because he was strong and had a good heart.

"I don't know," he murmured.

"Well, I do know. It's how it has to be. Somehow, we got to sneak her on the train. Or, if it's not too far, you can bring her."

"So we all sneak off when it's time for you to go," Levi said, thinking it out as he spoke. "Go to town, find out where you're off to."

She nodded and pushed loose hair behind her ear. It was a nervous habit she wasn't aware of.

"Maybe we can just get her a ticket once we know where you're going," he suggested nervously.

"Using what?" she scoffed, "Our good looks?"

He hesitated before admitting, "I maybe got some money."

24

For an instant, Susanna felt nothing but shock. Then she noticed Nate glance back at them and she realized that he knew. Not only that, but he was looking to see her reaction. Breath-stealing fury was her reaction, because it could have only come from one place since they didn't get any money of their own.

"You son of a—" she said through clenched teeth.

"I didn't have a choice, did I?" Levi interrupted angrily, leaning into her, his expression every bit as fierce as hers. "How long have we been saying we got to get away? Only how were we going to do it without any money?"

She couldn't help seething, even if he did have a point. "Why didn't you tell me?"

"Cause Cheever would have smelled it if she knew we was lying. It was better to keep y'all in the dark. Safer that way."

"Wasn't safer for Lily, was it?" Susanna retorted furiously.

His expression darkened. "I didn't know she'd do that. I wanted to kill her."

Susanna turned away. She was still seeing red, but the thing was done now and at least they had money. They could get Lily to wherever she would be stationed and, from there, she'd find a way to make sure she was taken care of. There would only be one more day to get through in this hellhole.

"Go on," Susanna said to Nate. "Go wash up." Nate obeyed at once, like usual. "Where will you go?" she asked Levi.

"Don't know."

"We got to make this work," she said in a low voice. "None of us can get caught."

He nodded grimly. "Don't plan on getting caught."

25

Chapter Four

They couldn't all risk disappearing from the farm at the same time or showing up in town together, so Nate and Lily snuck away first. They would start toward town together, but Nate would hang back at a designated spot in the woods and wait for Levi, while Lily continued on alone. She would get to the depot wearing a woolen scarf over her head and trying not to be noticed.

"You think we'll make it?" Nate asked Lily uneasily when they were close to his stopping point.

"Of course, we will. We have to."

"Think we'll wind up together?"

"I hope so."

"Me, too." He'd reached the spot he was to wait at, so he stopped. So did she. "Be careful," he said.

She nodded. "You be careful, too."

He sighed. "I wish I wasn't sayin' it, but … bye, Lily."

"Bye," she returned thickly. They exchanged an awkward hug and she walked on. It was hard to walk on without him. Her chest felt tight and she began crying.

She wouldn't turn back because she didn't want Nate to know she was being a crybaby, but she reached the bend in the road and thought it was far enough away that he wouldn't be able to tell. She turned back to find him still watching her. He waved. Smiling through her tears, she waved back and felt a little steadier as she continued on. When she rounded the next bend in the road, she began to run.

~~~

Susanna gave it roughly a quarter of an hour before she straightened from her hoeing and looked around. She took a few steps away, dropped her hoe and walked away as calmly as she could, although the force of her beating heart was causing an ache in her chest. She could feel it in her head. In her throbbing temples. She reached the road and broke into a run.

~~~

Levi was a nervous wreck as he chopped wood. He kept at it for as long as he could, hoping the sound would keep Cheever from growing suspicious. The woman slept with one eye and ear open, satisfied only when they were working.

When he finally made a break for it, having waited as long as he could, he snuck to the road and then ran full out. He only slowed his pace once he reached town. A stitch pulled in his side, but he pressed a hand to it and walked on, knowing the four of them would either pull off a miracle and get away or they would pay with flesh and blood.

When he neared the depot, he saw Susanna talking to a businessman, which was a relief. Maybe this would all go as they'd hoped. He looked around and saw Lily hovering at the backmost corner of the station, pale with fright. There was good reason for it, but he gave her a nod of reassurance.

Reaching the depot, he looked back to where Susanna had been and found her headed straight for him. He'd never seen her rattled before, but she was now. Had the man changed his mind about hiring her?

"Green Valley, Virginia," she said when she reached him.

"Okay, I'll get her on the train," he pledged.

"Well, hurry up," she snapped. "It's about to leave!"

He nearly snapped back at her, but there was no time to bicker. Especially when the reason for it was that they were both on edge from raw nerves. He turned and took long strides into the depot. He'd never bought a train ticket before and he was anxious about it. They weren't caught yet, but it would be a problem if someone noticed them and word got back to Cheever, and then she was able to trace them.

Given their ages, he didn't think Cheever had any right to make Susanna return, or maybe even him, for that matter, but it was possible she could force the younger ones back. Which he would never allow. Nor would Susanna.

Inside the station, there wasn't much of a line. Thank Goodness. He kept shifting his weight from foot to foot and looking out the window, dreading the sight of a livid Ruth Cheever or the train starting in motion before he could get a ticket.

"I need a ticket for a child," he said when he reached the window.

"How old's the child?" the man asked.

"Thirteen."

"That's the same cost as an adult. Where to?"

"Green Valley, Virginia," he replied, stammering in his nervousness.

"What accommodation?"

Levi frowned in confusion. "Beg pardon?"

"First class? Second?"

"The cheapest one, please."

"That'll be five dollars and sixty cents. The train will arrive late tomorrow evening."

Levi concentrated as he counted out the money and passed it over. It cut into their meager funds, but there was no choice. A ticket was handed over, Levi nodded his thanks, and hurried back out.

The train was belching smoke. Susanna looked about ready to soil herself, which might have been funny in other circumstances, but not now.

"Here," he said, handing the ticket to Lily with a trembling hand. "Go! Fly! You ain't got much time."

Lily threw her arms around him and hugged with all her might. Tears glistened in her eyes when she looked up at him. "Write to us," she said breathlessly.

"I will. Go on, now."

Lily dashed to Susanna, who held out a hand for her. Levi watched Susanna look around for Cheever before helping Lily up and following her onto the train. Turning back, she gave him a significant nod, but she still looked scared.

He knew the feeling.

"All Aboard," the conductor called.

There were two short toots of the horn and the train started moving. The slow, rhythmic sound of wheels clacking on the rails was better than music to his ears. Levi took a step backwards as gratitude filled his chest. He and Nate were not out of the woods yet, but the girls were on their way and that was a big victory. "Go," he breathed as he watched the train pick up speed.

~~~

Susanna and Lily found seats together in the second-class car. Lily took the window seat and looked out to where Levi was still watching. Lily put her hand to the glass, but he didn't see her.

When the train moved, Susanna exhaled in relief. "I still half expect her to show up and run alongside the train, screaming at us."

Lily grinned. "She'd have to run pretty fast."

"Or maybe fly her broom there. I always said she was an old witch." Lily giggled and Susanna gave in to a smile because, unless something changed, they were getting away. Now if only Levi and Nate would be as lucky.

"I'm going to pray for them," Lily said, as if she'd heard Susanna's thoughts.

"Yeah, you do that," Susanna rejoined.

"Do you really never pray?" Lily asked quietly.

"God's never done me no favors. I don't see why I'd go talking to him now."

"He did me a favor," Lily stated. "He put me with you."

The words got to Susanna, so she crossed her arms and looked around the car at the other passengers, trying to discern who they were and what they were doing.

Some were going visiting was her guess. One was going to see a sick relative. Bad sick, maybe dying. None of the others were running for their lives. She was pretty sure of that.

"I wonder what Green Valley will be like," Lily said wistfully.

Susanna wondered, too. She wondered a lot of things. Most importantly, how would she provide for Lily? But where there was a will. "We'll find out soon enough," she replied. "Long as it's better than this place. Right?"

Lily nodded and smiled. "It will be."

~~~

Ruth Cheever woke abruptly after dozing in her rocking chair on the porch. It was quiet. Too quiet. She should have heard the sounds of the rebuilding of the chicken coop. "Levi," she hollered.

There was no reply.

She stood and her right arm tingled unpleasantly because she'd leaned her elbow too hard on the arm of the chair. She straightened it out as she bellowed for Sue.

Not getting an answer, she started toward the barn, getting angrier with each step. Peering inside, she saw the horse was there, but no one else. "Levi? Where the devil are you, boy?"

She marched over to where Sue and Lily should have been hoeing. They weren't there and dark suspicion turned into a *knowing*. They'd run. They had all run. "Nate! Lily! You better come out!"

Moving fast, she went to hitch the horse to the wagon. She was shaking with fury, but she would damn well keep calm enough to do what she needed to do. Once the wagon was hitched, she went back for an item of clothing from each of her charges and rode out.

~~~

Crouched behind a thicket, Nate waited and watched the road. He held his breath at the sound of an approaching horse and wagon

30

from the direction of the farm. Seconds later, he saw Cheever go by headed for town.

He felt sick to his stomach at the thought of her encountering Levi. Nate hurried to the road in time to see the wagon slow and turn on the rough road that led to the Korby place. A new fear seized hold. Lynn Korby was a hard man who raised bloodhounds and used them to track people. That was how they'd caught Axel.

Cheever finding out they were gone this soon and the use of the hounds changed everything. Before he could decide on a course of action, he saw Levi running toward him. Good God in Heaven – Levi had just missed Cheever. Nate waved his arms frantically.

Levi was breathless when he reached him.

"Cheever's gone for Korby! She just passed by not two, three minutes ago."

Levi turned away from him, still working on catching his breath. "All right," he said. "Let's go."

Nate was stunned when Levi started back in the direction of the farm. "Where are we going?" he asked as they broke into a run.

"You gotta' trust me."

Nate only trusted a few people in the whole world and Levi was at the top of the list. Still, it was sickening to reach the farm when he'd hoped never to lay eyes on it again. Were they going to pretend they hadn't left?

"Go use the outhouse if you need to," Levi said. "You won't get another chance for a while."

Nate didn't need to, so he followed Levi into the house and watched as the older boy began rummaging through cupboards. "What are we doin'?" Nate asked desperately.

"Gotta hide where the dogs caint reach us," Levi replied, handing him a wooden pitcher from the back of the cupboard. "Rinse it and fill it with water. And hurry."

Nate rushed to the pump outside, keeping his eyes peeled and listening for sounds of the dogs. He could barely breathe for the anxiety that filled him. He pumped with all his might, filled the jug part of the way and rushed back in. Levi had a half-filled burlap bag in hand and was going toward the front of the house.

31

"Don't spill any," Levi warned.

Nate didn't understand what they were doing or where they were going, but he followed. Levi opened the door to a front room, a spare bedroom no one used. Nate came through and Levi closed the door behind him. With tears of apprehension pooled in his dark eyes, he asked, "What makes you think they won't find us here?"

"Not here," Levi said. He pointed to the ceiling. "There."

Nate looked and saw a barely noticeable square in the ceiling.

"Put the pitcher down. I'm going to lift you up and you're gonna push the panel out of the way and climb on up inside. You'll see a ladder," Levi said, talking with urgency. "Send it down."

Nate set the pitcher down and stepped into Levi's cupped hands. Levi lifted him. "Get on my shoulders," Levi grunted.

Nate managed to kneel and then stand on Levi's shoulders. His knees hadn't felt right all day, but he maintained his balance and slid open the panel. Drawing on all his strength, he hoisted himself up and inside the hole, sneezing from the dust he'd disturbed. He found and dropped the ladder to Levi. The sides of it were rope, the rungs thin pieces of wood.

He wiped his nose with his shirt sleeve and then dropped to his hands and knees and reached for the pitcher Levi handed up to him. Next, the bag was handed up. Nate backed up as Levi clambered up the ladder and pulled it back up behind him.

"I never knew this was here," Nate marveled.

Levi squatted. "Yeah. We found it a long time ago." He slid the panel back into place, instantly making the space darker. Levi stood and glanced around. "Sooner or later, the dogs'll come tearing back here. I'm hoping they'll think it's just because we lived here, but even if they don't, Cheever won't let them in the house. She hates dogs."

Nate was relieved there was a plan.

"Bloodhounds got the best noses in the world, but they ain't smart. They'd get us outdoors. They'd find us in the loft or under the house or up in a tree. But the attic? Nah. Cheever won't let them in. Like I said, she hates dogs. A stray came around once, it was a sweet thing, and she bashed in its head with a shovel."

Nate knew this because the others had told him. It's why they always tried to shoo off any strays that came around.

Levi sat and brushed off his hands. "What I figure is, they'll search all day and then call it off when it's late. Maybe they'll start again in the morning. Depends on how much she's willing to pay."

"Then what'll we do?"

Levi thought for a minute. "Late, after midnight, we'll take the horse and get ourselves a town or two away. Maybe get on a train. Buy as much distance as we can."

Nate nodded. He liked that part of the plan.

"For now, find a place and get comfortable because we cannot move around once she's back. No coughing or sneezing. Nothing. You got to hold it."

Nate nodded. He sat and looked around. "Where'd the girls go?" he asked quietly.

"Virginia," Levi replied.

Because of the light that filtered through the cracks in the walls and roof, he could see clearly now that his eyes had adjusted, although there wasn't much to see. There was a chest, a box and a coat rack lying on its side because of a broken base.

"A town called Green Valley," Levi added.

"Sounds nice," Nate said longingly.

"Yeah. I hope it is." Levi got up, went to the box and began pulling out the contents. There was nothing but old clothing. "We looked through this a long time ago," he said.

"Who?"

"Me and Matthew while Susanna kept a lookout. I guess we were about ten or eleven at the time." He pulled out a thick shawl and smelled it before tossing it to Nate. "Don't smell good, but you can use it as a pillow. Better than not having one, I reckon."

"I wonder how Matthew's doing," Nate said.

Levi shrugged. "I figure he probably got hired on at a farm somewhere and he's doing just fine."

Nate watched Levi open the chest. It made a creaking sound.

"Won't shut that again," Levi murmured. The contents of the chest were much the same, plus there were worn boots, hats and moth-eaten bolts of cloth. He picked up a bolt of flannel,

33

unwrapped it and threw it around his shoulders. Next, he stuck a flattened man's hat on his head. "What do you think?"

Nate grinned, despite the nauseating tension he felt.

Levi came closer and sat, still wearing the getup. "Damn. I hoped we'd be on our way by now."

Nate had, too. With all his heart and soul. "You reckon we'll hear the dogs?"

"Oh, yeah. We'll hear 'em alright."

"Maybe we'll get away tonight."

"Yeah."

"And the girls got away, for sure?"

Levi grinned. "I watched the train leave with them in it."

Nate looked up at the dusty timbers slung with spider webs.

"I remember when old man Cheever died," Levi mused. "He was a drunk. He was about as mean as her, *except* when he was drunk, and then he just didn't give a tinker's damn about nothin' or nobody."

"Oh yeah?"

"Yeah. Once he was drunk, he'd talk gibberish. Make up words. Sometimes he'd talk in rhyme. 'You must have fell on your head, fell on your head. You oughta' be dead, but you're here instead.' He said that one a lot." Levi paused, thinking about it. "Did I ever tell you how he died?"

"You said a huntin' accident."

Levi grunted. "Yeah. He went hunting this once, probably got drunk off his ass and got caught by a bear. He was torn up something fierce." Nate cringed and Levi nodded in grim confirmation. "Never saw her shed one tear over him. What she did was to tear the place apart looking for where he'd hid money."

"He had money?"

"Aw, who knows? He used to make moonshine and she thought he'd made a pretty penny at it. She had us dig holes all over the yard, and she searched the house, the cellar, the barn, the damn chicken coop. We heard her up here. That's how we knew about it."

"I remember, this one time, her asking him where some money was he'd just gotten paid. He said, 'It's up then down and

34

all around or maybe I buried it in the ground.' He said that one lots of times, too."

"Think she ever found it?"

"I think he drunk up every cent ever come his way."

"Up then down and all around," Nate repeated.

"Yeah. Sounds like it could be up here, right? That's what we thought. That's why we searched it all those years ago."

"Where did you look?"

"Every inch of the place. The chests and crates, of course. Seems like there was more back then, but I could be wrong. We looked in between all the rafters. It ain't here. I can tell you that."

Nate looked around. Only the center of the attic was floored, most of it was bare rafters. "Up then down," he muttered thoughtfully.

"Hell, could be anywhere," Levi said. "He had stills in the woods. Or it could have been in a tree stand or in some abandoned shack. When he went to brewin', he'd be gone for days at a time. There ain't no tellin' where he got to."

"You sure we'll hear 'em when they come this way?" Nate asked worriedly.

"We'll hear," Levi assured him. "You remember Axel."

Nate experienced a painful chill up and down his spine. He remembered what happened to Axel very well. Too well. He wished he didn't remember.

"Once we hear the first bark, we keep real still."

Nate nodded.

"You hungry? There's some food in the bag."

Nate shook his head. His belly was too full of fear to be hungry.

A quarter of an hour later came the sounds of dogs baying and barking, and the reactions of the boys could not have been more different. Levi settled back, put the hat over half his face and folded his hands atop his stomach. Nate stared out, trembling and breathing raggedly. The dogs were close, all around the house by the sound of it. There were sounds of horses and men shouting, too. They were surrounded.

"Whatcha' got there?" a man yelled. "Anything?"

"Check the barn," another shouted.

Nate couldn't make out all the words. For one thing, there was a rushy, roaring sound in his head. He'd never realized terror could be so noisy.

"They been here," a man called.

Nate began praying, his lips moving with the words of his silent pleading.

"Course they been here," Cheever shot back angrily. "They live here! Get them dogs of yours movin'!"

"Dogs don't lie, Miz Cheever. They got the scent."

"We need to search the place, top to bottom," another man called.

Please, God, Nate prayed, squeezing his eyes shut. *Please. Don't let them find us.*

"They're not in the barn," a voice called.

"Caint you hear?" Cheever yelled. "Are you stupid? They were here an hour ago and then they run off. Now you get those damn dogs movin!"

"We can follow the others toward town, Miz Cheever, but I wouldn't recommend leavin' yet. We should search the place. The dog stopped here which means they're here."

I'll do anything, Nate bargained with God. *At least, save Levi. He only came back for me.*

"I was *here* when I found them *gone,*" Cheever retorted furiously.

"They coulda' come back, ma'am. Or maybe you just thought they was gone."

"Either get them dogs moving or give me my money back!"

"Alright, then. Have it your way." A sharp whistle sounded and Korby hollered for his dogs. There was more barking and baying, men's voices calling to one another, and the sounds of hoofbeats.

Were they leaving?

The sounds were getting fainter. They *were* leaving. Unless it was a trick.

"It's alright," Levi whispered.

36

Nate released a slow, shuttering breath and opened his eyes to find Levi watching him warily.

"Didn't know you could turn so pale," Levi teased quietly.

Nate turned his face away, ashamed of being so close to tears.

"It's gonna' be alright," Levi said reassuringly.

~~~

"Wake up," Levi whispered, nudging Nate awake. He watched as Nate sat and struggled to get his bearings. The attic was striped with whitish moonlight from the spaces between boards in the roof overhead. It was strange looking. Levi hadn't meant to doze, but he had, so he'd experienced the same disorientation Nate was feeling.

Nate rubbed his eyes. "What time you figure it is?" he whispered.

"I don't know. Two or three, maybe. Time to go."

Nate nodded.

"We're gonna' move real slow-like. No noise if you can help it." He began scooting toward the access door. "Scoot this way, a little bit at a time." Even moving slowly, the floor creaked and they inwardly cringed with each sound. No matter what, they had to go and keep going.

Levi reached the access door and opened the panel silently, setting it aside far enough to be out of their way. He picked up the rope ladder and lowered it until there was no more. "You go first and take it slow. When you get to the bottom, step aside and wait for me. You hear anything, anything at all, just stop."

Nate nodded.

Levi watched Nate start down the ladder, moving stealthily, despite being stiff from sleeping on the floor. He reached the bottom, stepped off the ladder and looked up. Levi handed down the bag of food and started down.

Reaching the floor, he took a moment to breathe. "Gonna' try to open that window and crawl out," he explained in a whisper before going to the window and positioning himself to raise it. The effort met with resistance and then the window gave a fraction of

37

an inch with a scraping sound. Levi cursed under his breath, hesitated and then tried again.

The window yielded a few inches, enough to get his fingers underneath. No matter what, they had to go and keep going. The sound was not loud and yet it was nerve wracking enough to make his mouth go dry. Nate was so nervous, Levi could hear his labored breathing and sense his fear as if it was a third presence in the room. He got the window halfway up and then stood back and gestured for Nate to go first.

Nate got in position. He bent, put a leg over and then deftly squeezed through the opening. Levi let out a relieved sigh that they'd managed that much. He handed Nate the food bag before following.

It was a tighter, uncomfortable squeeze for his larger frame and he ended up pushing the window open further, but then he was out. Standing on the ground under a starry sky, the cold, night air had never smelled sweeter, and a sense of jubilance coursed through him.

He led the way to the barn, stepping as softly as he could. Inside the barn, he hurriedly saddled the horse and walked him away from the stall and the farm and the town and the hounds of Korby Lane. They walked until the house was out of sight and then climbed on the horse and rode at a trot and then a cantor.

The dirt road glowed under the moonlight, but when the path became surrounded by looming trees that cast erratic shadows, they had to slow to a walk. Later, when the sky began to lighten, Levi relaxed his grip enough to realize how stiff his fingers were. He flexed them. "Think I may have crippled my fingers," he muttered.

"You think we'll get away?" Nate asked hopefully.

"I think we just bet our lives on it."

Chapter Five

Mrs. Simpson, the manager of Wiley's in Green Valley, made a practice of watching new hires arrive without their knowledge. Their true character showed that way. Not like the show they often put on to try and impress her.

She was always given notice when a new girl was to arrive, and this time was no exception, although the telegram she'd received had been unusual.

New girl arriving on the 8:10 tonight. Stop. Likely more of a challenge than some. Stop. Please give her a chance. Stop. Let me know how she does. Stop. D.D.

It was from Mr. Dennis, and he'd said to let him know. In other words, he'd made a unilateral decision to hire this particular new girl. She'd only met Mr. Dennis once, but she had liked him and trusted his instincts. She'd met his partner, Mrs. Gaines, more than once and hadn't cared for her. The lady put on airs and felt herself superior.

Simpson stood back and watched as passengers disembarked from the train. She hadn't been told what the girl looked like, but she could always spot them. Without fail, they were of a certain age, attractive, nervous, and yet they held themselves just so. Generally speaking, they were image conscious and looking for adventure.

It wasn't rare for a girl to be looking for a husband or a sweetheart in a new place. As long as it was after a solid year of good service, that was fine with her. Anything less was a waste of her time and effort.

She was still mulling over Mr. Dennis's phrasing when a young woman with pale red hair stepped from the train. Simpson guessed it was her new hire until the young woman took hold of the hand of the girl of eleven or twelve who'd climbed from the train first, a lovely girl with fair hair. They might have been sisters, she supposed, except there was no physical resemblance between them. Had the younger girl been better dressed, the elder might have been a governess, but both were exceedingly poorly dressed.

Simpson focused her attention upon each passenger as they stepped to the platform, but she saw no other possibilities. She started back to the restaurant, wondering what had become of the new recruit. Occasionally, a girl got off at a wrong stop or simply changed her mind at the last minute. Perhaps that was it.

When Simpson arrived back at the restaurant, the redhead was waiting for her. Her young companion was nowhere to be seen.

"Mrs. Simpson?" the redhead inquired. There was no coy smile. No simpering. She was not the usual hire.

"I am."

"I'm Susanna Jones," she said, producing her letter of introduction.

Mrs. Simpson took it in hand and looked it over. "From West Virginia," she read. She looked up at Susanna. "Born and raised?"

"Far as I know."

Mrs. Simpson gave her a sharp look. "Yes, ma'am? As far as I know."

Something flashed in the girl's eyes. Something that might have been defiance, although perhaps the fickle light from the streetlamps was playing tricks with her vision.

"Yes, ma'am," the girl parroted with a droll expression. "As far as I know."

Simpson had not imagined the obstinacy. Likely more of a challenge indeed! She slipped her key in the lock. "How was your journey?"

"Fine. Ma'am."

The older woman opened the door and motioned the younger through. There were still lights on in the restaurant. Some were always left on as a matter of appeal to passersby. "Have a seat," Mrs. Simpson said, gesturing to a table.

Susanna sat obediently, but her expression was highly guarded, almost defensive.

40

Simpson sat across from the young woman. "Tell me about yourself."

"I'm eighteen."

"Something other than what I can read on this paper."

"There isn't much more."

"Why do you want to work here?"

"Guess you could say I need a new start."

"What was wrong with where you came from?"

Again, something flashed in Susanna's eyes. "Where I came from wasn't my choice. Nothing's ever been my choice. I want that."

Simpson studied the girl and waited for her to continue.

"I don't mind working hard. I'll work harder than anyone you got."

"Quite a statement, given that you don't know any of my other employees."

"Doesn't matter. I'm used to working, and I got more to work for than most."

"Oh? What's that?"

Susanna clammed up. She finally relented when it became obvious the manager was content to wait on an answer even if she had to wait all night. "It's like I said. I want to be able to make my own choices."

"Who is the girl?"

Confusion and then alarm registered on Susanna's face. Hers was a rather plain face, but also pleasing in its symmetry and simplicity. Her skin was pale but clear, other than a smattering of light freckles. Her hair was hard to judge, pulled back as it was, but it was an interesting color. Susanna Jones had never worked at being attractive; of that, Simpson felt sure. She probably didn't even realize she had the potential of being so.

"What girl?" Susanna stammered, looking decidedly guilty and more than a little spooked.

"The one you got off the train with. I was at the station to meet you."

Susanna was too shocked to speak.

41

"Perhaps the truth would be best," Simpson suggested. "Starting with where is she?"

Susanna suddenly looked ill. "She's on a bench across the street aways."

"Who is she?"

"Her name's Lily. I ... take care of her. She's my sister."

"But not a blood relation," Simpson guessed.

Susanna frowned. "I don't have any blood relations that I know of and neither does she." She paused and then blurted, "I couldn't leave her behind."

"And yet how did you think you would manage?" Simpson demanded. "Did you think I wouldn't notice? Where did you imagine she would live?"

Susanna swallowed. "I ... hadn't figured it all out. I just couldn't leave her. That's all."

Simpson huffed, because she'd never encountered the like. "Go and get her," she snapped.

Susanna looked miserable as she rose and left the restaurant.

"More of a challenge, indeed," Simpson muttered as she rose. She took off her coat and strode to the kitchen because she'd heard Susannah's stomach growling. She got out a bowl and cracked eggs harder than necessary and then began whisking them for an omelet. Obviously, the girls had to be fed.

By the time a chagrined Susanna and Lily stepped back into the restaurant, Susanna obviously having shared the news, dinner had been set out for them. The girls' collective gaze went to the food. "Sit. Eat," Simpson ordered.

Susanna looked even more miserable, if that was possible, but a grateful smile lit Lily's face. "Thank you," the younger girl said.

Some of Simpson's ire slipped away. The girl had a sweet disposition if first impressions could be trusted, and hers generally could.

"Thank you," Susanna repeated, although she didn't look at Simpson when she said it.

They still hadn't moved a muscle. Lily clutched her hands in front of her, Susanna stared at the floor. "Would you care for milk to drink?" Simpson asked.

"Yes, please," Lily replied.

Simpson went back into the kitchen. When she returned with two glasses of milk, the girls were seated. She set the glasses down in front of them then stepped back and crossed her arms. "You'll eat and be given a room for the night." She looked at Susanna directly. "Not in the dormitory. I'm not sure you will ever see the dormitory because I'm not at all certain you will be allowed to stay."

Susanna didn't reply and Simpson turned and went back into the kitchen to clean up. Before she'd finished, the girls carried their dishes into the kitchen, having eaten quickly.

"Thank you for the food," Susanna said without any visible emotion. She was a tough thing, used to a hard world and making do on her own. Simpson knew her type. In fact, she, herself, had been the type many years ago. Fortunately, she'd been given a place in the world with Wiley's. Of course, she hadn't shown up with a ward in stow and a chip on her shoulder.

"It was really good, ma'am," Lily said.

"We'll wash and dry these," Susanna said, moving toward the sink.

"Leave them," Simpson snapped. "Follow me." She picked up a pitcher of warm water and led the way to the corridor and toward a narrow back stairway. She'd already lit the lamp at the base of the stairs and one in the room above. "The room upstairs will do for tonight."

No one spoke again as they climbed the shadowy stairs. They crossed a small landing and entered a room used for company officials when they made a site visit or for a waitress who suddenly took ill. It was a plain room with two beds, meant for nothing other than a convenient place to sleep.

Simpson walked over and left the pitcher next to the ewer. She turned back to face the girls, and found their expressions to be telling. Susanna's was utterly closed off. Lily's was beseeching. She was worried for herself as well as Susanna.

43

"Do you want to tell me anything before I go?" Simpson challenged. She waited but neither girl spoke.

Lily glanced at Susanna and then dropped her gaze to the floor.

"The truth about where you came from, why you're here, what you were thinking," Simpson added crossly.

"I already told you," Susanna said.

Lily looked back up at Simpson. "Please let her stay."

Susanna looked at Lily. "Shush! I'm not staying anywhere without you."

"Lily cannot stay here," Simpson said equally sharply. "I have no idea what you were thinking. Our girls work a five-hour shift, take a rest break, then work another shift. It is *work*. This is a place of business. There is no place for a girl her age."

Susanna scoffed bitterly. "She's been working more than that and harder work than this for years. But you know what?" Susanna's chin shot up. "Thank you very kindly for the food and the place to sleep and we will be on our way in the morning."

The sheer audacity of the girl – being angry at her! "And do what? Go where?"

"We'll find something," Susannah replied curtly.

Lily watched the tense interaction with her breath held.

"She has no other family? No one else?"

"No!"

Simpson directed her attention to Lily since Susanna was clearly going to ruin whatever chance she might have been given. "Lily, come with me please," she said as she turned toward the door.

"She's not going anywhere with you," Susanna said, taking a protective step forward.

"Oh, but you were content to leave her across the street, sitting by herself in the cold!"

Lily touched Susanna's arm. "It's alright," she said, beseechingly.

"We are only going downstairs," Simpson said to Susanna, not withholding any of her displeasure for the stubborn girl. "Come," Simpson said more gently to Lily, and the child followed. Simpson

44

had no doubt as to the daggers Susanna Jones was staring into her back right now, but she didn't care. She led the way downstairs and into her office, where she turned up the lamp on the desk. "This is my office."

"It's nice."

"Please, sit," Simpson said. Lily sat, her hands folded tightly in her lap. Simpson also sat. "I apologize that I didn't introduce myself properly. My name is Annabelle Simpson. People generally call me by my surname."

"Annabelle's a pretty name," Lily said.

"Lily is a pretty name, too. And you are lovely. Any family would be lucky to have you as a part of it."

Lily lowered her head as if to study the pale hands clenched in her lap.

"Will you tell me about yourself?" Simpson asked. "I want to understand your situation. And Susanna's. I know I can come across as ... hard."

"Oh, no ma'am," Lily rejoined. "We don't think that, at all."

"Stern, then. But I have to be. This is a business, for which I'm largely responsible."

Lily nodded.

"So, will you explain your situation?"

Lily thought about where to begin. "I used to live with my mother but, she got sick. When she died, my aunt and uncle brought me to the Home. They didn't want to, but ... they couldn't afford to keep me. They have six children of their own."

"I see. How old were you?"

"When I went to the home? Almost nine. My aunt said a nice family would come for me, so I'd be better off there."

"Is that where you met Susanna?"

"No, ma'am. Mrs. Cheever showed up and took me."

"Mrs. Cheever?"

Lily nodded. "That's where I met the others. Mrs. Cheever had taken them, too. To work on her farm."

"I see. Who are the others?"

"Besides Susanna, there was Levi. He's almost grown. And Nate. Cheever usually called him Darkie."

"Darkie?"

"On account he's half negro." She paused. "Cheever called it his everlasting shame."

Simpson frowned. "Did she?" she murmured.

A quick smile broke through on Lily's lips. "But Susanna said meanness was Cheever's everlasting shame. Levi used to say she was ugly inside and out. 'At least you ain't ugly.' I mean, Levi said that to Nate. He said ain't. I don't. Mama said not to, cause people would think you're not very smart if you did. But sometimes Susanna uses it and she is smart."

"Is she?"

"Yes, ma'am," she replied, nodding fervently.

"So the two of you left Mrs. Cheever's. Without her knowing, I assume?"

Lily looked away. "Umm—"

"You must have had a reason," Simpson said.

The office door opened wider, and Susanna stood there. Obviously, she'd been eavesdropping.

"You want to know the reason?" she asked with an icy anger. "We worked fourteen hours every single day. Make her mad and she'd refuse you meals. Or take a stick to you. Or whatever else she could lay her hands on. You want to know the reason? We'll show you the reason." She looked at Lily. "Let her see your shoulder."

Lily looked stricken, but she stood obediently, turned and unbuttoned her blouse, then slipped it down several inches. A threadbare shift covered most of her back, but a scar near one shoulder was visible. The scar was ugly, the skin raised from where it had been gouged by the looks of it.

"That was done with a belt buckle," Susanna said. "Cheever didn't like none of us, but she had a particular dislike of Lily. Most of us she took from the home to work like mules. Lily she took for no other reason than to be cruel to."

Simpson shifted in her seat, highly uncomfortable. "Lily, you can cover yourself."

"It was high time for me and Levi to move on," Susanna said. "But no way we were leaving Lily and Nate to pay for it."

46

"So Levi took Nate and you took Lily," Simpson surmised.

"That's right."

"You could have told me when I asked," she snapped.

Susanna stood in stubborn, rebellious silence, so Simpson looked at Lily. "I am sorry you were treated so unkindly. That sort of cruelty is … inexplicable and inexcusable." Lily was also silent, clearly at a loss for how to respond. "Why don't you go on up to bed and get some sleep? I'm certain you're tired from your journey."

"Yes, ma'am," the girl said quietly. "Goodnight."

"Goodnight."

Lily started from the room and Susanna moved aside to let her pass, then followed, giving Simpson one last chilly look. The meaning was clear. Do what you will; I'll take care of her. The young woman was infuriating, and this was not the way Annabelle Simpson should have been spending her evening.

Chapter Six

Doll Summers Shaw, five feet four inches tall and weighing a hundred and seventy-five pounds, was not known for skimping. Not on affection, not on portions she dished out as cook of the Martin-Medlin farm and not on matters of opinion.

On this early morning, as she placed her supply of goat cheese in front of Simpson, she eyed the woman critically. They were both about the same age, give or take a few years, and Simpson usually looked sharp and ready for battle. This morning, however, she had dark circles under her eyes, and she looked lost in thought and not happy thoughts, either.

Kitchen preparations were going on around her with the usual fervor, but Simpson stood in a daze. "You look like five kinds of hell," Doll stated.

That snapped Simpson out of it. "I beg your pardon?"

"You don't have to beg; you got it. You still look like you've been a week without sleep."

"I have been *one night* without a great deal of sleep," Simpson retorted. "Although it's exceptionally rude to comment on it."

Doll was unfazed. "Why don't you take a load off your feet, and I'll fix you right up," Doll said as she went toward the pots of coffee brewing on the stove.

"I can get coffee in my own kitchen if I want it," Simpson replied, and yet she walked over and sat at the table where the staff took their meals when on duty.

Doll poured two mugs of coffee and then poked around shelves and cupboards, adding a spoonful of this and that to the coffee. The kitchen staff gave her free rein, even Peg, the head cook, although she surreptitiously watched the preparation.

"What is this?" Simpson asked when Doll set a mug in front of her. It was light with cream and there was a scent of cinnamon and something else she couldn't quite identify.

48

"It's good, that's what it is." Doll waited for Simpson to take a sip and approve, even if she didn't say so, then she sat catty-corner from her. "So why couldn't you sleep? I come here week in and week out, and I've never seen you with all that luggage under your eyes."

"Luggage?" Simpson repeated wryly.

"Some people get bags, but you got a whole set of luggage."

Simpson rolled her eyes and sipped more coffee. "What's the spice?"

"That brew is to perk you up and loosen your tongue. So?"

Simpson sighed tiredly. "So, a new girl showed up last evening with a child."

"You mean a babe? She had a babe out of wedlock?"

"No, no," Simpson replied irritably. "The child is a girl, twelve years of age or so, I would guess. A … sister, if you will."

"What does that mean? A sister-if-you-will?"

"It means they're not blood related. They were adopted by a woman. An exceedingly cruel woman who used them for farm labor. Susanna, she's the new hire, was old enough to move on, but she refused to leave the younger girl there."

Doll nodded.

"Lily is her name and she is a lovely child, sweet as can be. I feel for her, for both of them really, but a girl that age cannot stay here, of course. I've thought and thought about other suitable arrangements."

Doll nodded again, her expression thoughtful.

"I don't think orphanages take in girls her age," Simpson continued. "Besides, Green Valley doesn't have one. The closest might be in Roanoke, and Susanna wouldn't agree to that."

"Interesting," Doll murmured. "They got here last evening and you already care this much?"

"I didn't say I cared," Simpson snapped. "But it is a problem. And I'm not without a heart, you know."

"I guess I know it now," Doll teased.

Simpson started to make a sharp reply when she accepted it had been said in jest.

"Why don't you bring her to meet me?" Doll said. "Or I'll go with you. They at Wiley House? Maybe I can help you out."

"How would you help?"

"We could probably take her in. We always got more to do than we can get done and it's a good place. You know that. Em can always use a hand with the little ones."

Simpson gasped softly and sat up straighter, her eyes wide. "Oh, it could work, couldn't it?"

Doll shrugged. "I'd think so."

Simpson stood, suddenly all vim and vigor. "I'll bring her down. They're just upstairs." She tried to hold back a smile as she started from the kitchen with a brisk step. "Before you leave," she called over her shoulder, "I want to know what went into that coffee."

Doll chuckled. "I'll bet you do." Doll looked over and exchanged a smug smile with Peg.

Simpson was back shortly with the girls following. "Lily, this is Mrs. Shaw."

Doll, who'd been chatting with Peg, turned to see a fair-haired, too thin and yet beautiful girl in a raggedy, ill-fitting dress. Behind her, was a young woman who looked highly suspicious.

"Call me Doll," she said as she offered her hand to Lily, who reached out and took hold uncertainly. Doll gave it a firm shake. "It's a real pleasure, Lily. And you must be Susanna," Doll said, turning to her and sticking out her hand.

"Ma'am," Susanna said, taking hold.

Her handshake was firmer, her skin more callused, but the greeting was no less tentative and far less friendly. Lily's stance was stiff, her expression one of worry because she thought she was being judged, which she wasn't. Doll liked the girl at first sight and would likely love her dearly in no time.

"No one calls me Mrs. Shaw," she said with a wink. "I got hitched a couple of years back, if you can believe that, but I caint get used to having a different name."

Lily gave her a shy smile.

50

"I'm married to Wood," Doll continued. "That's his name. He's not actually made of wood." Lily smiled full out and it was like a burst of sunshine that made Doll grin. "Although he can be stubborn enough that he might as well be."

Peg had gone back to her work, and activity continued all around them as breakfast preparations were in full swing.

"I got a place for you to live if you want," Doll continued. "I think you'll like it. I know I do. We all do."

Susanna folded her arms and frowned darkly.

Clearly, the young woman was a wall of resistance that might as well be handled, so Doll looked at her. "I know you're worried about her, but she won't be far off. You can come visit when you can and we'll see you here, too. I bring a batch of goat cheese on a weekly basis, usually. How would that be?"

"It sounds wonderful," Simpson replied.

Susanna didn't speak.

"Lily?" Doll asked.

Lily nodded.

"Good. Well, you've got your work to get to here," Doll said to Susanna. "And we'll be off to get her settled in at the farm."

"The farm?" Susanna repeated sharply.

"The Martin-Medlin farm. It's a good place, honey. You don't need to worry."

"How much will you make her work?" Susanna snapped.

"We all have chores. We all have our jobs to do, and she'll be no exception. But it won't be too much. It'll be helping me in the kitchen or helping with the little ones." Susanna's expression and stance didn't alter, and Doll considered for her a moment before saying, "Simpson here tells you I'm good people, and you already know she is, since she didn't toss you out on your hind end when you broke the rules. Am I right?"

Susanna didn't answer.

"I'm telling you my people are good people, so how about you show a little faith?"

"I want to," Lily said softly to Susanna.

Susanna looked conflicted which caused Simpson's patience to snap. "Honestly! You create an impossible situation and then

51

you are presented with the most perfect of solutions and all you do is glower."

"C'mon, Lily," Doll said. "Let's skedaddle out of their way and I'll tell you about everybody on the way home," she said, starting for the door.

Lily ran to Susanna and threw her arms around her, hugging her tightly. Susanna patted Lily's back while looking at Doll with a *you'd better take care of her* look.

Lily next hugged Simpson. Simpson smiled warmly at the girl. "You'll like it," she whispered. "I promise."

Across the kitchen, a cook by the name of Gladdie flicker her hand at another cook, who looked up from the potatoes she was peeling. Gladdie nodded toward Simpson, having rarely seen such a soft side to the woman.

"You got belongings to fetch?" Doll asked Lily.

"Just my coat on the hook," Lily replied.

"In that case, we'll go pick you up a few things you'll need at the store," she said. "Then we got to get, because I got the noonday meal to get to. Did I tell you I'm the cook?"

Lily shook her head.

"You like cooking? You ever learned how?"

"Yes, ma'am. I can do it, but I'm not very good at it."

"Maybe you didn't have the right teacher."

~~~

Simpson and Susanna watched the interaction as Doll and Lily left. Simpson realized Susanna felt bereft, although the young woman would never have admitted it. The best thing to do was to get her busy and keep her busy. "Beth," she called to one of her girls who had just entered the kitchen.

Beth was the ideal girl to take charge of Susanna. She had a pretty face, curly dark hair, large brown eyes and the best disposition of any of her girls. She was one that genuinely wanted to help.

"Yes, ma'am?" Beth asked, coming closer.

"This is Susanna Jones. Susanna, this is Elizabeth Baker.

Beth smiled at her. "Everyone calls me Beth. It's nice to meet you."

"Nice to meet you," Susanna repeated, although it didn't sound terribly sincere.

"Do you go by Sue or Susie?" Beth asked.

"No," Susanna replied firmly.

"Take her to the dormitory and get her set up," Simpson said to Beth, irritated at Susanna who was clearly looking a gift horse in the mouth. "Go through the menu with her and explain our procedures. You will be her trainer."

Beth lit up. "Yes, ma'am. I'd be happy to do it, but I have my shift this morning."

"We'll be fine. This is more important. By the supper shift, I want her to shadow you, and I would like her on the floor no later than Friday."

Beth nodded eagerly and looked at Susanna with a bright smile.

Susanna remained stoic.

"Go," Simpson said brusquely, and the girls went. Beth began chatting amiably about who was who and what was what, while Susanna looked lost and unhappy. Oh, yes, Simpson thought. They would be a perfect pairing. Complete opposites.

"We have a right nice farming operation," Doll said as she drove.

The day was cold, but Lily felt a warmth unlike any she'd ever known. Doll had bought her new things, including a new coat, gloves and hat, which she was wearing. Besides her new winter wear, a thick wool blanket stretched across their laps. All around them was beautiful country with mountains in the distance no matter which way she looked.

Doll talked a lot and laughed easily, and she'd seemed to enjoy buying the things at the store. Doll had the storekeeper put the items on her tab, but Lily saw the prices. She couldn't believe what Doll had spent.

"We grow wheat and tobacco and corn and barley. We change up what we grow and where we grow it. They call that crop rotation. We have some livestock and just a real nice operation. It's owned by Tommy and Emeline Medlin, and you will love them. Emmy was the niece of Ben Martin, who first owned the farm. That's why it's called the Martin-Medlin Farm."

"Oh."

"When he passed, Em tried to keep it going all by herself, but it was real hard and she didn't have enough money. But then she and Tommy started working together and they fell in love." Doll winked at her, and Lily smiled. "Now they have three little ones, a little girl name Caty who's six, Julianne who's four and a baby boy named Ben who's a year and a half."

"After her uncle," Lily said.

"That's right."

"That's nice to name a baby after somebody. Were you named after somebody?"

"Nope. Apparently, I was such a little doll when I came into the world, that's what they called me. Still am, some say."

Lily giggled.

"Caty is shy as can be. She looks just like her daddy. Our little Jewels, on the other hand, looks like a cross between her mama and daddy. She has her daddy's dark hair and blue, blue eyes, but her mama's nose and smile. She's a sweetie, of course, but considerably more apt to get into mischief than Caty ever was.

"Then along comes Baby Ben, and he looks like Emmy. He wants to hurry everywhere and climb on everything. Not a day goes by that he doesn't have a lump or a bump from some fall. He just refuses to stay in one place. Wears us all out."

It sounded wonderful to Lily. "I like babies," she said.

Doll gave her a smile. "I do, too."

"In the home, I helped in the nursery sometimes. I know how to change diapers."

"That's good. That'll come in handy. I'm not a bit sure Ben will be their last little one."

"Sometimes the babies died," Lily recalled as she looked out to the mountains. "One of the matrons, Mrs. Palmer, she could tell which ones were going to die and she told us not to bother with those."

Doll frowned, troubled by the notion.

"Sometimes I would, anyway if she wasn't around. They were so little. It wasn't their fault they were there."

"No, it wasn't," Doll agreed. "You are right about that. Well, Ben's not so little. He's a handful."

"Do you like being married?"

Doll chortled. "Yeah, I like being married. The man plum chased me till he wore me out, but we're good together. We were kind of like an old married couple since the day we met, so I thought why not? We moved into the original farmhouse because Tommy and Em built themselves a bigger house. The farmhands all live in what we call the long house. That's where I cook and serve meals."

It took a few moments before Lily got the nerve to ask. "Where will I be?"

"I figure with Wood and me. Upstairs in the house is a nice bedroom. I think you'll like it. It used to be Em's when she was your age."

"I never had my own room."

Doll reached over and patted the girl's hand. "I think you'll like it."

Lily sat ramrod straight as they drove up the long driveway. The white-washed farmhouse that Doll pointed out as theirs was picturesque, and the other buildings were nice, too. There was a big, pale-yellow house in the near distance with a porch on the first floor and a veranda on the second. It was beautiful, but she liked the smaller, white farmhouse even better.

"That's Tommy and Em's place," Doll said, pointing at the yellow home.

Lily couldn't look hard enough at everything. There were horses and cattle and men working in the field, although nothing was growing yet. A large dog slept on the porch of the farmhouse.

"That's Doon," Doll said. "Big ole worthless dog, but we love him. And there's a cat named Pritty and another mutt we call Bob.

Creatures just seem to find us. It's like they know we're an easy mark."

A stomach-hurting worry had taken hold because the thought of living here seemed too good to be true. "It's so pretty," she managed to say.

"Well, thank you, honey."

A dark-haired little girl came running around the corner of the long building across from the farmhouse and stopped short when she saw them.

"Hey, Jewels," Doll called cheerfully.

The girl turned abruptly and ran back the way she had come.

Doll chuckled with delight. "It's exciting to have news to share. Give it about a minute and here'll come the rest of them."

Doll parked the wagon, and they climbed down. Lily's knees felt funny and springy, she was so nervous. She turned around and saw a pretty lady carrying a baby and coming toward them with her young daughters trailing behind.

"Hey, sweetie," Doll called. "I hope you don't mind, but I went and got me a girl of my own," she said playfully.

Em was surprised; Lily could tell, but she didn't seem upset.

"I thought you were just getting supplies for the week," Em replied teasingly.

"This is Lily," Doll announced, putting an arm around her. "Lily, this is Em and Caty and Julianne and Little Ben."

Lily couldn't breathe very well. "Hello," she managed in a small voice.

"Hello, Lily," Em returned with a smile. Em was beautiful.

"Caty, honey," Doll said. "Why don't you and Jewels show Lily the house?" she said with a backwards jut of her thumb. "Especially the loft. That will be her room."

Caty nodded eagerly and the little girls started forward, so Lily followed them. She realized the women wanted to talk without her hearing. Em seemed kind, but it was possible Doll would have to drive her right back to town again if Em didn't want her to stay.

Where would she go then?

"This is the kitchen," Caty said as they walked through.

56

Lily hadn't known a kitchen could be so pleasant. A fire crackled in the hearth, and the room smelled wonderful, like cinnamon and apple. There was a table with a lacey tablecloth and a fat red jug full of wildflowers. Copper pots gleamed cheerfully and there were brightly colored rag rugs on the floor. She realized the girls had walked on, so she followed them into a cozy parlor.

The wood floor gleamed and reflected the light from the windows as well as the burning fire. There was a sofa, chairs and tables placed perfectly in front of the hearth and there was a bedroom to the left as well as a staircase leading up to a loft. It was the most perfect house. The girls were already heading up the stairs to the loft.

"Wood and Doll live here," Caty said. "We used to live here, but we live in another house now. We can show you that next."

The loft was comprised of two rooms, both with slanted walls. One side had two beds and the other had one. If she got to stay, if she got to choose, she'd choose the one with one bed and a desk and chair, a chest and a wardrobe, but it was best not to think on it too much since they might want her to leave.

"Do you like it?" Julianne asked.

"Oh, yes. It's so pretty here."

The girls smiled at her.

Lily smiled back and walked to the window peering past the curtains that matched the bedspread to the view beyond. It reminded her of a picture in a book. But why *would* they let her stay?

"Do you want to meet our cat?" Caty asked.

Lily grinned and nodded. "I sure do." She followed them from the room saying, "Thank you for showing me around."

"You're welcome," the girls said in chorus, their young voices clear and sweet.

Chapter Seven

The dormitory for the waitresses, or Wiley House, as it was known, was two blocks from the restaurant. The exterior was brick and of simple design. The interior had started out equally plain, but over the years, the young women that passed through had adorned it with personal touches – artwork, pillows, colorful curtains and objects of decor that gave it a feeling of eclectic, whimsical warmth.

Downstairs housed a kitchen, dining hall and laundry, plus a parlor for the girls' use and for receiving guests. Upstairs, there was a communal lobby and a series of bedrooms with two beds per room.

Susanna had never experienced living arrangements other than the orphanage and Cheever's farm. She'd wrongly thought the dormitory might be similar to the orphanage with narrow beds lining both sides of a stark, colorless hall. In the orphanage, someone had always been coughing. Someone had always been crying into a musty-smelling pillow, flattened by too many years of use.

She'd learned to stop crying there after the sound of it angered an older girl who then made her a target for her own misery. Susanna had indulged in tears just once more, at Cheever's, after cutting her hand on an ax that had been left in a wood pile. It was nearly dark and she hadn't noticed it until stinging pain followed the shock of blood. Or had it been the other way around?

"Staunch that," Cheever called, having seen it from the porch. "And dry up them tears or I'll give you something to cry about."

Then the old witch had taken a razor strop to Matthew who'd left the ax out. He'd just finished chopping to carry a load of wood inside, but Cheever didn't care. Her newest ward wouldn't be fit to work much for the next day or so, so there was a price to be paid.

Susanna knew then that Cheever was without mercy. More importantly, she wasn't a baby. She could take whatever the witch dished out without crying one more tear.

Wiley House was not like anyplace Susanna had seen or imagined. It was nice. It was pretty. There were cheerful-looking checkered curtains of gold, orange and green in the downstairs parlor and dining room, and several sofas in the parlor, plus upholstered chairs, and shiny, dark-wood tables with fancy claw feet.

There were colorful glass lamps and candles in brass holders and strange little knickknacks and pretty glass bowls for flowers or candy. One held peppermints.

"Want one?" Beth asked as she gave the tour.

Susanna shook her head as if indifferent, but discreetly grabbed a few when she passed and shoved them into her pocket.

Beth introduced her to the other girls, who all seemed interested and curious about her. Susanna couldn't say the same. She didn't remember even half the names because they weren't important. She'd save her memory for what was important.

Besides, she was finding the place disconcerting. It was filled with the sounds of female voices and laughter. Sounds that were strange to her. She wondered what could be so funny or if they were just nitwits. Laughter wasn't the sort of thing she'd ever be able to share in. It was just too foreign to her.

The housemother, Mrs. Geraldine Beard, was surprisingly young, perhaps thirty. Beth confided that she'd been a Wiley's girl who'd met a man and married him. Sadly, he'd died shortly afterwards.

"It was so sad, him dying, but I think she's happy here. She's got a nice suite on the end of the first floor. She said his family would have kept her, but she didn't want to be beholden. And maybe stuck," she added sheepishly. "She was only married about a year. Isn't that sad?"

"A lot of things are sad," Susanna commented dryly.

"I guess so. I wouldn't want to be beholden either. I'd rather do what she does than be stuck somewhere where you really weren't wanted. Or happy. You know what I mean?"

Susanna could have laughed at that since she'd never known any other sort of existence.

"I sometimes wonder if I'm ever going to find the right man to fall in love with and get married to," Beth chattered on. "If I don't, I wouldn't mind being a housemother. I'd like it."

The upstairs lobby was a favorite spot of the girls. It was smaller and less fancy than the parlor downstairs, with only two sofas, a few other chairs and tables, plus card tables and chairs. There was a chest full of games and decks of cards. A place for gathering and play – yet more foreign concepts to Susanna.

By the time, they reached the room she'd been assigned to, Susanna was convinced this arrangement would never work. At least, not for long. She was just too different than the rest of the girls. She was a big, ugly sheep among pretty, soft lambs. They wouldn't let her stay for long.

Her assigned roommate was Jean, a dark haired, dark-eyed woman of twenty who was about to complete her year and leave immediately thereafter. She was friendly enough, but standoffish.

"It's because she's counting the days," Beth shared quietly.

Beth asked Jean if she'd mind switching rooms with her, but Jean refused. "I'm not upping and moving everything when I'm leaving in a month. You can move in then."

Beth conceded cheerfully. In fact, she did everything cheerfully, which was a source of bafflement to Susanna. She was a good teacher, though, and she took mentoring seriously. Only an hour into working on the menu, she noticed Susanna didn't write quickly or particularly well, often misspelling words, so she taught her a number system to use instead.

"Every day, we have the whole menu to choose from, but there's also a special. We almost always have the same specials on the same day every week, and people come to expect it. I'm telling you, we up and have something different one day?" She rolled her eyes. "Lord in Heaven, you have all but *ruined* their day.

"So you rememberize," she stopped short and laughed at herself. "I mean, *memorize*. Mrs. Simpson has worked so hard to break me of that habit, so don't tell her I slipped. Anyway, you *memorize* the specials, and you just have to write a big S and circle

60

it on the ticket. For all the other meals, we'll figure out a short version you write down. Like chicken livers and gravy can be—" she jotted Chic Liv and showed it to Susanna.

Susanna shrugged. "All right."

"Shepherd's Pie?"

"SP," Susanna said.

"I'd put—" Beth wrote Shp pie. "See we have at least a dozen things on the menu, so you want to make it simple but also clear, so you won't accidentally order the wrong thing."

"I won't order the wrong thing," Susanna stated.

"I know you have a good memory, but you have to write it so the kitchen knows what it is, too. See?"

"All right."

"You want to try on your uniform to make sure it fits?" Beth asked with a smile.

"Are you always so happy?" Susanna asked.

They were seated cattycorner at a card table in the upstairs lobby. From one of the sofas where a young woman named Lorna was reading, a chuckle was heard. They glanced over and saw her watching them.

"She is," Lorna said with a smile.

"You better try on your uniform," Beth said. "You have to shadow me later, so—"

"That means, follow you around?"

Beth nodded as she stood and stretched. "You try on your things and I'll get us a drink. You like cider?"

"I do," Susanna said uncertainly as she stood. All this freedom and happiness made her feel off balance, like a rug was about to be ripped from under her feet, knocking her to the ground and splitting her head wide open. Then they'd probably show her to the front door for making a mess on the floor.

As she walked to her newly assigned room, it occurred to her that this would be the perfect place for Lily, once she was more grown up, but not her.

"You want something, Lorna?" she heard Beth ask behind her. "I can bring a tray."

Susanna rolled her eyes and kept walking.

"I'll go with you," Lorna replied as she rose. "She's so sour," she whispered as the two of them started downstairs.

"She'll be alright," Beth whispered back. "I have a feeling she came from a really bad place."

"Yeah, I can see that. Her clothes," Lorna said, making a face. "It's just a shame you had to get stuck with her."

"I don't mind," Beth replied earnestly. "I really don't. She's trying."

Lorna gave her a look. "Simpson will not put up with that temperament of hers, which is not your fault. I can't believe they let her stay this long."

Beth chewed on her bottom lip as she went down the stairs. She could teach Susanna to waitress, but how to be pleasant? How could she teach that?

~~~

Susanna walked toward her bed, curious about the good-sized paper bag sitting there. Peering inside, she saw an envelope on top of nicely folded clothing. She glanced around, feeling slightly panicked. This was the room and the bed she'd been told was hers, wasn't it? She didn't need to get in trouble for snooping or stealing. Jean wasn't there, but there were items in the room that she'd noticed before, including a pillow on Jean's bed embroidered with a J. This was her room.

She turned back to the bag, reached in and pulled out the envelope, relieved when she saw her name written on it in pretty penmanship. She opened it and blinked in surprise to see money. She quickly pulled out a notecard and opened it.

Susanna,
I took the liberty of using some of your signing bonus
to purchase some things you'll need. It is early for the
bonus, but I feel confident you will come through your

*training well. The remainder of the money is for anything
I might have forgotten.*
   Cordially,
   A. Simpson

Mouth ajar, her heart beating faster, she walked to the straight-back chair on her side of the room, taking the bag with her. She sat stiffly and set the bag on the floor and the note in her lap before reaching in to pull out a cotton nightgown, allowing it to fall open. It was pale blue, brand new, still with fold lines. She'd never had anything so nice.

She draped it over her arm and pulled out warm stockings, a hairbrush, a toothbrush and tooth powder. In the other bag was a new blouse, a skirt and undergarments.

Astonished, she brought the clothing to her nose and inhaled appreciatively. They smelled new. They were *new* and they were hers. Unless they changed their minds and wanted her gone right away; then she wouldn't be allowed to keep them. She clutched the armful of clothing to her chest, too dumbfounded to do anything else for the moment.

Chapter Eight

T he cold night wind stung Lawrence Hastings' eyes as he walked toward town hall at a brisk pace for the council meeting.

Stepping inside, he was surprised to find no one chatting in the foyer as usual. Hearing a voice from the chamber, he walked on, stopping short to see the six individuals of the town council sitting around the mahogany table. He was not late so, clearly, they had convened early.

Without informing him.

He looked accusingly around the table. At either end were rich men and business owners Greg Howerton and J.P. Smythe. In the middle, sat T. Emmett Rice, Henry Waters, the president of Green Valley Bank, Reverend Stephen Thompson, and April May Blue, an unmarried woman of at least sixty, who'd somehow won the position despite the fact that no woman had ever sat on the council.

Some called her the mule lady because she took in mules from the mines that were past all usefulness. He called her a pain in the buttocks. "What is this?" Lawrence asked.

"Have a seat, Mayor," Smythe said. The man was well into his sixties with thinning gray hair that he wore slicked down, and a long, well-coiffed mustache. He was rarely seen in anything other than a gray suit and a red string tie. He was not a particularly well-liked man, but he was respected for his shrewdness and success. It was speculated that his net worth exceeded two million dollars.

To Lawrence, the suggestion or perhaps invitation had sounded too much like an order, which no one had the right to do. He moved to the open chair in middle of the table between the Reverend and the banker and across from Emmett and April May, unbuttoning his coat. He sat, but immediately felt pinned in. He was used to sitting at the head of the long table, his rightful place as mayor. "You were all here early, I see. Why?"

"Because the people in this town have a problem with your sons," Greg Howerton said in his characteristically blunt style. He was the owner of a large cattle ranch, thoroughbred horses, and mines. He was an impressive looking man in his late thirties married to a woman doctor with both beauty and class.

"What problem is that?" Lawrence asked coldly.

"They're troublemakers," April May Blue said. "And they've caused enough grief around here. It's time they made their way somewhere else."

Lawrence worked at remaining expressionless. It was no wonder the woman hadn't married. No one would have her.

"Everyone knows they were responsible for the attack on Trentwell," a deep voice spoke from the back of the room. It was the sheriff, having just entered. Maybe he'd been listening all along.

"They were not responsible," Lawrence retorted angrily, turning to glare at the man. "As I made clear to you. And since when do you attend council meetings?"

"Then there was the fight that got them barred from The Corner Saloon," Howerton spoke up. "The other guy lost an eye in that one, if I'm not mistaken. And the fight with … what's the baker's kid's name?"

"Alford," Emmett replied. "You know all this, Lawrence," he added in a placating tone. "Something has got to be done."

The mayor seethed. He could not conceal it and no longer cared to try. "You cannot force my sons to leave."

"Force," Howerton mused as if the word intrigued him. "That may be true. Or maybe not. Question is, do you want to be reelected?"

So *that* was it? The threat of losing his position? "My post is one the public will decide on. I won quite handily, if you'll recall."

"A lot's happened since then," Howerton stated coolly.

Lawrence glared at him. "How dare you."

Howerton shrugged. "Your boys can make it on their own somewhere other than here."

65

"It's not simple mischief we're talking about," Reverend Thompson said solemnly in his deep, resonating voice. "We realize this is not an easy thing to hear."

"It's horseshit," Lawrence exploded, pounding the table. He stood, trembling with anger. "My sons haven't been convicted of anything except your bad opinion." He took a step back, knocking over his chair. "Shall I tell you what you can do with that … or can you hazard a guess?"

Howerton smirked, which was too much. Hastings turned on his heel and strode from the chamber with his gloves clenched in his fist.

~~~

"That went about as well as expected," April May commented in the silence that followed. "So what's our next step?"

Smythe leaned back in his chair and fixed Howerton with a look. "Who we going to put up against him, if need be? You or me?"

"Emmett," Howerton said. He looked at Emmett, who was clearly taken aback. "T. Emmett Rice. Mayor of Green Valley."

"Hear, hear," April May seconded enthusiastically.

"It's not that I don't appreciate the confidence," Emmett rejoined. "But let's give Lawrence a little time to come to his senses. He's a bit of a show horse, but he's not a bad man. "And if only Lonnie leaves, I think we could all live with that. He's the problem."

Howerton shrugged. "It'd be a start."

~~~

It wasn't until Lawrence reached for the knob of his front door that he realized he hadn't put his gloves back on. The nerve of those fools!

He went inside, threw his gloves on the table, put his hat on the rack, and went directly to the sideboard in the front parlor where he poured himself a glass of whiskey and downed it.

Marian, his housekeeper, came for his coat. He set his glass down, shrugged it off and passed it to her.

"Do you need anything?" she asked in her usual, cool tone.

"No."

She bowed her head ever so slightly and left. She always had an ever so slight frown on her highly attractive face, although her behavior was unfailingly proper. She'd been with them more than twelve years now.

She was the wife of Darren Boyd, his former clerk, and had been their daytime household help from the time his wife passed on until the time her husband suffered a fit of apoplexy that left him a senseless invalid. After that, she'd moved into a room on the first floor along with her husband. It was a damn shame the man still lived since he was a constant burden to her. Of course, she had chosen to marry a man who was considerably older than herself.

Her unspoken and yet chronic unhappiness was due to her disapproval of how Lawrence handled her husband's affairs, but what he'd offered was more than fair. The Boyd's had a room in his home. Naturally, he'd docked her pay a bit for it, but they ate his food. He provided the necessities of life. They had a perfectly sufficient room in a home on the best street in town.

This house, built in the thirties, was a grand old thing, although creaky and drafty. Lawrence liked its grandness, but detested the drafts, especially in winter. Still, there were many worse off than Marian Boyd.

He poured another drink and looked at himself in the mirror above the sideboard as he sipped. He was a fine figure of a man. He had a successful business, this lovely home, two healthy, handsome sons, and he was mayor. It was quite a list of accomplishments, and no one was going to dictate what he would or would not do.

He gave a satisfied if grim looking nod at himself and went to his chair. "Where are the boys?" he called to Marian.

After a few moments, she appeared at the door. "Timothy is upstairs, I believe. Lonnie went out."

"Where?"

"He didn't say."

67

He gave a wave of his hand dismissing her and she tipped her head ever so slightly and bid him goodnight before walking on. Lonnie had developed some bad habits, including spending entirely too much time gambling. He also drank too much.

The apple doesn't fall far from the tree.

He could well imagine Imogene, his deceased wife, saying it. She would have said it sweetly with a loving expression on her face. She'd been a good wife. She'd known him and accepted him. He'd failed her a time or two, but he'd been genuinely sorry for each instance and she knew that.

Imogene. She'd been the perfect woman, really. Attractive, but not so beautiful as to be vain. She'd been content to be on his arm when required and to take care of his home and children without complaint.

His firstborn and namesake, although they'd always called him Lonnie, was only nine years of age when they lost her. Timothy had been a mere three years of age and had no memory of her. Lawrence sighed, thinking of it, and got up to refill his glass again.

Looking at himself in the mirror, he did a quick assessment of himself as a father. It wasn't his fault their mother had passed. She might have instilled a more sympathetic nature in them, he supposed, but it wasn't his fault she'd died. They'd never missed a meal or known hardship. He'd done the best he could. All in all, he'd done a fine job.

On occasion, boys would be boys. Drink too much. Fight. Gamble. Lay with loose women. It's not as if they'd robbed a bank. He carried his drink upstairs and to Timothy's room. He hesitated a moment and then knocked.

"Yes?"

Lawrence opened the door to see Timothy seated at his desk, writing. He'd taken to writing stories at an early age. It was a harmless enough diversion, especially in that he never let it get in the way of his responsibilities. Unlike his brother with his diversions.

As a child, Timothy had anxiously shared each story he'd written. It had been a relief when he grew out of that incessant need for approval. Now, though, with his shirt collar loose and his hair tousled, Lawrence was reminded of the young boy Timothy had been. "Where did your brother go?"

Timothy glanced at his father for the first time. "I have no idea."

Lawrence considered his son. It was odd, but Timothy suddenly seemed like someone he didn't know well. It was absurd, of course. A trick of the light from the desk lamp or some such thing. "Come have a drink with me."

"No, thank you. I'm in the middle of something."

"You're writing one of your stories," Lawrence retorted scathingly. Timothy turned and looked at him without response for several seconds, expressionless, and Lawrence got the uncomfortable pang again. "Come on," he urged good naturedly. "Come have a drink with your old man."

"Fine." Timothy put down his pen and rose.

The son followed his father downstairs without speaking, the tension between them palpable. When had it gotten to be like this? Why? Timothy had been the sweetest boy ever when he was young. At the bar, Lawrence looked at his son, determined to turn the conversation and the mood around. There was no reason they shouldn't enjoy a pleasant half hour conversing. "Is whiskey all right?"

"Fine. Thanks."

Lawrence poured a glass and handed it over. "What's your story about?"

Timothy accepted the led crystal glass and sipped. "What is it you want?" he asked a moment later. "Because it isn't to hear about my *story*. You've never cared the least bit about my writing."

The words stung and then needled. "I had an interesting town council meeting this evening," he stated coolly. "Well, not a meeting exactly. The meeting had apparently taken place before I arrived."

"Oh?"

"That's right," Lawrence said. "When I arrived, the other members *declared* that you were to go." Confusion and perhaps even alarm passed over Timothy's face, which was satisfying to see. At least it was a reaction.

"To go?"

"Yes. You and your brother."

"Ah." Timothy turned and walked to the hearth and looked down at the flames as the seconds ticked by.

"Well? Have you anything to say?" Lawrence demanded.

"About what?" Timothy asked calmly.

"About *what?* What about being detested in this town? What about the fact that if I don't see you gone, they'll elect another mayor."

Timothy turned back to face his father with a smirk. "So, *that*'s what this is about. Your political career."

It was said with such scorn, Lawrence felt the sting of it again which made him angry. "What happened with the blacksmith? Trentwell?"

"You asked Lonnie," Timothy replied. "I know because I heard it. You asked, he told you, and you were satisfied with his answer." Timothy paused, but his father said nothing. "If I remember correctly, Lonnie said something like … 'We came straight home. I swear. There was no fight. It wasn't us.'"

"I recall the answer he provided," Lawrence replied through a clenched jaw. "Now I'm asking you."

"Why now?"

"Tell me!"

"He said it wasn't us, and it's true," Timothy said with great deliberation.

Lawrence heaved a sigh of relief.

"It was him," Timothy added with relish. "And whoever came back with him from Jackals."

Distress flickered on his face, but then his expression filled with repulsion. "You're just saying that," he said under his breath.

"Come now, you're not that naïve, father." Timothy moved to the middle of the striped settee and sat with apparent nonchalance. He took a drink before continuing. "I was there at DeWitt's that evening. We'd both had too much to drink. I lost at blackjack. He

70

lost at poker and got loud about it. He spit on someone." Timothy canted his head. "You've seen him lose a game."

Lawrence swallowed and stared hard at his youngest not willing to concede the point.

"Anyway, once he was kicked out, I left, too. He was livid, drunk, so I tried to talk him into coming home, but I've never had any luck at that. He does exactly what he wants to. You know that, too. That night, he went on and on about teaching the cheater a lesson. Meaning Trentwell."

"Did he cheat?"

Timothy scoffed. "Of course not. DeWitt's is a professional gambling establishment. They smell a cheater from a mile away and show him the door. Lonnie was irate because he lost. Not only did he lose all his money, he threw in grandfather's gold pocket watch and lost that, as well."

Lawrence felt hot and then cold fury. That watch had been his, part of a meager inheritance. He'd given it to Lonnie last Christmas, but it had meant something. He'd hoped it would be the start of a worthy tradition. And Lonnie had bet and lost it in a drunken card game?

"When Lonnie went for *the boys,* meaning jackals from Jackals … since I wasn't 'man enough to help teach the hayseed a lesson,' his words, mind you, I knew what would happen. No," he immediately recanted, recoiling a bit. "I don't mean to say what actually happened. I thought they'd jump him. Land some blows and take his money. I never imagined the brutality of the attack. That they'd smash the bones in his hands to bits."

Lawrence grimaced.

Timothy looked straight ahead. "So I am partially responsible."

"No, you are not!"

Timothy glared at him. "I should have gone back in and warned Trentwell. I could have alerted someone, but I didn't. You'll never know how deeply I regret that. It eats at me," he declared pounding his chest with his fingertips."

Lawrence clenched his free hand into a tight fist at his side, detesting himself for how much he hadn't seen.

"When I learned what happened to him, what my brother and his goons had done, I was sick to my stomach. I vomited. And then I cried. It wouldn't have been a proud moment for you," he added bitterly. "Not how a real man behaves, is it?"

"Why should I believe you?" Lawrence asked weakly, despite what his gut told him.

Timothy stood. "Believe me or don't," he said. "I don't care. I can tell you that I was home long before him, and I wasn't covered in blood as I imagine he must have been." He walked back and handed the glass to his father.

Without thinking, Lawrence took it.

"I agree with the town council," Timothy stated. "It is time we left here. Will you offer some financial support to get me started in another town? I'll pay you back, of course."

"I told the town council what to do with their demands! No one chases my sons out of town. I have not worked my way to this position to—"

Timothy turned and started off. "Goodnight."

"Timothy!"

Timothy stopped and turned back to face him.

Lawrence shook his head, overwhelmed by a sense of loss and confusion. "What has happened to you?"

"Tonight? Nothing much. Or did you mean over the last—" he paused and blew out a breath as if in deep concentration. "Let me think. How long has it been since you asked that. Oh, I know. Never. You've never asked." He paused for effect. "You never cared. Don't bother starting now."

Timothy walked on and this time Lawrence let him go. He felt unsteady as he walked to the closest chair and sank into it with Timothy's words ringing in his ears.

~~~

The next morning, before the clock struck the seven o'clock hour, Marian walked into the kitchen and halted, stunned to see Lawrence sitting at the kitchen table. The vain man who took great

72

pride in his appearance, hadn't slept or changed his clothing from the day before. "Are you unwell?" she asked.

"The night that young man was attacked, the blacksmith—" he began in a hoarse voice.

Shocked by the words, she abruptly turned to the stove. "I'll make you some tea."

"Did you see my sons return home that night?"

How strange that he was actually asking her. "No," she replied hesitantly. "Not exactly."

"What does that mean?" he snapped. "Either you did or you did not."

She turned to face him. Crossing her arms, she said, "I was warming some milk when I heard someone come in that night. Within moments, there was a banging of sorts and I went to see to it." She paused. "Timothy had tripped going up the stairs. He was inebriated, but he said he was fine."

"What time was it?"

She thought about it. "Eleven. Perhaps quarter past."

"And Lonnie?"

"I heard him come in later. He used the backdoor. He was … noisy."

"How much later?"

"It was nearly one."

His eyes narrowed as he observed her. "Go on. You're not saying something."

She was suddenly nervous. He might penalize her for what she said, and she had nowhere else to go. She loathed the man, but she needed this job to survive. Who else would take her in with an invalid husband?

"Sit," he ordered. "Please," he added more civilly.

She pulled back the chair across the table from him and sat, holding herself erect. He seemed miserable. If he was a better man, she might have felt sorry for him.

"You heard him come in," he repeated. "But you didn't see him?"

She nodded. She wondered if he would let it go at that.

"Do you have any reason to suspect he had something to do with the attack on Trentwell?"

So, he was using the young man's name now. She'd encountered Garrett Trentwell a time or two and he was a fine young man. So much better than Lonnie. "There was a smear of blood on the door," she said. "And that night, he burned his shirt in the fire." She paused before adding, "I noticed he was wearing a different coat the next day, an older one. I wondered why. Then I saw his coat was wet where it had been washed, but it was still stained. Blood stained. Ruined. I haven't seen it since, so he may have burned it, as well."

Lawrence considered in silence until he remarked. "That could all mean something else entirely."

Now *that* was the Lawrence Hastings she knew.

"I'll take that tea now," he said coolly.

~~~

When she rose to make tea, he got to his feet and went upstairs. He stopped in the hallway and looked at each of his son's closed doors. He'd heard Lonnie come in at two in the morning, insensible with drink. He had waited up to speak with him but there was no point when he was liquored up.

He walked on to his own room feeling hollow and sad, especially about Timothy. He'd never told anyone, but, for years, he'd been burdened by a reoccurring nightmare in which he suddenly realized he had left his young sons for a lengthy period of time. Lonnie was young in the dreams, Timmy a mere infant. When he hurried back into the home, Lonnie seemed unscathed, but Timothy was frail, wearing a soaked, soiled nappy. The remorse that descended was all consuming. When he picked Timmy up, he weighed practically nothing. He'd done this terrible thing. He'd been negligent, and it broke his heart.

Lawrence shook his head and muttered, "No." He would not indulge in these maudlin musings. Perhaps he hadn't been the finest parent, but he had been an excellent provider, and he could still provide them a good and fitting life.

74

Lonnie needed reining in, and he would see to that, but he would not give them up! There was a path forward and he would find it. He had not worked this long and hard to fail now.

Chapter Nine

Jemima Bullock walked into the smithy with what felt like the weight of the world on her narrow shoulders. She was forty-three but she knew she looked ten years older. She ran a boarding house to support herself and her children, her husband having left them long ago. Left and never looked back.

The blacksmith she'd come to speak with, Wayman Brock, was not yet forty, but he looked younger. He was considered the finest blacksmith in town and had the workload to prove it. He enjoyed his business and those that worked for him. He had great responsibilities including a wife and four young children, not to mention an ailing father who had recently moved in with them. He considered his apprentices and journeymen his responsibilities, as well which is why Jemima was there.

Wayman looked at her with a wary expression. It was unusual for him to be in the shop by himself, but she was glad he was. There was no point beating around the bush. "Garrett is a fine young man," she began with tears in her eyes.

Wayman set down his tools. "Yes, he is."

"But I'm not running a charity," she said softly. "I'm simply not in a position to."

"I know."

"I wish I was," she added. "I feel terrible for him. He sits alone in his room, barely touches his food. He's not a bit of trouble or worry, but I need the room for the income."

Wayman sighed. "I understand. You're not a charity. Nor am I, but we've got to do all we can for him."

"I have," she rejoined earnestly. "That's what I came to tell you. I have to take his room back. I … was hoping you would tell him."

Wayman looked away and ran a hand over his chin before looking back at her. "Can you give me until tomorrow to find a place for him?"

She nodded and started to leave but turned back after only a few steps. "Those Hastings ought to have to pay for what they've done," she said bitterly. "They ought to have to pay for him for the rest of his life." She let out a shaky breath and walked on.

Wayman didn't disagree, but it was a futile statement. People like the Hastings never had to pay for damage they caused. Poor Mrs. Bullock looked in distress as she left the smithy, passing Albert and Dan, his apprentices, along the way. The boys were returning with buckets of coal, one of their never-ending chores.

With the loss of Garrett, he'd have only one other journeyman, Fred, who wasn't nearly as talented as Garrett. It wasn't the most important consideration at the moment, but it was a consideration. Already, the workload for all of them had increased and the output was not the same as before. Garrett had been even more of an asset than he'd fully appreciated.

"Fred's headed back," Dan reported. "Shall we build up the fire?"

"Yes," Wayman replied. "We've got jobs to finish this day. Build it up and make it hot."

"Did Miz Bullock say how Garrett was?"

"The same," Wayman replied before turning his back to them. He leaned onto the worktable with a heavy heart. The small rooms the apprentices slept in held just enough space for their beds and few possessions. There was no place for Garrett here or at his home. But there *had* to be a place for him somewhere.

"I'm going out for a while," he said. "I need to see Reverend Thompson."

~~~

Late the next morning, Jemima Bullock opened her back door to admit Reverend Thompson and April May Blue with a grateful

77

smile, having received a note of explanation from Wayman. The pair came in and she shut the door behind them. "I brought a tray to him last night and again this morning," she said quietly. "He didn't touch it. Not either of them."

"I'll go and speak with him," the pastor said.

"No offense, but why don't I do it?" April May suggested. "I have a way with stubborn mules."

"He's wounded," the pastor reminded her. "Body and soul."

She nodded in agreement. "They all are," she said, before starting off.

"Upstairs," Jemima called to her. "Second room on the left."

April May reached the room and knocked. "Garrett?"

There was no response.

"I'm opening the door."

She tried it, half expecting it to be locked, but it wasn't. She opened the door and saw him sitting in a chair, staring out the window. "Good," she said. "You're up and dressed."

Obviously surprised by her appearance, he stood and turned to look at her as she came closer. He held the wrist of his partially amputated hand. It was the fingers and part of his thumb that had been taken. The stump was still bandaged.

"I think you know me. I'm April May Blue."

He started to speak, but his voice caught. He cleared his throat. "Yes, ma'am. We made that pitchfork for you last year and a few other things."

"You shore did." Garrett had always struck her as a good-looking lad, but her heart ached to see him now. He had fair hair that curled softly, and evenly placed features. There always seemed a shyness, almost an innocence about him. He'd always been lean, but now he looked frail and ill. "You're probably wondering why I'm here."

He shifted on his feet, unsure of how to answer.

"You know my sister and I have a small farm. Fact is, we could use some help and I hear you could use a roof over your head." She shrugged. "Seems like a perfect arrangement, don't it?"

He was clearly uncomfortable. "Why would you do that for me?"

78

"Why would you do it for us?" she countered. "Why not, when we can help each other out?"

His expression was one of doubt and shame. "I'm not sure what help I can be, ma'am."

"Well, truth be told, me neither. Why don't we just take it day by day and see?" He stood utterly still, unsure what of to make of her. *You wouldn't be the first,* she thought with wry amusement.

"Look, nobody is gonna' hold anybody prisoner," she said. "We realize you need a little time to get back on your feet, but I'm guessing you're going to be able to do more than you think. I'm thinking you can be a whole lot of help to a couple of old ladies. And if I'm wrong and you want to hit the road, won't be nobody to stop you or even hold it against you. So what do you say?"

"I—"

She turned for the door. "Good! I'll be downstairs when you're ready," she said cheerfully. She walked out, shut the door behind her and kept walking. It seemed important that he hear her walk away. "I could shore use a cup of that delicious smelling coffee, Mrs. Bullock," she said as she marched back down the stairs.

~~

Moonlight eked through the lace curtains and made a fascinating design on the walls and ceiling. Susanna stared up at it, nowhere close to sleep. She'd made it more than a week waiting tables without any catastrophes.

At first, the cooks had griped about her penmanship and Simpson told her to write neater, but that was it. No one slapped or hollered when an order was wrong or a something was spilled. They didn't even withhold pay when an apron or uniform got ruined.

The food was really good, and the bed was the most comfortable she'd known. The dorm was warm, heated by a contraption called a radiator. When the others complained about the hard work and long hours, she could have laughed in their faces. She imagined Cheever leering. *I'll show you hard work and long hours.*

Susanna's main worry was Lily. She'd brought her all this way only to hand her off to someone else, someone who might be treating her poorly or starving her or working her like a dog. Sometimes the fear of it caused a burning in her stomach.

"What's wrong with you?" Jean asked.

There had been little conversation of consequence between the roommates, so little, in fact, that in a month's time, each would be forgotten in the mind of the other. "Nothin'," Susanna replied tartly.

"Then why all the heavy sighs?"

"Didn't know I was," Susanna said defensively. It grew quiet, before her curiosity got the better of her and she asked, "Are you leaving to get married or something?"

"Sure am."

"Did you meet him here?"

"Nah, he's from back home." Jean yawned. "I was only here about a month when he wrote and wanted me to come back."

Susanna turned onto her side to face Jean. "Did you stay to get the bonus?"

Jean shrugged a shoulder. "Not at first. I just thought it was a good thing for him to miss me for a bit. See, before I left, he developed a fancy for a girl named Dottie York. When I left, I told him not to write me again until she was out of his system. He wrote after only a few weeks, whining and wanting me to come home, but I thought it'd be good for him to wait awhile. Then enough time went by that I decided to stick it out for the bonus."

"Did you like it here?"

Jean scoffed. "Up at five for the breakfast shift? That's the worst. Farmer's daughters don't mind it, but I wasn't a farmer's daughter. You ever figured out how many hours a week we work?"

Susanna knew it was a lot less than she'd ever worked.

"I saved up some money, though," Jean said. "I'm going to buy this dress and hat at Miss Simmon's and still have some for a private stash he doesn't need to know a thing about. If he thinks I'm gonna' be under his thumb, he's got another thing coming."

Susanna had seen Miss Simmon's store with its pink and white striped awnings covering windows filled with mannequins in the loveliest gowns and accouterments she'd ever seen or even imagined. Eleanor Simmon's spelled her shop s-h-o-p-p-e. Susanna wondered why, but she wouldn't ask for fear of being thought ignorant. "What's the dress look like?"

"It's blue and white with the prettiest sleeves you've ever seen. I'm going to wear it when I go back home." She yawned again. "Did you leave a sweetheart back home?"

"No."

"Well, maybe you'll meet someone special here," Jean said sleepily.

Susannah rolled onto her back, thinking of how little she cared about meeting someone special. What she wanted was independence. "I ain't lookin'," she murmured.

<u>Chapter Ten</u>

A pril May walked into the kitchen to see her sister agitated and pacing the floor. "You perturbed?" Cessie turned to face her with her hands on her hips. "You have him fixing the wagon?" she demanded.

"Needs to be fixed, don't it? It's not like I'm not helping the boy with it."

"He has one good hand!"

"And he needs to learn how to use it. If you think we're going to keep him around to throw out chicken feed and set the table—"

"He's only been here a few days."

"He's been here a few weeks and he's looking better and getting stronger every single day." April May poured a glass of sassafras tea and took a drink before speaking again. "I know you mean well, Princess, but babying him will not do him one bit of good. Nor will he appreciate it."

Cessie huffed, knowing she was going to lose the argument.

"He knows when he's done a good day's work. He's used to it and he wants to. Granted, he doesn't have all his strength back yet, but it don't just float back like a feather in the wind. You got to work it back."

Cessie frowned and folded her arms.

"Physically, he's mostly healed," April May continued. "Correct?"

"Yes," Cessie admitted, although April May could hear the discontentment in her voice.

April May reached for another glass and filled it. "I know what I'm doing," she added as she headed for the door. "Don't you worry your pretty head about it."

"Are you paying him extra for—"

"He is getting fair compensation," April May interrupted, turning back. "Furthermore, I told him we want him to take his wages and get hisself to town for a meal or two a week."

Cessie looked horror struck.

"Now, you cannot think it's good for him to spend all his time with the likes of us," April May said. "He *needs* to go to town. Have a meal. Have a drink. Play a card game."

"Have you forgotten that's what—"

"No, no, no you don't. It wasn't a card game that cost Garrett those fingers. It was a rotten-to-the-core individual or two. It was a crime, a sin and a terrible thing, but Garrett's life still goes on, and we need to help get him back to it. His every day and night are not going to be spent here with us. We're just a little ole' stop on his way. Now, if you will excuse me," she said as she started for the door.

"I am not for this," Cessie called.

"Why don't you bake him some cookies or something?" April May returned playfully. "Ain't nothing like some fresh baked cookies to fix what ails a body."

"Cookies," Cessie huffed under her breath. Then, again, it wasn't a bad idea. Garrett especially liked gingerbread snaps.

~~~

Garrett was in the barn, hewing the new axle, his shirt sweated through in places. April May offered him a glass of tea and looked appreciatively at his work. "Lookin' good."

He set the chisel down and then took the glass. "Thank you." He drank most of it. "That's good, too."

"Feel right to have tools in your hands?"

He nodded. "Different than before, but ... yes, ma'am. It does. Course everything takes longer."

"You've got all the time you need." She walked over to pet Ibsen, a white and gray stallion friend of thirty-five years. "You miss the smithy?"

"Seems like a long time ago since I was there."

"It wasn't so long ago." She turned back to face him. "What was it like to work there?

He set the glass aside and took the chisel in both hands and began smooth, steady strokes to finish shaping it. "The day starts early," he said. "As an apprentice, you live in the back. It's just a little room. Usually there's two of you, which is a good thing since you've got each other to complain to," he said laughingly.

She chuckled.

"Complain all the time about how hard it is. But you're loving it, too. You part of an operation you're proud of."

She grinned and nodded.

"Early in the morning, it's just the apprentices there cleaning out the forges. Breaking up and hauling in charcoal. Got to have at least two or three bushels to start. Then they start fires and *then* they get breakfast."

"Probably good and hungry by then," April May commented.

"Yes ma'am." He shifted the chisel to his left hand, his stump, and felt the wood with his right, judging the smoothness of the surface. It was apparent he was caught up in the recollection. "I did a lot of the instructing of the apprentices."

"Oh, yeah?"

"Yes, ma'am. It's rewarding when they understand how something works for the first time." He turned to her. "But the best thing was when Wayman and I were working something together. You gotta' imagine that the flames are high, the others working the bellows to keep it hot. The two of us swinging sledges on a big piece, him and then me, hitting one right after the other—"

She'd seen it and been amazed that their instruments never collided, as fast as they got going.

"It was like we were of one mind," he continued. "White sparks flying with each strike. The slowly changing shape of the piece. People used to gather and watch."

She nodded and waited for him to go on.

"I love when a finished piece goes into the water. The sizzle of it, and then the water steams. I mean, water that was just cold. And, besides us that worked there, there were always people stopping by to visit. Ordering something new or checking on the progress of something they'd ordered. It was … good."

"I know Wayman misses you," April May said. "But he'll find others. Maybe not as good as you, but he'll make do. What you need to do is think about what's next for you."

He nodded slowly, his expression somber.

"You're young, Garrett. I know it may not feel like it when you've lived what must feel a lifetime in these last weeks, but you are. You can still choose a whole new direction and do whatever you want to do."

"That's nice of you to say, but I don't have all that many choices. Besides, all those years I spent—" he said quietly, turning back to the wood he was working with.

"What?" she asked gently. "You feel like they were wasted?"

She'd hit too close to the mark and an expression of pain crossed his face. He turned further away from her and he may have wiped a tear from his eye.

She turned back to Ibsen who nuzzled her, as if to offer reassurance. Ibsen knew she cared even if she did sometimes go too far. She patted his neck. "Personally, I don't believe anything we learn is ever a waste," she said. "And that's the God's honest truth. A doctor, a great surgeon, who suddenly loses his hand in … say a carriage accident. Can he operate anymore? No, but he still got all that knowledge. How can that be anything but good?"

Garrett nodded, but he didn't look like he believed it or wanted to say more.

"You need any help with that right now?" she asked, sensing she should let him be.

"No, ma'am."

"Alrighty, then. I best go tend to my herd of wayward asses."

He grinned a cockeyed grin. "Guess I'm just another one, huh?"

She was chuckling as she left the barn, because he'd said it in good humor and that was a good thing.

~~~

85

Susanna was relieved to step into the back entrance of the restaurant because the cold wind whipped right through her coat. When she got enough pay together, she'd buy herself a decent one. Well, first she'd get Lily one, and then she'd buy herself one.

She took off her coat and hid it beneath others, as she always did. She went to the supply closet and donned a fresh apron, an order pad and a sharp pencil, glancing at the chalk board where names of girls working each shift were listed along with their assigned section of tables.

She was prepared to start the shift, but when she entered the kitchen, Peg, the portly head cook, waved her over and handed her a mug of hot cocoa so fragrant that it made her mouth water.

"Simpson's in her office waiting for you," Peg said. "Take this."

"Why?" Susanna asked worriedly as she took the mug. "Am I in trouble?"

"Well, if you are, the chocolate should help," she replied with a wink. "Go, before it gets cold."

Susanna walked on, wondering what Simpson wanted with her. She reached her office door and knocked.

"Come," was the response.

Susanna opened the door. "Peg said you wanted to see me?"

"Yes." Mrs. Simpson replied distractedly as she put her pen and ledger aside. "Come in."

Susannah walked in and set the chocolate down on the desk in front of the lady. As she did, Simpson picked up an envelope and handed it over. "This is for you," she said. "Doll was here this morning."

Susanna's smile was instantaneous. "How's Lily?" she asked anxiously.

"Sit and read for yourself," Simpson said, as she stood. "The letter is from her, and the cocoa is for you."

As Simpson started for the door, Susanna felt off balance. She still found kindness hard to accept, much less get used to. "I thought I might be in trouble."

Simpson turned back from the door. "You're doing well," she reassured. "Make yourself comfortable and enjoy your letter. I got a good report from Doll, so I feel confident you will, too."

It took a moment after Simpson had gone for Susanna to collect herself enough to sit. She reached for the cocoa and sipped, and it was just as delicious as it smelled. Setting the mug down, she opened the envelope and pulled out the letter. Lily's familiar writing was wonderful to see.

> *Dear Susanna,*
>
> *I hope you like Wiley's and Green Valley. I <u>love</u> it here so much. Doll said Mrs. Simpson's bark is worse than her bite and that I'm not to fret because you'll be as fine as a baby's eyelash. She says all kinds of funny things like that, but she's not wrong very often. That's what Wood said, although he said for me not to tell her he said so.*
>
> *They are both funny and so, so kind. You just won't believe how good they are when I tell you everything. I have my own room in the loft. I hope you can see it soon. Doll said we can go to town and I can come see you on Saturday. We're going to have lunch there.*
>
> *There are a lot of people who live here. I can't wait to tell you about them all, especially Em and Tommy. They have two little girls and a baby boy and I help with them. Em calls me her helper and says she doesn't know what she did before I was here. I love helping them.*

Susanna could feel Lily's happiness exuding from the page. It was such a relief. She smiled and sipped the cocoa as she read further.

> *My favorite thing is that every night, Doll comes up at bedtime and asks me if I'm warm enough. Then we talk about the day until Wood calls up and says to let me sleep. Then Doll makes a face and then leans over to kiss me and says 'Sweet dreams, beautiful girl.'*
>
> *I have a new best friend who is in my grade at school.*

"School," Susannah said. "They have her in school." She was in a nice place with nice people, and they had enrolled her in school. Susannah's eyes tingled.

> *Her name is Rebecca and she's helping me with arithmetic and geography. We're reading a book called* Ivanhoe *and I read a chapter to Wood and Doll every evening after supper. It's about a man named Wilfred who lived a long time ago and he falls in love with Lady Rowena, but his father gets angry and makes him leave on account of him wanting a different king. There are jousts and wars and a man named Robin of Locksley, who becomes Robin Hood. I'll tell you all about it when I see you if you want.*
>
> *I miss you and the boys, too. Will you write to me and tell me if you have gotten a letter from Levi? I'm so happy here. The only thing that would make me happier is if you and Nate and Levi were here, too. I wish we could all live here.*
>
> *Cordially and with all my love,*
> *Your sister,*
> *Lily*

Susanna squeezed her eyes shut, full of relief and gratitude that she'd been right to come here and to bring Lily. Lily was happy and that meant more than anything.

Chapter Eleven

arrett kept his head over his menu long after he'd chosen what he wanted to eat. It was strange to be here. For one thing, he'd never been much of a restaurant eater. For another, he'd received lots of nods and supportive murmurings from people he passed in the street on the way here and from the other diners. It made him uncomfortable. It made him wish he'd stayed at the Blue's or at least chosen a less busy time to come to the restaurant.

He was also dreading possibly seeing Bella, a pretty waitress who'd snubbed him a few months back. He hadn't been good enough as a two-handed journeyman and he would be even more undesirable now. Not that he worried over her opinion of him, but he didn't want to ever experience that sort of disdain again.

Luckily, he'd gotten a window seat, so he looked out the window and watched the passing traffic, only looking up when a waitress stopped at his table. He'd never seen her before, but the name embroidered above her shapely breast was Susanna.

"You know what you want?" she asked without a lot of interest and certainly no sympathy.

"The meatloaf," he said. "Just water to drink."

She jotted it down on her pad. "Anything else?"

"No, thank you."

When she moved on, he noticed Mrs. Simpson watching. He didn't want to see or have to speak with anyone else, so he went back to staring out the window.

Susanna was back in no time with his meal. "You like biscuits?" she asked quietly. "Cause that's what I brought. I was supposed to ask."

"It's fine," he said, taking his hands from his lap for the first time. She saw the stump and her eyes widened in shock. "You must be new in town," he commented.

"What happened?" she asked.

"Got attacked. Lost half my hand."

"Least it's your left hand," Susanna offered.

His face flushed and he gave her a look, galled by the words. "I am left-handed," he snapped.

She might have paled a little bit and he expected an apology. Instead he got, "Not anymore." The response was so unexpected, he couldn't form a reply. Not that it mattered because she'd turned and walked off.

Mrs. Simpson was definitely watching and she looked disturbed. He wondered what Susanna would admit of the encounter. Everyone knew it didn't take much to get in trouble with Mrs. Simpson. He looked at his meal. *Not anymore.* He couldn't believe she'd just said that. Cessie would be scandalized, but April May would probably get a good laugh out of it. He cut into the meatloaf with his right hand and took a bite. It was hot but good.

"Is everything all right?" Mrs. Simpson asked him, perfectly timing it between bites.

"Yes, ma'am. It's good."

"The waitress is relatively new," she began.

"I thought so. I mean, I didn't recognize her." Mrs. Simpson still looked troubled, so he added, "She did fine."

"I thought … perhaps she'd said something."

"No. Well, just offered to help," he said.

"I see."

He noticed she looked relieved, and he was glad he'd covered for the girl. Everyone deserved a break now and then. She hadn't meant any harm.

"Enjoy your meal," Mrs. Simpson said before walking on to inquire after another customer. She would ask a few more, so he wouldn't think he'd been singled out. Sometimes he knew things like that. It was amusing and even touching to see it play out as he'd guessed.

90

He'd eaten half his meal, savoring every tasty lump in the mashed potatoes, when someone else stopped at his table. He expected to see Susanna but looked up into the face of Lonnie Hastings. A painful chill traveled up his spine.

"Having any trouble cutting that?" Lonnie asked with mock sweetness, slurring slightly. Garrett could smell the alcohol on his breath.

"If he is," Susanna said, shoving in fast and forcefully enough that Lonnie was pushed aside. "I'll help him. You can move along."

Lonnie gave her a scathing look. "You must be new."

"Oh, must I? Why's that?"

"Cause I move along when I feel like it. Waitresses don't push me. You might want to ask around about who I am."

She looked pained. "I know a pesky fly when I see one. I don't need to ask nobody. I just swat it dead."

"Aren't you a funny one?"

"Go laugh about it outside."

"You think you can kick me out of here?"

"I think I just did. You've filled your belly and had a snoot full by the smell of it. Now, get the hell out."

Mrs. Simpson was suddenly there, looking incensed behind a forced-calm exterior. "Mr. Hastings," she said, gesturing to the front door. "Please."

Lonnie sneered and started to the door, weaving unsteadily, and Simpson followed, but only after scowling darkly at Susanna.

"Probably shouldn't have done that," Garrett said to Susanna. He felt sick and shamed and way too warm, all the sudden.

"Was I wrong? Was he a pesky fly or wasn't he? Plus half drunk. I know people."

Garrett pushed his plate away. His appetite was gone, replaced by a hard swelling of anger in the pit of his stomach that he'd let Lonnie Hastings razz him and done nothing about it. The waitress had stood up to him, but not him. What the hell was wrong with him? "Oh, yeah?" he asked dryly. "You know Mrs. Simpson?"

Susanna turned in a huff and walked back to the kitchen, and he fumbled for his money, resentful of how difficult every task was. He put the money on the table, but then froze as he experienced a flash of memory.

Of DeWitt's.

That night.

It was clear enough and powerful enough to cause a moment of dizziness and disorientation.

Sounds of laughter, glasses clinking, and voices. The smell of cigar smoke and whiskey. Emerald green curtains in the window and lush, oriental carpets under the gaming tables.

He'd won a hand of poker. Or had he won several? Lonnie Hastings called him a cheater.

"Only thing worse than a loser," a fellow card player said, "Is a sore loser."

Garrett blew out a slow breath. The return of the memory had left him shaken and he had to give himself a moment to stand.

Susanna walked back to the kitchen, wondering if she'd just lost her job. She damn well knew who Lonnie Hastings was, although she wouldn't have given him the satisfaction of letting him know that. More than a few of the waitresses were loony over him because he was good looking and rich. The mayor's son. Those girls were stupid. He was the kind who'd catch a butterfly just to pull the wings off. The type who'd kick a lame animal for no reason other than meanness. She knew people.

"What happened?" Beth asked worriedly, having walked up to her.

She deserved to know and so Susanna told her. Beth's eyes filled as she listened; she was so sure Mrs. Simpson would send her packing.

"What did you say to him?" Bella Byrd demanded angrily, shouldering past Beth.

Bella was one of the prettiest girls Susanna had ever seen, a blue eyed, honey-haired beauty. The girls all said she wanted Lonnie to ask for her hand in marriage. Furthermore, she expected it and for good reason. She'd always gotten what she wanted.

Susanna was more affronted that Bella had pushed Beth than the way she'd spoken to her. "I said he was ugly and hateful and to clear the hell out, that's what. Because he was stinkin' up the place."

Beth's jaw dropped, and Bella seethed. "*You* stink up the place," she uttered furiously. "I can't believe they let you work here." She gave Susanna a derisive once over and then turned on her heel and walked off just so that her ponytail swung back and forth.

"Susanna," Beth scolded. "You can't say things like that!"

"She *pushed* you and she said I stink. She's lucky I didn't say worse or punch her right in her face."

Beth didn't know whether to laugh or cry. "You are impossible."

"I know," Susanna conceded.

"I'm sorry that occurred," Mrs. Simpson said to Lonnie. Her tone was cool and businesslike, her hands clutched primly, as if she were about to recite a verse or launch into a grand aria.

"You ought to back in there and fire her."

"She should not have spoken so. I do not allow cursing from my girls. Her lapse in judgment and protocol will certainly be addressed."

"Uh, maybe you didn't hear everything, because she tried to kick me out. Her cursing was the least of it."

"You're wrong, sir. Rough language is not allowed at Wileys."

He shook his head wondering if the old cow was deaf or just slow. "You heard the part about she told me to get out?"

"Yes. I heard you and I heard her. Quite clearly."

"Well, why didn't you say so?"

"Because cursing is unacceptable. I thought it worthy of acknowledgement that that sort of language will not be tolerated or repeated. I'm very sorry it occurred."

"Yeah, well I don't care about that. Question is, what are you going to do about her trying to kick me out?"

"Oh, she was correct in that. You are no longer welcome in Wiley's."

Was it a joke? She couldn't possibly mean it. She couldn't get away with it. "What? I didn't do anything."

"You disturbed a diner. Several, in fact. Something else we do not allow."

He could only shake his head in utter bafflement.

"Good day, Mr. Hastings." She turned and started back inside.

"We'll see what my father has to say about this," he said, louder than necessary.

~~~

Garrett had reached for the door to leave Wiley's when it happened again. He was suddenly reliving that night.

Starting home, thrilled because he'd won something like forty-six dollars, enough to pay for his room and board for months. The night was black and freezing, but he'd won.

"Hey, cheater," a voice taunted. Lonnie's voice.

Then pain and blackness crashed upon him. What had he been hit with? No one had ever said. But he remembered hearing Lonnie's voice.

Hey, cheater.

Garrett stepped outside the restaurant feeling strange – as if he was at one end of a long tunnel. He passed Mrs. Simpson but was unsure if she said something to him. He saw Lonnie walking away and started after him, walking fast. He knew others were around, but his sole focus was Hastings. "Hey," he called just before he reached him.

Lonnie turned and Garrett's left nub flew. He didn't have to make a fist, Lonnie had arranged for a permanent one. The blow caught Lonnie's jaw, sending him reeling sideways. Garrett went after him and drove a fist into his gut.

Lonnie raised his own fists, but Garrett's jab made contact with his nose, bloodying it. His next blow knocked the wind from his assailant. He was assailing his assailant. He swung again and again and again.

94

"Garrett! Stop!"

A strong arm was around his chest and arms, forcing him back. It was Sherriff Swanson. Behind him was Bella, who was nearly hysterical.

"That's enough," the sheriff exclaimed.

"Aw, leave him, Sheriff," a man shouted.

The red fog lifted enough that Garrett could see that Lonnie was on the ground, trying to get up, his nose bleeding profusely. How many times had he hit him?

"Easier to beat a man when you knock him out from behind first," someone called. "Ain't that right, Lonnie?"

Garrett could hear his heartbeat in his ears. His body thrummed with it. The crowd seemed to be pressing in and they hated Lonnie. They would have let him kill him. They would have welcomed it. The thought sent a chill through him.

"Be on your way," the sheriff said to Garrett.

"I remembered," Garrett said to him, still breathing hard. "That night. I remembered."

"What do you remember?"

"Playing cards. Then in the alley. He called to me," he said, nodding toward Lonnie. "He called me a cheater. Then I got hit."

Swan glanced down at Garrett. "He attacked me," Lonnie yelled. "Are you blind?"

"You had it coming," someone called. "And more!"

"Payback's hell, ain't it?" someone else chimed in.

"Hardly payback," another said. "Not when he's still got both his hands."

"Be on your way," Swan called to the mouthy onlookers who'd gathered. "All of you!"

Garrett swallowed hard, shaken that a crowd had gathered. When had that happened? It was as though he was missing time. He turned and walked away, feeling lightheaded and dizzy and more than a little sick. Men and women alike patted him on the back or shoulder as he passed and offered words of support. It was the strangest feeling, almost as if he was outside himself.

~~~

Lonnie struggled to his feet, stunned by the attack and the animosity of the people around him. He fumbled for his handkerchief and held it to his nose to staunch the bleeding. That hayseed had snuck up from behind him, but *that* was just fine? The bunch of hypocrites! Not one of them knew who had beaten up Trentwell. They hadn't been there. They all just assumed it was him.

Somehow, he'd get back at all of them. He reached for his hat on the ground and had to battle dizziness on the way back up. He glared at the sheriff and started toward home, knowing none of them could touch him. Not really. They may have wanted to, but they couldn't touch him.

Bella took an unsteady step backwards, and then turned and hurried back to Wiley House, close to tears. Her shift had not yet ended, but she was too upset to go back to work. Lonnie had just *glared* at her, and the crowd had taunted him. They'd hated him. It felt as if the foundation of her future had suddenly and unexpectedly developed deep, dangerous fissures.

She made it back to her room and slammed the door, leaning against it as she began to cry. Lonnie was the son of the mayor. She'd assumed he'd have a successful career in the family business and then probably become mayor himself one day. She was planning to become his wife. She'd figured that out after only a few weeks of coming to Green Valley. It was her destiny.

She walked to her vanity and sat down to study herself. None of the others had a vanity like this one, because her parents had ordered it and had it delivered there. The mirror was large and three sided, the outside corners sitting at an angle that allowed her to see the back of her hair with use of a handheld mirror.

She sniffed and then reached for a hanky. She couldn't marry someone that everyone hated. She needed to marry someone who was respected. As a banker, her father was respected, but not to the degree her uncle was. He was a congressman. How many times she'd wished she'd been born to him. He had two daughters, but her cousins were nowhere near as pretty as she was. She sometimes wondered if he wished she was his child instead of them.

She dabbed at her eyes and worked to collect herself. Lonnie hadn't meant to glare at her – he'd just felt the animosity surrounding him. She took a few deep breaths. Maybe the situation wasn't so terrible. The mayor would stand up for his son and people would forget. Lonnie was right for her, and she was right for him. She rose, still watching herself. She was still too upset to go back to work, so she'd lie down until she'd recovered her composure.

~~~

A livid Annabelle Simpson cornered Susanna in the kitchen. "We do not curse in this establishment, as you well know!"

Susanna hadn't known exactly what Simpson was going to say, but *that* would not have been her guess. Of course, she wasn't finished yet.

"What are the rules?" Simpson demanded.

"Maintain good hygiene and a pleasing appearance," Susanna dutifully said just as she had ten times before. "Be honest, respectful and cheerful to superiors, coworkers and customers. Be on time, work hard and fulfill all duties. No cursing and no slang. Always use good manners. Say 'yes, sir,' 'no, sir,', 'yes, ma'am,' 'no ma'am', 'please' and 'thank you,' and obey dorm rules."

Simpson crossed her arms tightly. "What was that about cursing?"

Susanna's gaze dropped. "Don't do it," she muttered.

"Excuse me?" Simpson said sharply.

Susanna looked up at her, fully chagrinned. "Don't do it." She paused before adding a sincere, "I'm sorry."

"If it happens again, you are gone," Simpson warned, lowering her voice, but looking no less stern or angry.

Susanna was too surprised and grateful to respond. She'd thought for sure she was getting the ax. She nodded stiffly.

"You will stay after your shift and make sure everything is in perfect order," Simpson continued. "Every sugar bottle filled and shined. The tables spotless. Floor swept clean. Not one crumb," she said, holding up a finger, "—had best be left."

"Yes, ma'am," Susanna said with all the voice she could muster.

"I will be in my office," Simpson announced to all the other listening ears, and there were plenty of them.

After Simpson walked off and her office door closed behind her, a body could have heard a pin drop in the large kitchen.

Looking around, Susanna saw she wasn't the only shocked individual in the room. Beth's eyes were closed in a silent thanksgiving, her hands were actually pressed together. It was a surreal moment because, for one thing, Susanna realized she was looking across the room at a friend. An actual friend.

For another, she was experiencing a heady rush of relief. Perhaps it was time to admit she liked this place and this job and she liked having a friend. She liked her new life.

More than liked it.

"Susanna," Peg, the cook said, snapping her back to attention.

Susanna went to the heavy-set woman, who usually seemed harried and serious. "Yes, ma'am?"

"You've got a lot of work ahead of you today," Peg stated firmly. "Which I would take seriously, if I were you."

Susanna nodded miserably. It didn't feel like she was out of the woods yet.

"But after," Peg said quietly. The woman sniffed and glanced around the kitchen before looking back at Susanna. "There'll be a big ole' piece of cake waiting for you," she finished with a wink.

Did Peg realize what she'd actually done and said? Did Simpson know or was more fallout coming? "I told the mayor's son to clear out," she admitted just above a whisper. She couldn't take not knowing if she was about to be fired because they didn't know what she'd really done.

"Only in more colorful terms, I heard. Wish I'd been standin' there. Go on, now," Peg said, flicking the back of her hand at Susanna's rump. "You got work to do."

Susanna walked on numbly. When she went through the door, Beth linked arms with her. "I'll help you," she pledged.

Susanna squeezed Beth's arm, which was all she could manage in the way of thanks at the moment. In the dining room, she saw her one-handed customer had gone. "Do you know who he was?"

Beth nodded. "I'll tell you all about it later."

~~~

"Garrett," Albert, the youngest apprentice, called joyfully when he saw him walk into the smithy. The rest of them, Wayman, Fred and Dan, turned and started toward him, all talking at once.

"It's so good to see you," fourteen-year-old Albert said. "We miss you."

Fred reached him first and shook his hand, then laughingly pulled him into a bear hug.

Wayman reached him and clapped his shoulder before noticing the odd look on Garrett's face. "What's happened?" he asked, getting right to the point.

Garrett's smile dimmed. "I just pounded Lonnie Hastings."

Fred cheered. "Good for you! Bastard had it coming."

"Wish I could have been there," Dan called.

"Why?" Wayman asked Garrett with a concerned frown. "What brought it about?"

Garrett released a shaky breath. "I was at Wiley's and he came up to me, half drunk, and asked if I needed him to cut my food for me."

Wayman sighed as he shook his head in disgust.

"I didn't say anything back, but this … feeling started building. Shame, I guess. That I'd just sat there. This girl, this waitress, defended me, and I just sat there like a damned lump of coal."

99

"Because he took you by surprise," Wayman reasoned. "It would anyone. What decent human being says something like that? They don't!"

"Then, all the sudden, I started remembering that night." He paused. "It was him, Wayman. I remember him calling me a name right before I was hit."

"You're certain?" Wayman asked.

Garrett nodded. "I remember. He said, 'Hey, cheater,' and then I was hit." He swallowed. The thought of what had transpired still made him feel sick to his stomach. "So when I left the restaurant, I saw him walking away, and I … went after him."

"He deserved it," Wayman stated calmly. "And he provoked it." He looked at the others. "Get back to work," he said evenly. "We've got deadlines to meet."

Complaining as much as they dared, they went back to their tasks, and Wayman gestured Garrett to his office. Once there, they sat, and Wayman pulled out a bottle of brandy. "To steady your nerves," he said as he poured. He offered Garrett a glass.

Garrett accepted it and waited for Wayman to fill his before they lifted the glasses to one another and drank. The amber liquid warmed his innards as it went down. It felt good to be back in the presence of his friends and his mentor. The familiar sounds and smells of the smithy soothed his nerves far more than the brandy.

"How is it at the Blue farm?" Wayman asked.

Garrett nodded slowly. "It's good. I was worried at first it might just be charity on Miss Blue's part, but there's plenty to help with."

"I'm so glad to see you, Garrett. You look better."

"I feel better. Stronger. Cessie and April May are seeing to that. Hey, Wayman, I know I owe you for paying—"

"No, you do not. Truth is, with you here, I got jobs done I can't come close to now. You don't owe me a thing and that is the truth. I probably owe you back pay."

Garrett grinned and then he stared into his glass and waited for the emotion that swelled in him to subside. "I miss it."

"We miss having you here."

There was a rap at the door and they both looked at Dan standing there. "Sorry to interrupt," Dan said, directing it to Wayman before his gaze shifted to Garrett, "But can you talk me through something before you go?"

"Who's on bellows?" Wayman demanded irritably.

"Albert took over. Geez, Wayman, my arms were about to fall off."

Garrett grinned, because some things never changed. It was good that he'd stopped in. He felt calmer and more like himself again. "Sure, I will," he said to Dan. "Happy to."

~~~

Lonnie stepped inside his house feeling more humiliated than he'd been in his entire life. He burned and prickled with humiliation. He trudged upstairs to his room. The mirror above the vanity revealed a cringe-worthy image. His face was red and blotchy; his eye was already swelling, his nose and lip bloodied. *By God,* he would get back at Trentwell if it was the last thing he did!

He poured water into the bowl, bent, and repeatedly splashed water on his face. The more the water turned pink, the more he swore he would get both Trentwell and the waitress who'd talked to him like he was a nobody. He would get them both.

"What happened to you?" his brother asked from the doorway.

Lonnie glared at Timothy through the mirror. "I got jumped, that's what."

Lonnie looked alarmed. "Who jumped you?"

"Trentwell."

Timothy blinked in surprise. "Trentwell? With one hand?" Lonnie whirled around and went at him, and Timothy quickly backed up, his hands raised in defense.

Lonnie stopped, but still looked like he might pounce. "I'm going to get him," Lonnie swore through clenched teeth.

"You did get him," Timothy retorted. You got him first, for no other reason than losing to him."

"Get out!"

Timothy shrugged and walked away.

Chapter Twelve

Susanna sat cross-legged on her bed that night listening as the girls filled her in on what had happened to Garrett Trentwell. Try as she might, she could not get his boyishly handsome face out of her mind.

Beth was perched on her knees in back of Susanna determined to fix her hair in a more flattering style. Across the room, Jean lay in her bed on her side. Callie Jo perched at the end of the bed with her legs drawn up. It was nearly lights out and they were all in their nightgowns.

"Why wasn't Lonnie Hastings arrested?" Susanna asked when she'd heard the story.

"They couldn't prove it," Callie Jo said with a shrug. "He denied it and his daddy backed him up."

Susanna rolled her eyes. "Of course, he did."

"What did he say to Garrett today?" Callie Jo asked.

"He asked if Garrett needed help cutting up his food. Smirkin' the whole time."

"That is so mean," Beth declared. "I think he's maybe the worst person ever."

"Don't say that to Bella," Callie Jo warned.

"She doesn't care what I think, anyway," Beth said mildly. She reached around and handed Susanna a hand mirror. "What do you think?"

Beth had parted her hair on the side and pinned it back in small strands, leaving it fuller and softer looking. It looked so good that Susanna hardly recognized herself.

"You should wear it like that," Jean said.

"Timothy is not the same as his brother though," Callie Jo said. "He's so much nicer."

"I knew you liked him," Jean laughed, kicking Callie Jo's leg playfully.

"I didn't say I liked him," Callie Jo said as she blushed. "I just said—"

"That you wanted him to kiss you," Jean interrupted. She smacked her lips in obnoxious air kisses, and Callie Jo leaned over to smack her friend's rear end.

"And hug you," Jean laughed, undeterred. "And whisper sweet things in your ear."

Susanna couldn't tear her eyes away from her reflection. Never before had she liked what she saw in the mirror. It was still peculiar to be in this place with friends, leisurely chatting while someone fixed her hair, but it was getting less so every day.

She'd never had friends her own age. The orphanage hadn't allowed it because they claimed it led to mischief making. At Cheever's, she'd grown close to the others from the experience of shared misery, but they'd been more like siblings.

Here, they were on equal footing. All different personalities and backgrounds, but all doing the same thing and earning the same pay. They were all independent to some degree and most of the girls were nice and supportive. The few who were spiteful and two-faced were well known and easily avoided.

"Lights out in ten minutes," Mrs. Beard called.

"Thank you," Susanna said to Beth, who smiled happily as she climbed off the bed. "I like it."

Beth bent to press a quick kiss to her cheek.

Susanna stiffened, unaccustomed to tender physical touch, but Beth was oblivious to her discomfiture.

"It might even be alright in the morning if you don't toss and turn too much."

"Nighty-night, girls," Callie Jo said, as she rose. "Sleep tight."

"Sweet dreams of Timothy," Jean sang, then smacked a few more air kisses.

Callie Jo giggled, and Beth left saying, "I'm on first shift."

"Thank goodness I'm not," Jean said.

Susanna rose and set the hand mirror on Jean's vanity, catching another glimpse of herself in the tilted oval mirror above it. In the high-necked nightgown and new hairdo, she hardly recognized herself. She looked almost pretty.

"Turn out the lamps, will you?" Jean asked climbing under the covers.

Susanna turned out the lamps and then went to pull the curtains together, but hesitated. The moon was full enough to permeate the blanket of fallen snow and make it luminous. She could still see snowflakes tumbling down in the light of the streetlamp below.

"Is it still snowing much?" Jean asked sleepily.

"It's slowed down."

"Everyone was talking about the almanac today. We're supposed to get another big storm before winter lets up. Probably soon."

Susanna wondered how anyone could know that. All she knew was that it was strangely thrilling to look out on a bitterly cold night when it was warm in their room. The radiator was a miracle, as far as she was concerned.

She thought of Lily, Levi and Nate and hoped they were all warm enough. There was no way of knowing where Levi and Nate were. She'd hoped to hear something by now, but she hadn't. She tugged the curtains closed and went to bed, silent in her stockings. Once there, she settled back trying not to muss her hair as she pulled the covers to her chin.

"Did you really tell him to get the H-E-double L out?" Jean asked, still marveling over the story.

"Yes, I did."

Jean giggled. "How is it Simpson hasn't fired you yet? Have you got something on her or something?"

"No!"

"I can't figure it. She fired a girl for scowling once. She's fired them for cursing. She fired a girl once because she smelled bad."

"I don't smell bad," Susanna objected.

"I didn't say you did, but you cussed at the mayor's son and told him to get out."

Worse than that was that she'd said something about Garrett *only* losing most of his left hand. She could still remember the look on his face when she'd said whatever asinine thing she'd said. The look had been half disbelieving, half … what? Insulted?

Yes.

She'd insulted him. She hadn't meant to, but she had. She hadn't known he was left-handed. Not that it mattered, she thought as she looked at her own hands in the dark. What if she lost most of a hand? Either hand?

She had to apologize. She was off until the dinner shift tomorrow, so she'd do it in the morning no matter how cold it was. She'd learned a lot about him, including where he was staying. "Yeah, well, the mayor's son is a horse's ass," she stated, finishing the conversation.

"I'm glad Simpson hasn't fired you yet," Jean said as she turned over in bed. "Night."

Susanna grinned. "Goodnight."

Chapter Thirteen

There was a sound. Cooing? No, whining. And then a sharp barking began. Close. By his ear. Levi struggled to open his eyes, but he was aware of only a few things.

Cold.

Pain.

Something sharp in his back … and terrible trouble breathing.

He couldn't reason beyond the cold and pain to figure out where he was or what had happened. God, almighty, he was hurt.

Nate! Where was Nate?

A rush of fear for Nate roused Levi to full consciousness. He was lying on his back on cold, hard ground somewhere. He was inside, not outside. He had a strong sense of being enclosed.

Grunting, he rose up on an elbow, although the effort caused lightheadedness and agony. He nearly collapsed again, but he panted and stayed semi-upright. A dog was jumping around and barking. It was a small thing.

He was in darkness; the smell of damp earth was strong and he was surrounded by walls. A cellar? He could make out steps close by and so he scooted to them and managed to pull himself up onto the first, although he had to bend forward and put his head between his knees in order not to pass out. His skin was cold, then hot, and he felt so terribly sick.

Nate stayed behind! he suddenly remembered. Relief made him weak with gratitude, and it was tempting just to lie back down on the ground. Wherever he was, whatever had happened to get him hurt and possibly imprisoned, Nate was safe and would make his way with the assistance of Mister … *What was his name?*

He could clearly picture the man's face. He could remember how they'd been directed to his place. They were near the Potomac River. In Riverton! Yes, that was the town. The man, *Colmer*, Joseph Colmer, had been a man of perhaps fifty with pockmarked skin and the palest blue eyes Levi had ever seen. Colmer had been suspicious of them at first, but charitable in the end. Which made sense once they understood his story.

Levi sat up, trying to remember everything that occurred from the time they'd run from Cheever's. They'd ridden for days, slept in fields, scrounged for food. They'd briefly found themselves in Pennsylvania and then back in West Virginia.

They'd bought goods at general stores when they could, but they were few and far between, so they'd stolen eggs and a few chickens along the way. They had killed squirrels and rabbits with his slingshot, caught fish and frogs and cooked and eaten them.

They'd found themselves in a vast wilderness it felt they couldn't escape, especially when everyone they encountered looked at them as if they were villains or worse. Once, men had chased them and they'd barely gotten away. They'd kept to the woods for days after that.

When they reached the next town, they began to ask for work, and they got a day's worth here and there. In Pendleton County, more than one person suggested they seek a man named Colmer at a place called Gibbons House Farm. It took two days to find the neatly kept farm with an impressive three-story Victorian home, the grandest either of them had ever seen.

A black maid, old enough that her hair was beginning to gray, answered the door and coolly instructed them to wait on the porch. There were rocking chairs on the porch as well as a swing, but they didn't dare sit since they hadn't been invited to.

Looking out on the enviable vista, Nate had whispered. "Can you imagine?"

The answer was no, although Levi didn't say it. He couldn't imagine possessing such wealth and privilege.

The maid was back in short order with glasses of lemonade and pieces of strange looking cakes, saying only, "You boys look hungry."

"Yes, ma'am," they said in unison, their eyes going to the food. "Thank you."

"Mr. Colmer been fetched. Make yourselves comfortable. He'll be here presently."

"Yes, ma'am," Levi replied. "Much obliged."

The cakes were light brown, long and slightly rounded and nothing had ever tasted better. They sat, ate, and agreed the journey had been worth making, even if Colmer told them to get off his land.

The maid came back with a pitcher and another plate of bread, saying, "Josephine's my name." She set the plate between them and refilled their glasses for which they thanked her.

"What is this?" Nate asked, holding up a piece of cake.

She gave him a puzzled look. "Shortnin' bread. Ain't you never had no shortnin' bread?"

"No, ma'am. But it's the best thing I ever tasted.

She huffed a small laugh. "The two of you looking for work?"

"Yes, ma'am," Levi replied. "We are."

Her head cocked slightly. "You brothers?" she asked with a thoughtful expression on her face.

Nate's jaw dropped and he looked at Levi, wondering how he'd take such an insult.

"I think of him like a brother," Levi said carefully.

Again, her gaze went from one to the other of them. She gave a sort of grunt and left again.

Colmer, when he appeared a quarter of an hour later, asked their business. At first, he seemed offended that they'd been directed to him, but he listened and then agreed to put them up for the night. The next morning, he told them he'd grant them a few days' work to help them on their way. It was after the third day that he invited them into his home for supper.

It was at supper, served in Mr. Colmer's own dining room, that they finally understood. They'd already been told that Colmer's wife had passed on, but his pretty, blue-eyed, dusky-skin daughters, nine-year-old Yvonne, and fifteen-year-old April, were present – and mulatto. For Nate, it was a revelation. He'd always felt alone in his biological makeup.

They'd stayed a few days more, grateful for the pay, when Colmer offered a permanent place for them. Without hesitation or reservation, Nate wanted to stay, but with equal conviction, Levi needed to press on. It was unsettling to leave Nate behind, but it also felt strangely right.

As for himself, perhaps he'd never make it to Green Valley, but he wouldn't end up in West Virginia, either. That much, he'd sworn to himself. The horse had grown slower than Levi could walk, so Levi left her in Nate's care and left on foot, catching a ride on the back of a wagon whenever he could.

Waynesboro!

That's where he'd been last. It had proven to be exciting for a couple of reasons. Mainly, because he'd finally made it to Virginia. Also, the town, known as the Iron Cross because it was the junction of two railroad lines, was where he'd be able to catch a train to Green Valley.

He had eight dollars and change left, since Nate had insisted that he take all the money they'd earned, so he indulged himself in a much needed meal in an inn. He also planned for a bath and a night's lodging in a real bed. It wasn't the best of inns. In fact, it was pretty shabby and old, but it was clean. And his meal of roast duck and vegetables was delicious.

He'd struck up a conversation with two men and they'd bought him a scotch whiskey. His first. It hadn't tasted good, but he liked the fuzzy warmth that enveloped him from the inside out. There had been several scotch whiskeys bought for him, come to remember.

Now, the little dog stopped barking and cocked his head at Levi as he reached for the wood banister and managed to stand on wobbly legs. Levi reached for his purse, fearing its absence.

It wasn't there.

Stolen. Gone.

He felt so ill, he had to sit again. Those men had robbed him. They'd hit him with something, robbed him and threw him down here. Wherever *here* was. A spot in his back hurt terribly and was bleeding, he could feel the warm trickle of it.

He tried to stand again and failed, and the little dog began barking. On a second attempt, Levi managed it. He turned, found the railing, and dragged himself up, but each step seemed a mountain, and he was so dangerously lightheaded.

Halfway up, light flooded the place and he squinted up at a shapely figure.

110

"Wha—" a woman exclaimed. She hefted her skirt a few inches and started toward him. "Oh, Lord! I wondered what had become of you," she said disapprovingly. She clucked her tongue as she slipped an arm around him, supporting him as they moved toward the top of the stairs. "I damn well knew those two were up to no good!"

He lacked the strength to say anything. He was putting his all into staying conscious.

"Jim," she hollered as soon as they reached the first floor. "Jim! Come quick!"

Levi realized he was going to pass out. He was falling. The woman tried supporting him, bracing his collapse as best she could.

Chapter Fourteen

Susanna trudged down Crooked Tree Lane staring over the long, white fence at the farmhouse belonging to the Blue sisters. It was heartbreakingly lovely on the late winter's morning. White, two-storied and spacious with trim and the front door painted navy blue. Smoke curled lazily from chimneys, white gray against a deeper gray sky. Snow sparkled brilliantly as did the ice cycles hanging on the wide front porch.

She was plagued with second thoughts, because how bad was it to show up to speak to a man? Would the elderly sisters think she was ignorant and uncouth? She hesitated as she reached the long driveway to the house, but she'd come this far on a freezing day. She would go on up and apologize for hurting Garrett Trentwell's feelings.

At least, she would if they would allow her to speak with him. If not, she'd be damn well near frozen by the time she got back to the dorm.

Halfway up the drive, a small gray and brown terrier came tearing toward her barking up a racket. She gasped and came to a standstill. Dogs frightened her because she'd never been around them. The little dog stopped a yard away from her but kept barking.

When she saw a large golden hair dog coming for her, she would have hightailed it except for the lady calling to them from the front porch.

"Wags! Sheeba! Come here!" the lady ordered, clapping her hands. "I'm sorry, honey," she called. "They won't hurt you, I promise."

Susanna started forward uncertainly, and the dogs trotted alongside her, the little one occasionally barking as if to boast about what it had found.

"They don't get a lot of excitement," the lady called good-naturedly, stepping further out on the porch. "So they like to announce callers." The lady was at least fifty, but she still had a pretty face. It was apparent she had been a great beauty in her day.

"I was hoping to speak with Mr. Trentwell," Susanna said when she got closer. She was so cold that her jaws weren't working well and she sounded odd.

"Come on in, but be careful of the steps. It's pure ice out here."

Susanna pulled her hands from her pockets and reached for the icy banister.

"Oh, honey," the lady fretted. "Where are your gloves?"

Despite being cold through and through, Susanna's cheeks grew hot with embarrassment. The steps were icy, but she reached the porch without mishap – and then slipped. The lady reached out to steady her and, in doing so, her fingers went right through the worn spot in the arm of the coat.

"Let's get you in and warm," the lady said, pretending she hadn't noticed. "I'm Cessie Blue."

"Susanna Jones," she bit out, stammering from the cold. "I work at Wiley's."

"It is nice to meet you, Susanna. My goodness, you had a long walk on a cold day."

As Susannah stepped in and her eyes adjusted to the dimmer light, the room before her came into view. The fire burning in the hearth of the parlor illuminated a charming room with mismatched settees and chairs that somehow went together perfectly. "Your house is so pretty."

"Thank you. Sister and I were born and raised here, so we are fond of it. Where are you from?"

"West Virginia, ma'am."

"Your family still there?"

"I don't have any to speak of. At least, no one who's there anymore. A girl who's like my sister came here with me. Her name's Lily."

"We know Lily," Cessie exclaimed. "Which means we know you, too. We just hadn't met yet. Lily's the best of friends with our Rebecca."

Suzannah nodded. "She told me about Rebecca," Susanna said as best she could with a jaw stiffened by the cold.

"Rebecca and her brothers and sister are like our grandchildren. Lizzie, their mama, is a daughter to us. They live just past here, and the children almost always stop in after school. Oh, Lily is such a sweet girl. We just love her."

Susanna nodded. "I'm so glad she's happy here. She deserves it."

"Of course, she does. So do you."

Susanna wondered how much Lily had shared with them.

"Why don't you have a seat and I'll call Garrett," Cessie suggested. "He's out back with April May bedding down the animals for the storm that's coming."

"Oh."

"Sister says it is coming this afternoon and she's more often right than not about these things. Make yourself comfortable, and I'll make you some tea. I'd offer to take your coat, but I'm going to let you warm up first." She walked away.

Susanna felt awed by the lady, both her beauty and graciousness. She wondered if she would ever be as gracious when she was older. She'd never be as good and kind as Lily or Beth, but she was improving.

She walked further into the parlor wondering what it would have been like to be raised in a home like this, surrounded by family who loved one another. What might she have turned out like had that been the case?

~~~

April May and Garrett had spent the morning stocking stalls and moving in the herd, one ornery animal at a time. The almanac had the storm starting no sooner than tomorrow, but April May felt it coming in her bones. Given the dropping temperature, the smell

114

of snow, and the daylight getting strange, it felt like it could begin any minute.

As they worked, they discussed an aged donkey named Handsome Harry that had been suffering from donkey flu. In the last few weeks, he'd stopped eating altogether and grown frail. It was time to put him down.

"Had him for five years," April May said as they trudged toward the barn, each leading a mule by a rope wrapped around its stout neck. "We've talked about a lot of things over the years, he and I. Solved some problems. Told some good stories. He's got a dry wit, that one."

Garrett grinned as he followed April May into the barn where it was immediately warmer. The wind had a stinging bite to it. They'd been trying to get the necessary jobs finished, but it was slow go since the ground was icy and had to be trod carefully. Garrett put his mule in a stall with another. "You said he's nine years old?"

"About that. That's old for a mule, especially one who's been a slave in a mine." She looked to Mildred the mule who was in a large stall with two others. "Now, y'all get along. Hear me?"

"I'll do it," Garrett offered, turning back to face her. "Put Harry down, I mean."

April May stomped and clapped her gloved hands together to keep the blood flowing. "I may just let you," she said. "I never want any of them suffering needlessly. When there's no hope, why linger and suffer? Makes no sense. Still, it's hard to do it when they're a friend."

"Garrett," Cessie called from the house. "Susanna is here to see you."

Garrett stopped breathing for a second and April May smirked. "You been holding out on us?"

He frowned with anxiety. Why in the world was *she* there and on a day like this? "She's the waitress."

"The spunky one that said you weren't left-handed anymore? Oh, I have got to meet this girl."

"Don't keep her waiting," Cessie called.

115

April May grinned. "Don't keep her waiting," she repeated teasingly. "We're about done here, anyway."

"Alright, then," he muttered. And he started inside, his heart beating fast.

"It's all right," Cessie said soothingly when she saw his anxiety. "I'm making a fresh pot of tea and we'll serve some slices of that oatmeal cake you like."

"Why is she here?" he whispered.

"She said she wanted to speak to you," she said quietly. "Go on, now. She seems like a nice girl."

He gave her a look. "Maybe we're not talking about the same person, then."

Cessie chuckled and turned back to arranging the tray.

Garrett took off his coat, gloves and hat and went upstairs by the back staircase to wash up and comb his hair. Most of the rooms on the floor had been shut off in preparation for the storm. Hope for the best, prepare for the worst. If it was a bad storm, they would not waste fuel keeping unnecessary rooms warm.

He hurriedly cleaned up, changed his shirt, and made it as far as the main stairs before he stopped to take a breath to calm his nerves. It was probably silly to be nervous, but a girl had never come calling before. What in the world did she want?

He walked on and found her sitting with her hands folded in her lap watching the fire, although she looked up at him the moment he stepped into view. His heart did a strange lurch at the sight of her; she looked so pretty. He hadn't remembered she was that pretty. "Hello," he said, coming further in.

She looked uncomfortable. "Hello."

Cessie had already brought the tray, although Susanna hadn't touched it. He sat on the far end of the settee, so they could both reach the tray, and then wondered if he should have sat across from her.

"I know I probably shouldn't have just … showed up," she said.

"I'm sure you got your reasons."

She nodded but didn't voice them.

116

"You want some tea?" he asked and then felt foolish, since it was sitting right in front of her.

She nodded though. She poured a cup and began preparing it as she liked, so he did the same, accidentally sloshing some on the saucer and the white doily.

"Want me to do it?" Susanna offered.

"I can do it," he replied quickly and a little snappishly. He felt badly about it as soon as it was out of his mouth, but it was too late to take it back and not make it worse.

"I only meant—"

"I'm awkward. I know."

"No, Mr. Smartypants. I meant … I thought … the lady is supposed to fix the tea. Not that I know anything about anything like that."

"Well, neither do I," he said edgily. This was stupid. Were they already arguing?

"Look, I come to apologize," she said, turning to face him. Her faced was flushed and she looked sincere and so pretty, he couldn't even breathe right, much less think of what to say. "For what I said," she continued. "Sometimes I just open my big mouth and say things. Then, later, all I can do is think about what I said and wonder why I said it. What is wrong with me?"

"We all do that sometimes."

"I don't think everybody does it," she retorted. "In fact, I know they don't."

Did she just want to disagree with everything? She'd come there on a below-freezing day to apologize, and then she seemed to want to make it hard. "Yeah, they do," he insisted. "We all do."

She rolled her eyes. "Anyway, I'm sorry."

"I know you didn't mean anything by it. Let's forget it." She looked uncertain and he wasn't sure what else to say. "The cake is really good, if you want some," he offered.

She took a piece. "I've never had such good food before coming here. I'm probably going to get fat."

"I doubt it. You probably work too much."

"Not near as much as I used to. A lot of the girls complain, but you won't catch me griping about it."

"So you like it there?"

She nodded. "I like it fine."

"I guess I wouldn't mind if you handed me a piece," he said, nodding to the cake slices.

She bent to the task and placed a slice of cake on a delicate, blue-rimmed china plate, then put a fork on it and handed it over. "Miss Blue seems nice."

He took the plate and fork in hand. "She is. They both are. The way they took me in?"

"Did you know them before?"

"Not well. They just learned about what happened and wanted to help. They're like that."

"I never knew anyone like that until coming here. Except for the man who helped me get here."

The words jarred him for some reason. "What man?"

"The one who works for Wiley's. Who sent me here. See, there was these other two ladies choosing girls, and they didn't think a whole lot of me."

"I doubt that's true."

She gave him a look. "I don't lie. One of them looked at me like I was dirt beneath her feet."

"Why would she do that?"

She shrugged. "Cause the other girls looked better. They were dressed nicer."

"I think you look fine."

"She thought I was dumb, too."

"Maybe you just think people think bad things about you."

"I think it when they do," she retorted. "I can always tell. I know people. What they think. If they're good, bad or rotten to the core."

He took a bite of cake to buy time. And then another. It was easier than coming up with a response.

"So, did you really wallop Lonnie Hastings after you left yesterday?"

He frowned as he poked at the remainder of his cake. "He had it coming."

"I know. Hell, everybody knows."

He looked up at her because her response surprised him. It was the second time she'd cursed in front of him. Not that he cared, but it was a bit startling. The fact was, she was trying to be nice, although she wasn't very good at it. "You didn't get in trouble because of … that whole thing?"

"She told me I'd better not cuss ever again."

"That … that's good. I mean, that that's all she said."

"Yeah," she agreed. "Personally, I think it's good you knocked him flat on his—"

She stopped so abruptly that he laughed.

"I guess cussing just comes natural to some," she said sadly. "Me being one of them. I'm trying not to."

"I worked in the smithy. There was plenty of it there."

She took a bite of the cake and nodded with appreciation. "That is good."

He relaxed a little. "Where are you from?"

"Just a state over. But I am never going back."

There was heat in the reply and a sort of darkness in her gaze when she declared it. "Well, this is a—"

"Garrett," Cessie called urgently.

Garrett practically flung his plate aside, jumped to his feet and rushed from the room.

"Hurry! It's April May!"

"What's wrong?" Garrett called.

"I don't know, but she's on the ground," Cessie cried, halfway out the back door already without bothering to put on her coat. The wind had grown stronger and it buffeted her.

He grabbed his coat and rushed around Cessie toward April May, sliding more than once on the icy ground. The change in conditions in the last few minutes was alarming, but not as frightening as seeing April May lying crumpled on the ground against the fence. "April May," he called midway to her. Damn it, he couldn't move fast enough.

"I'm alright," she called back.

"I'm coming!"

"Dad blamed ass gave me a swift kick and sent me flying into the fence," April May hollered. "Got my arm but good."

Garrett grabbed the fence post and used it for balance to round himself around and reach her. He knelt beside her, staring at her arm, which was clearly broken between her elbow and wrist. Even in a coat, the forearm was at a sickeningly unnatural angle.

"Oh, no," Cessie cried when she reached them and saw the arm.

"We'll get her inside and I'll go for the doctor," Garrett said.

"Damned ass," April May complained.

"I hope you're talking about the mule," Garrett said as he considered the best way to get her up without further injuring the arm. She was extremely pale and there was a sheen of sweat on her face despite the bitterly cold precipitation blowing in their faces.

Susanna joined them, breathing hard. She had Cessie's coat with her, which she helped the lady into. "How can I help?"

"Let's get her into the house," Garrett replied urgently, talking loudly enough to be heard over the wind. It had grown a lot louder. "Cessie, get her something for the pain. We'll be right there."

Cessie nodded frantically and started back to the house.

Susanna knelt beside April May.

"So you're Susanna," April May said to her.

"Yes, ma'am."

"On second thought, just let me get her," Garrett said, positioning himself to carry her.

April May waved him off with the gloved fingers of her left hand. "I don't need to be carried," she declared. "I'm too heavy. Just help me up."

"For once, don't argue," Garrett said as he scooped her up.

She moaned as he lifted her. "Damned ass," she muttered.

"Watch it now," Garrett grunted. After only several steps, the effort of carrying her was causing his muscles to quake. She wasn't exactly light weight, and he hadn't fully recovered his strength. "Susanna here doesn't cuss."

Susanna, walking alongside them, ready to catch her if he slipped, snorted. "I *said* I can't cuss at work anymore."

April May chortled despite the pain. "I like this girl."

The walk seemed to take forever. It was an immense relief to reach the back steps and even more so to get inside the house. The

120

temperature outside had dropped sharply since he'd come inside earlier and that couldn't have been more than a quarter of an hour.

It was tempting to lay April May on the kitchen table, but he continued into the parlor and set her on the wide Victorian sofa where Cessie had prepared a place. He stepped back, breathing hard, and Cessie moved in with a blanket. A small, dark bottle of laudanum and a glass of wine had been placed on the table.

"Oh, honey," Cessie fretted. "Lay on back."

"We need to get her coat off first," Susanna said.

Cessie nodded. "Yes, help me."

"I'm going to go for the doctor," Garrett said urgently, backing up. "It's getting bad fast. We got no time to waste." Without waiting for a response, he headed for the front door.

Susanna unbuttoned April May's coat. "We'll take out your good arm first."

They heard the door open and close.

"Here, honey, have a swig of this first," Cessie said, handing April May the bottle of laudanum.

April May took a swig and then grimaced. "That is pure awful."

Susanna got the older lady's good arm from the coat, but the movement of the coat on her broken arm made April May's breath catch. But once her left arm was free, the coat was eased from around her and carefully pulled off the broken arm.

The break was as expected, midway between wrist and elbow.

The front door suddenly banged open again, driven by the force of the wind. As Cessie hurried to shut it, Susanna considered how to stabilize the break.

"Garrett!" Cessie called.

Susanna looked to where Cessie stood in the door.

"He's fallen," Cessie called, glancing back at her. "It doesn't look like he's moving!"

Susanna gawked. "Don't try and help him up on your own," she called. "I'll be right back," she said to April May.

"Bet you're glad you came over today," April May commented weakly. She squeezed her eyes closed and moaned. "I think I'm gonna be sick."

Susanna reached for a pretty, cutglass bowl full of wrapped peppermints. She dumped the candy on the table and handed the bowl to her. "Use this, if you need to."

She rose and hurried to the front door where Cessie stood, shocked motionless by the ferocity of the storm. In the last few minutes, it had become a whiteout. Susanna stared breathlessly but couldn't see Garrett at all. "Where—" she started to say, and then she saw a form.

Staring at it, she stepped out, but the freezing air sucked the breath from her. It was like nothing she'd ever felt. She could barely breathe and the wind seemed to carry shards of ice in it that stabbed the skin.

In the next moment, she saw Garrett was face up, unconscious from where he had obviously slipped and hit his head. He was already covered in snow and there was blood on the snow beneath his head. He was visible one instant, lost from sight the next.

She felt a new sort of fear she hadn't experienced before. That Garrett could be lost. That they all could be lost in this killer storm. It felt like a living thing that was out to get them one at a time.

"You can't get him by yourself," Cessie said, coming out behind her, hunched against the assault of the wind.

"Let me try," she called back. She had to shout to be heard over the wind and even then, her voice was carried away. "It's safer that way." She hoped Cessie would heed the words because it was treacherous. Every moment, every movement. She turned and managed one careful step and then another, but on her third, her feet slipped right out from underneath her and there was no recovering her balance.

She fell hard on her back, hitting her head against the icy porch, which is exactly what Garrett must have done. For an instant, she couldn't move, but when Cessie called to her, she held up a hand to show she was alright.

She struggled to sit, finally managed it, and then she scooted forward. She reached the railing and the stairs, but having no visibility was disorienting. She reasoned that she had to be moving in the right direction and yet she had no sense of that direction other than Cessie's voice behind her.

Keep shouting, Cessie, she silently beckoned. She didn't have the strength or breath to call back. In fact, she couldn't seem to breathe in enough air.

She touched freezing railing and slid down the steps until her foot came into contact with Garrett. She reached out, got hold underneath his shoulders and pulled. But, instead of pulling him up, she slid toward him. Her face and ears were on fire from the cold, and her fingers had gone numb, but, *damn it*, they were not going to die right there on the steps to the house!

Gritting her teeth, she spread her legs apart so she could straddle him for leverage and tried again. She pulled and this time Garrett moved, although she suspected he'd done it himself. "Push," she called. "We gotta' back up!"

Again, she pulled and he pushed with his feet, and they gained a few, precious inches. Again and again, they worked their way back. It took what felt like an eternity, but, near the front door, Cessie got hold of one of his arms and helped pull him in.

Back inside the house, just enough to clear the door, Susanna laid back, breathing hard and flexing her fingers to get the blood flowing again. Garrett's head was on her stomach, her legs still straddled his body. What an impression she'd made today.

Cessie shut the door and rushed off for blankets. Returning, she covered Garrett first and then went to help Susanna who was attempting to get out from underneath him. "He doesn't look good," Cessie said, her teeth chattering. She pulled another blanket over Susanna. "Lay there and warm up."

Susanna stared at the ceiling until she could catch her breath. Seconds passed like hours until she was able to gather strength enough to scoot closer to Garrett. She was weak and clumsy, not yet in full control of her limbs. Garrett's eyes were open, but unfocused. The part of his face that showed above the bunched up wool muffler was bluish gray in color. The shock of it sent adrenalin into her system and she experienced a surge of strength.

She wiped the snow from his face and hair. His lips were blue, his eyelashes were frozen and there was ice beneath his nose. His muffler was icy so she pulled it off.

Cessie peeled one of his gloves off and rubbed his hand in between hers and Susanna sat and gingerly felt his head to see if it was still bleeding. There was a lump, but there was no warm pulsing blood. It had stopped bleeding, but would it start again once he warmed up?

"Just …n-need t-" he uttered as best he could with jaws that were locked.

"Shush, now," Cessie said, still rubbing. "You took quite a fall. You need to warm up."

"H-help April May," he bit out, stammering badly. "Puh-please."

Cessie and Susanna exchanged a look. "Alright," Susanna said, wanting him to relax. She patted his chest. "She'll be alright. Don't you worry." She put the other blanket over him.

Cessie helped Susanna to her feet, and they went back to April May. Susanna was rubbing her hands together to warm them. "We need something to brace her arm with and something to bind it," she said as best she could through chattering teeth.

Cessie nodded and went to get the necessary items.

"He going to be okay?" April May asked.

"Soon as he warms up," Susanna replied. "Cept his head will hurt. He clunked it good."

"How much we going to owe you for your doctoring services?" April May asked, her words slightly slurred. The laudanum had taken effect.

"A couple of those peppermints will probably do," Susanna said. "I got a weakness for them." She knelt beside the sofa, the best position to fix the arm. The longer they waited, the more the muscles would tighten and the harder it would be.

"You look half frozen," April May uttered.

"I'm thawed out enough to do this."

Cessie came back into the room. "I broke a yardstick nice and straight and I have strips of cotton for the binding," she said, speaking fast. Her eyes looked feverish. "Will that do?"

Susanna looked at it and nodded. "Yes, ma'am." April May was propped against pillows with her broken arm up against her, her fingers curled on her chest. "Close your eyes and breathe real

124

deep," Susanna said to April May. "I'm going to count to ten and, once I get there, I'm gonna pull on your arm to get the broken ends apart and then I'll put them back together again nice and straight. It's the only thing to do."

April May nodded grimly.

Susanna looked at Cessie. "Soon as I do that, hand me the splints and then help me tie them in place."

Cessie nodded nervously.

April May closed her eyes. "Do it."

It felt like cruelty, but Susanna felt the broken ends with her fingertips, making April May suck in a breath. "Here we go. One, two," she counted aloud. "Three," she said, positioning her hands on either side of the break where it felt right. "Four …" She pulled the arm on either side of the break, which made April May cry out. Gritting her teeth, Susanna fit the bone ends back together.

Cessie reached in with a splint. She put it beneath April May's forearm and Susanna grabbed hold and held it in place. Cessie placed another section of the broken yardstick atop the arm and Susanna took hold of that, as well.

Cessie reached for a strip of cotton cut from a well-worn sheet that had been in the basket to iron. She tied a loop around the splints at the wrist and began to crisscross it up the arm. When it was done and tied, the splints secured, Susanna sat back on her heels, breathing hard. Sweat had broken out all over her body from the strain of her efforts, both physical and emotional.

"What happened to ten?" April May asked weakly.

"How's your stomach?" Susanna asked.

April May grunted. "The pain isn't as bad now."

"That's good." Susanna managed to pull off her own coat. It felt as though she had no strength left. "Once you can sit up, we'll make you a sling to go around your neck and keep the arm up and still."

Cessie looked at Susanna in amazement and gratitude. "Have you done that before?"

"Seen it done," Susanna replied hesitantly. It was not a remembrance she wanted to relive. "And I helped."

They all looked over as Garrett struggled to his feet. His face was gray.

"Oh, honey," Cessie said, starting toward him. She helped Garrett to a chair, then tucked blankets around him. Susanna rose and made it to a chair herself. There was a soft, knit blanket on the back of it, which she put over her and hugged close without even asking permission. It felt like she might never be truly warm again.

"You alright?" Garrett asked April May.

"I'll live," she said sluggishly. "You?"

"I'm okay." He looked at Susanna. "Thanks to you," he said. "Thank you."

Cessie sighed tiredly. "I'm going to make us all some hot mulled wine. We could use it." This time, there was no spring in her step as she left the room.

"Aren't we a sight?" April May mused. "I think old Handsome Harry might have cursed us."

Susanna closed her eyes. The warmth of the blanket felt good as did the warmth of the fire, but outside, a blizzard raged. It was the strangest feeling because it was killing someone right this second, she was sure of it. But she was so tired and foggy brained, she could have fallen fast asleep.

Cessie sank into a kitchen chair, buried her face in her hands and cried. When the flood of emotion subsided, she felt spent, but calmer. She dried her face and blew her nose with a monogrammed handkerchief, and then rose to warm and spice the wine.

As the fragrant brew heated, she stared out the window, although there was nothing to see but white. She pressed her hands together and prayed because this wasn't the sort of storm everyone survived.

~~~

Tommy Medlin reached his front porch and turned just in time to see the signal from the front porch of the longhouse. Two long back and forth swings of the lantern indicated all was well and everyone accounted for. There was a pause and then the signal repeated, although he could barely see it through the wind-driven snow.

Tommy hefted his lantern up and down to let Wood know he'd seen the signal. When that signal was repeated, he went inside, knowing Wood would do the same. They were as prepared as possible for the storm. There was nothing to do now except wait it out.

He stomped to get rid of some of the snow from his boots and stepped inside. He shut the door against the wind and leaned against it relishing the warmth and quiet. But Caty calling out, followed by Em's panic-stricken voice calling the name of their youngest daughter propelled him back into motion. He hurried through the house and into the kitchen, nearly colliding with Lily, who was holding Ben. She quickly stepped out of his way, her eyes round with panic.

Caty, standing in middle of the kitchen, was white-faced with fear. Em had thrown open the back door and was frantically calling for Juliana. He went to her.

"She went after the cat," Em cried, clutching at the front of his coat. "I went upstairs for a minute, and she went out after the cat!"

"I'll get her," he pledged, already heading back out, grateful that he hadn't yet removed his outerwear. "Stay here." The last words were an afterthought, and the wind was so noisy, he didn't know if she'd heard him.

Lily set Ben down in the parlor and then ran to fetch Em's coat. She knew Em would stand in the doorway until Juliana was found, just as she knew she was glad for the coat, even though she didn't say anything as she snatched hold and put it on. Snow had blown in her hair and already her eyelashes shone with ice, because she was crying. Lily went back for Ben, coaxed Caty into the parlor, and the three of them huddled in front of the fast-burning fire in the hearth and began to pray.

"Jules!" Tommy yelled over and over, only to have the storm swallow the sound. It was a nightmarish, freezing madness. He couldn't see two feet in front of his face. The lantern only illuminated furiously blowing snow. He put his arm up in front of his face and stared out from beneath the crook of it, but it didn't help.

When he walked into a large limb of the apple tree, he was confounded, because he'd veered way left of where he thought he was. "Juliana," he called. God almighty, he couldn't lose her.

"Jules," Em called. "Juliana!"

Em's voice barely reached him, but it served as a guide. He needed to go back closer to the house because Juliana couldn't have made it far, as small as she was. Where would the cat have gone? Where would his baby girl look? He took clumsy steps back, buffeted by the wind and stinging snow. Christ in Heaven, Jules was out in this.

He heard Em's voice and followed it. When he reached the house, he dropped to his hands and knees to look under the porch. He saw a pair of illuminated eyes – the cat's eyes, but no Juliana. He reared back up, feeling desperation he'd known only a few times in his life. Only when Em's life was in danger.

Help me, he prayed.

He thought he caught a glimpse of something in front of him and scrambled forward. He hoped, but wasn't sure it was Juliana until he had his hands on her. She was clinging to the side of the porch. He grabbed her up tightly and started back inside, although every step took great exertion. Not that there was any question that he would make it. His baby girl was in his arms; he would make it.

Em cried out to see them. She reached for her child, even as she stepped back to let them in. The half frozen, very spooked cat ran in behind them, the door was slammed shut and they fell together, clinging tightly and crying unashamedly.

~~~

Cessie came back with a tray of filled mugs and offered the first to April May. "You're looking better," she said encouragingly.

"Better than what?" April May croaked.

Cessie smiled at her sister and then moved on to Susanna. "How are you doing?"

Susanna took a mug. "I'm alright. Thank you."

Cessie went to Garrett. "Maybe you should take a little laudanum, too," she suggested as he took a mug. He was still shaking, and his coloring was not right.

"No, ma'am. But this'll help," he assured her. "Thanks."

Cessie sat with the last mug and set the tray aside.

"To the blizzard of '88," April May said. "One we will not soon forget."

How true, Susanna thought wryly. She would never forget today. She'd never heard wind make a more mournful-sounding howling. The way the windowpanes rattled, and the boards and rafters shook, it would be a wonder if the place held together. Yet here they sat in the comfortable room feeling a thick lethargy.

The warmth of the mug was pleasing as was the scent of the brew. Cinnamon, cloves and a dark, complex, fruity aroma. The contrast of it all – sitting in a stupor amidst a deadly storm, was so disparate, it felt unreal, more like a dream than real life.

The fire in the hearth was burning hot and fast, the flames hissing and shooting from side to side. Were all the earth's elements angry? She sipped the warm brew and it warmed her all the way down to her stomach. She sipped again and again, liking it more with each mouthful.

"What a blessing it is that you were here," Cessie said.

Susanna looked over and blinked in surprise that the comment had been addressed to her. No one had ever said such a thing to her. What did she say back? It was nothing? I didn't really do anything? "I'm glad I was," she finally uttered.

Except for those few words, none of them spoke or moved for at least a quarter of an hour. Not until Garrett got up, setting his blankets aside and saying he was going to see to the other fires.

"It's embarrassed him that he fell," April May said when he was out of earshot.

Susanna knew it was true. Although anyone could have fallen, it *had* been foolish for him to rush out, given how bad it was. He'd wanted to be the hero, and it could have cost him his silly neck. Part of her wanted to tell him so.

"His balance hasn't been the same since—" April May added, although she didn't finish the sentence.

Once again, Susanna felt terrible for not having considered that.

"Tell us about yourself, Susanna," Cessie said.

"I don't have any good stories," Susanna said reluctantly.

It was quiet for several seconds before April May said, "Lily's told us some."

Susanna looked at her and then Cessie. "What did she tell you?"

"About the woman who took you from the foundling home for no other reason than to work you," April May said.

So they knew. She wasn't used to people knowing her business. "Makes no sense why she took Lily, though. Not that she didn't work her, but that wasn't the reason. She did it just to be vicious."

The fire popped loudly, setting off sparks.

"I think it's because Lily's everything she's not," Susanna said. "Pretty and good. She's got a pure heart. She's easy to love."

"Did the woman hate you, too?" April May asked.

"She didn't like any of us, but she liked how I worked. And I didn't have anything she hated."

"Oh, Susanna," Cessie said tenderly, "You are lovely and you have a good heart."

Susanna scoffed. "I'm not either. I'm plain and gawky—"

"Why do you say that?" Garrett asked heatedly.

Susanna jerked in surprise to hear his voice. He was standing in the doorway. She prickled with embarrassment that he'd overheard. "I know people and I know what I am, too," she replied crossly. "Good and bad."

"There's good and bad in all of us," April May stated. "And the bad is easy enough to see in you. You're on the short-tempered side. It's that red hair of yours, I imagine. And you're stubborn as all get out. Me, too, so I recognize it. In fact, I imagine we're quite a bit alike, you and me. You say what you think, sometimes without thinking it out real good. Am I right?"

For once, Susanna didn't mind hearing her faults laid out. Maybe it was the wine, but it was true, plus it was said with a sort of ease and acceptance. April May had just said they were alike. "Yes, ma'am."

Garrett was still watching her, and his expression seemed full of feeling, which made her feel strange. She looked down at the last of the wine in her mug. She knew the three of them meant well, but they didn't know her. They couldn't know how hard-hearted she really was. She wasn't like them. She hadn't been raised in a place like this.

"So what is the good?" Cessie asked tenderly.

Susanna shrugged. "When I care about someone, I have their back."

"*Mm-hmm.* Loyalty," April May said. "Me, too. What about a good singing voice?"

It was such an absurd question, Susanna almost laughed. "I don't have a good singing voice," she replied with a shake of her head.

"That's too bad," April May said. "We do like to sing around here. Do you know Sweetly Sings the Donkey?"

"Can't say I do."

The fire popped again and the flames shot high. The pull of the wind was making it roar.

"April May," Garrett said worriedly. "Did the animals all get put up?"

"All except Harry. He knocked me into the fence and made his getaway."

Susanna suddenly realized if she hadn't come over, he would have finished helping April May, and maybe she wouldn't have gotten hurt. Then there would have been no need for him to go after the doctor and he wouldn't have gotten hurt. It was all her fault – and they were grateful she was there? "I'm sorry," she said. "If I hadn't of come over—"

"One of my asses gave me a swift kick," April May said curtly. "Wasn't the first time and it won't be the last. It wasn't

131

nobody's fault. We just had a series of misfortunes. But we came through it, didn't we?"

"Yes, we did," Cessie said. "Thank the good Lord."

"A little worse for wear," April May said, "—but we will be just fine."

Cessie nodded. "May everyone be so lucky this day."

Susanna and Garrett glanced at one another and looked away equally fast.

"There's more wine on the stove," Cessie said.

"I'll get it," Garrett volunteered. "I was going to get some headache powder, anyway."

When he'd gone, Susanna set her blanket aside. "Would it be alright if I—"

"Of course," Cessie said, understanding the unspoken question.

Susanna stood and started toward the kitchen feeling slightly off balance. Hot, mulled wine was potent stuff. There was a fire in the kitchen hearth and a low blue flame burned under a pot on the stove. Garrett stood at the kitchen sink staring out at the storm through an icy collage on the windows.

"I've seen bad snows, but nothing like this," he said.

She came and stood beside him, feeling equally awed and frightened by the blizzard; it was so full of power. Even from the safety of the house, she felt its voraciousness. It seemed desirous of claiming and conquering, utterly heedless of killing.

"I guess you read about the blizzard a few months back on the plains?" he asked.

She hadn't read anything about it, but she wasn't about to admit it. Normal people knew things. They read papers and talked to others about newsworthy events. He turned to face her, and so she looked at him.

"They had a bitter cold winter," he said. "Then one day it warmed up. Really warm. Turned balmy. So everyone got out and did shopping and errands. They'd been cooped up, so children were glad to get back to school. But only a few hours into the day, the temperature was dropping fast and it started snowing hard enough that they stopped school and sent the children home.

132

"Then it got like this. Snow blowing so hard, you couldn't see your hand in front of your face." He paused. "Children couldn't find their way home or to any shelter. Temperatures way below zero. I read one account that said it was forty below."

Susanna didn't understand how cold that was, but it made her ache to think of it. She'd spent many a winter's night so cold she couldn't sleep for the way her muscles seized up. Teeth chattering, jaws aching. Everything aching. Being chilled to the bone hurt.

"Hundreds of children froze to death," he said. "That's why they call it the Schoolhouse Blizzard."

"That's awful," she murmured.

"Maybe I am, too," he said.

It was aggravating that he claimed such a thing when everyone knew he was a good person. Frowning, she folded her arms tightly. "Why is that exactly?"

"Because when I was recovering from—" he stuck his fingerless hand in the air. "I thought of that blizzard. I purposely thought about people who had it worse off than me." He looked miserable, like he'd just admitted a crime.

"You didn't cause that blizzard and I'm pretty sure you didn't cause this one either. I may not know you well, but I can tell you're not somebody who'd wish bad things on someone else. 'Sides, if I hadn't come over, you'd have been helping get ready for the storm and April May might not have got hurt."

He frowned back at her. "There's no way to know that."

There was no sense arguing the point, so she moved over to the stove. She picked up the ladle in the pan of mulling wine and stirred gently, knocking about the sticks of cinnamon. "Do you think they had school today?" she asked quietly.

"I don't know," he admitted. "But I'll tell you this much. A lot of people learned a lesson from the Schoolhouse Blizzard."

She looked at him. "What lesson?"

"If you have shelter, stay put and let help come to you."

She hoped that was the case.

"She'll be alright," he said. "They all will."

He came closer and her breath caught, thinking he might kiss her. Instead, "I'll take that," he said. She stepped aside, feeling foolish for what she'd been thinking. He reached for the pan but leaned close to press a kiss to her cheek.

Sensations shot through her at lightning speed.

His nose was still cold.

Her heart raced.

He blushed.

So did she.

"You know what occurs to me," he asked.

She shook her head.

"If you'd been a little later getting started today, you could have been caught out in this."

It was true. It was an unnerving thought.

"I'm glad you weren't," he said.

With his boyish handsomeness and goodness of heart, he made it hard to think clearly. "When you came into the restaurant, I didn't know," she admitted. "I didn't know anything. Some of the girls told me last night."

Something flashed in his eyes. "Which girls?" he asked guardedly.

It took a moment to answer because his reaction had been so odd. "Beth. She's my friend, and Jean is the girl I share a room with. And Callie Jo."

"Do you like most the girls?"

She shrugged. "Most of them. Some more than others."

"A few don't seem very nice."

"A few of them have been raised being told they were perfect, and they believe it."

A corner of his lips lifted. "It's one strange day, isn't it?"

"Upside down and inside out," she agreed. As she followed him back to the parlor, she wondered if she had ever felt so strange. She felt giddy and girlish, which she'd never felt before. She was as tired as if she'd worked all day, but it was only noon or a little after. She felt protected and safe, except that was crazy thinking in the middle of a killer blizzard. *Must be the wine.* And relief from getting past the morning's experiences. But mostly the wine, and she wanted more.

By half past five, it was fully dark, but, thankfully, the blizzard had finally abated, leaving a frozen world and an eerie silence in its wake.

April May was helped to bed, and a room was prepared for Susanna, although she wasn't shown to it until after supper and several games of backgammon, well after eight o'clock.

"Whose room was this?" Susanna asked Cessie as she looked around the enchantingly pretty room. It had a petite hearth, a bay window and two beds with curtain-covered canopies. The trim on the walls was a soft blue gray, and the mantle around the hearth was hand painted to match.

The paintings, vases, lamps and knickknacks seemed worth a fortune to Susanna. She couldn't imagine owning such fineries. In the flickering golden light of the fire and the oil lamps, it seemed splendid and luxurious.

"When I was a girl, I shared it with my next older sister, Scarlet."

"I've never seen such a pretty room," Susanna said wistfully.

"We truly loved it. In the spring and summer, we'd open the windows and the summer curtains would blow in the breeze. I remember us talking at night, telling secrets. Giggling. Sometimes our other sisters would hear us and come busting in. They couldn't stand to be left out of anything."

Susanna stifled a sigh. A happy childhood was a fluke of fortune and birth. "Do your other sisters live around here?"

"No, dear. They've passed. As have our brothers. It's just me and April May left."

"I'm sorry. It must have been nice to have a big family, though," she said carefully.

"It was. Oh, it was a blessing. It has always been a truly happy home, full of laughter and music and … family drama." She chuckled. "There was always plenty of that, too. When Lizzie came home with the children—" she broke off.

"I should tell you all about that sometime. It's quite a story. Anyway, when they came into our lives, this house came to life again. Not that it hadn't always been a nice place, but it's meant to be bursting at the seams with family and friends and … life."

135

Susanna smiled at the older woman. One day, Susanna wanted to know all about her life. It was obvious she'd been a great beauty, so why had she never married?

Cessie opened a dresser drawer. "There are nightgowns here. It smells like lavender because of the sachets. You might want to take one of them to bed with you, put it under your pillow. Anything else you need, just let me know. I think we've shown you where everything is."

"Yes, ma'am. Thank you."

Cessie came closer. "You were a godsend today."

Susanna still felt the day's events were actually her fault in a roundabout sort of way, but there was no point saying so again. Instead, she gave Cessie a wan smile. "Never been called that before."

"I'll see you in the morning," Cessie said.

"Night," Susanna said.

"Night, dear."

The door shut and Susanna stepped closer to the hearth and stared into the flames. Garrett had banked it to burn through the night. What a unusual day and night it had been, maybe the strangest of her life. She'd been made to feel truly welcome in this place.

And Garrett.

Had he taken an interest in her or was that just wishful thinking? She'd caught him looking at her more than once in a way that made her heart begin pounding.

She circled the room, stopping to look in the mirror above the vanity. She tipped it upward to better see herself. Was it possible he thought she was pretty? No one had ever thought that. She did look better since moving here because the girls had taught her styling techniques and tricks. Her clothes were nicer now and a better fit, too.

She opened the lid of a small, ornate box and discovered it was a music box. She smiled at the tinkling tune and then caught a glimpse of her smiling self. She wasn't exactly pretty, nor would she ever be, but there were moments when she wasn't bad to look at.

136

~~~

Garrett went room to room, hearth to hearth, making sure all fires were banked for the night. It was peculiar with Susanna here. He could *feel* her here. She was different than anyone he'd ever known. She was real and honest and pretty in her own unique way. She wasn't a beauty, like Bella Byrd, but Bella wasn't kind in the least. In fact, she was unkind.

After only one day spent with Susanna, all he really knew was that he wanted more of them.

As he set the poker back in its place, he frowned at his fingerless hand, wondering if she or any woman would consider him for a husband, given the defect. *Defect.* Was that the right word? It wasn't an injury anymore; it was his condition. A deformity. What woman would want to see that every day?

He hated Lonnie Hastings.

~~~

It was wonderful to be enclosed in the curtains of the canopy bed, and Susanna relished it for a few minutes, thinking this was what a princess's life must be like. She'd washed up, used some scented talcum powder and donned a pretty if old fashioned nightgown of pink. A lavender sachet was near her pillow, and she could make out the fire through the curtains.

It was cozy and she was safe, but the story of the schoolhouse blizzard stayed with her. The thought of children trying to find their way in the sort of violent, freezing madness she'd experience earlier was painful. What if it had been Lily? She couldn't possibly know if she was safe. And where in the world were Levi and Nate? Why hadn't she gotten word by now? It couldn't be for any good reason. Tears sprang to her eyes, and it was so unexpected and uncharacteristic, she sat straight up.

Her chest ached with worry and grief over all the children who had perished, which was foolishness when she didn't even know them.

Damn it.

She wiped her face with both hands. She would never get to sleep if she didn't rein in these feelings. She drew her knees up and hugged them.

Please, she thought. *Please let them be safe.*

Her breath caught when she realized she was praying. Or was it praying? No one had ever taught her to pray.

God's never done me no favors. The memory of her words came back mockingly. She also remembered Lily's response. *He did me a favor. He put me with you.* "Please," she whispered. "Take anything from me you want, just protect her and Levi and Nate. Please."

~~~

Lawrence Hastings finished checking the month's receipts, which had added up correctly. He was about to dip his pen to sign off on it when Lonnie sent the chess board flying from the table in a fit of fury, having lost the game to his brother.

"Pick that up," Lawrence snapped angrily. "Don't be such a horse's ass!"

Instead of picking it up, Lonnie glared at him as he stood and stomped from the room like a child. Timothy, on the other hand, watched his father with impassive disdain. Lawrence didn't know which behavior he liked least.

The blizzard had kept him on edge all day, Lonnie was drunk and behaving like a spoiled two-year-old, and Timothy seemed to have developed an all-encompassing hatred for him. He leaned back and squeezed the bridge of his nose.

Calm heads prevailed. Clear thinking prevailed and he had thought of a plan to salvage the Trentwell situation. He was going to offer Trentwell a good job where he could make a far better living than he ever would have as a blacksmith. Also, Lonnie would stop drinking and carousing like a sailor and he would take his position in the company seriously or he would be sent on his way.

Today hadn't been the day to bring it up, trapped in the house as they were, but he would address the situation very soon. The greatest unknown was Timothy. Lawrence sat forward again. "Fancy a game with your father?"

Timothy had leaned over, reaching for some of the pieces on the floor. "Why not?"

Lawrence rose and retrieved the board and the farthest flung pieces and returned to the table. The blizzard was over and the toll of it was impossible to know at this point, but they were safe and comfortable in the warmest room in the house. The heavy velvet curtains were drawn, and a fire blazed in the oversized hearth. "I'm going to have a drink."

"The port is good," Timothy commented as he began to set the board up. "The tawny is better than the red."

Lawrence walked to the sideboard and poured himself a glass. Maybe he would mention his plan to Timothy first. Get his take on it. His youngest had a cooler temperament and a better head for business, even if it was in the clouds with his story writing sometimes. Lawrence walked back and sat. "I'll be black, if you don't mind."

"Not at all." Timothy moved a pawn as did Lawrence.

"Have I told you much about my upbringing?" Lawrence asked.

Timothy glanced at him. "Some. Born and raised in New York. Mother, father, two brothers."

Lawrence nodded absentmindedly. Both moved pieces without comment and watched the board. "I was the middle son. Wedged between my father's favorite, the firstborn, and my mother's pet, although he was only fifteen months younger than I was." He took Timothy's pawn, which Timothy paid back in kind. "I suppose to get attention, I—"

"What?" Timothy asked when the sentence trailed off.

Lawrence shrugged but continued studying the board. "Tried too hard. Was loud. Brash. I particularly wanted my father's approval, but I never did get it. He told me once I'd never amount to much."

139

Lawrence looked up and caught something in Timothy's eyes. Something like empathy, but then his son looked down at the board, and Lawrence wondered if he'd imagined it. It was his move. His bishop took a pawn in order to get into position to take one of Timothy's bishops.

Timothy blocked the move.

"I think I've spent my life trying to prove him wrong," Lawrence continued. "Makes me the fool, doesn't it?"

Timothy didn't reply, but his frown had grown more thoughtful. They played several minutes with no more discussion.

"You enjoy the business, don't you?" Lawrence asked.

"I do." He looked up at his father. "But I don't enjoy being despised."

Lawrence sat back with a sigh. "It's not as bad as that, is it? Not really."

Timothy looked bemused. "I don't know how you can be so blind to it. I may not be *as* despised as Lonnie, but I am despised. So are you. Yes, it has gotten that bad."

"I am mayor of this town," Lawrence stated irritably. "People don't elect men they despise."

Timothy looked back at the board. "Check."

Lawrence looked down and saw it. He grunted and moved his king.

"I think moving away would be best," Timothy said slowly. "For all of us. I mean to say *my* moving away. It would be best for me."

Lawrence felt a deep chill, because Timothy was serious, not merely talking out of anger. "I don't want that," Lawrence rejoined. "I don't want that, at all."

"I know, but too much damage has been done."

"We can turn it around," Lawrence beseeched. "I know we can."

"Do you really have no idea how hated Lonnie is?"

"I'm learning," Lawrence admitted. "After the incident in the street. And there are ugly comments that seem to be getting louder. The situation with Trentwell—"

"It wasn't just that," Timothy interrupted.

140

"I know, but it certainly acerbated feelings." He paused. "Perhaps he should go abroad for a time."

Something closed off in Tim's expression and he looked back to the board.

"Or perhaps he should just go," Lawrence added. Damn it, if he had to make a choice of which son to work at keeping, he'd made his choice. "I want you to stay."

"Check."

"Timothy," Lawrence pleaded. "Please. Will you consider it?"

Timothy looked up and met his father's gaze. "I will," he finally agreed.

"I am sorry," Lawrence said. His voice broke and he had to look away to collect himself. He was suddenly exhausted. He looked at his son who was watching him with compassion, if not love. "I never meant to fail you."

Timothy shrugged. "Maybe I should have been *more* loud and brash."

Lawrence smiled wanly. "I should have been less so and you should have been more so. All hindsight, eh?"

"It's still check," Timothy said.

Lawrence grinned and moved his king again. "Not for long. Paint me into a corner and I'll usually find a way out."

"I hope that's true," Timothy said.

~~~

Em took her time tucking in the sleeping children, pressing a kiss to each warm cheek or forehead. She walked into their bedroom to find Tommy standing and staring into the hearth at the fire he'd just stoked.

The blizzard had subsided. Now there was quiet with an occasional high-pitched whistling of wind that made her feel the cold deep within her bones. Her baby girl had been swallowed up in the storm. For only a matter of minutes, but what if Tommy hadn't arrived just when he did? Of course, she would have gone after Jules, but would she have found her or been lost in the storm along with her child?

Em pressed herself to her husband's back and wrapped her arms around him as tears tortured the backs of her eyes. She'd cried enough. Crying did nothing, but how would she ever shake this feeling? The initial terror had passed, but not the residual anxiety caused by a thousand what ifs. If only she'd bolted the door, Jules couldn't have snuck out as quickly as she had. But Em hadn't thought. She hadn't protected her child well enough.

Tommy leaned back into the embrace while covering her arms with his. She exhaled slowly and squeezed her eyes shut, loving him so completely, she nearly couldn't breathe. She'd been drawn to him from their first meeting, a chance encounter in the livery. She'd found it baffling how anyone could be so handsome and yet so shy, but more baffling was that she could feel intrigued by any man after what Sonny Peterson had done to her. Sonny had taken her captive, forced himself on her, humiliated her, and kept her a prisoner. She'd barely escaped and returned home only to have him track her down.

It was Tommy who had saved her. Protected her. Loved her. It was Tommy who had brought her back to life. And then she'd nearly lost him. The pain of the memory was too much and she began to cry.

"Hey," he said softly, turning around to face her. He gently wiped her tears away. "It's alright, now. She's fine."

Em nodded and let herself be pulled into his embrace. "I should have b-bolted the door."

"Emmy," he said tenderly. "You couldn't have known. We never bolt the door."

What if she ever lost him? He was the foundation of her entire world. Her clutch was tight; it felt she couldn't hold him closely enough.

"Em," he breathed.

He did that sometimes. Just breathed her name. He loved her as she loved him, and that only made her heart ache all the more. She drew back enough to lift her head and kiss him, and he kissed her back with the same intensity. Slowly circling while kissing, clutching, and shedding their clothes, they moved toward their bed where they would make love until the anxiety of the day was wiped away by exhaustion.

Sometimes their lovemaking was sweet and slow, this was different. It was hungry, almost desperate. As kindling crackled and flames in the hearth licked one another ravenously, her hair tented his face as he gripped her hips, directing her movement. Her hands ran up the contour of his back, and then he moved them, climbing atop her to thrust as he needed. They were deep thrusts that made her moan, but she encouraged it with her hands on his sweat-slicked back and the rhythmic lifting of herself to him.

Later, when they lay under the covers, emotionally and physically spent, they still held one another.

"Next, blizzard," Tommy said, breaking the silence. "We'll bolt the doors."

Em blinked in surprise.

"Especially when Ben gets a little older," Tommy added. "No telling what he'd try."

Em grinned and then chuckled and Tommy did, as well. They were fine, after all. They were all fine.

Chapter Fifteen

L ionel was incorrigible. He was in his favorite waking
position, curled against Cessie's back, one arm
wrapped around her, his hand caressing her breasts.
Within moments, he was stroking the place that made her writhe. It
felt good and yet, "Too early," she scolded mildly.

"Never too early," he rasped softly. "Never too late."

She turned to smack him playfully and woke from the dream.
Blinking up at the ceiling, she relished the quickly fading feeling
of lying next to him. Lionel Greenway. The autumn love of her
life.

Had destiny played out like it should have, there was no
question that she would have married John Yardley, the boy she'd
loved as a girl. They were as meant to be as any two people ever
were. Even when John became ill at the tender age of eighteen, she
was certain their love would overcome whatever his ailment was,
but his affliction persisted and worsened, weakened him and
finally ended his life. The grief of losing him had devastated her.
He was the springtime love of her life. With his death, she found
herself thrust into a long and terrible winter of melancholy.

Eventually, she made it through mourning. She had
opportunities to choose another path. Some wonderful men vied
for her hand, but her heart felt untouchable. She had long since
reconciled herself to spinsterhood before Lionel Greenway
happened into her life. Who chose to up and move to a new place
when he was fifty years of age? She thanked Heaven that he had.

Lionel had been a unique man whose hair had turned white
prematurely. It was soft and he wore it long. He sometimes grew
his facial hair out and she teased that he looked like Father Time.

"I am Father Time," he would return gravely in his lowest
voice.

In fact, he had turned back time and made her heart race. He'd
made her laugh like the girl she'd once been. He'd introduced her

to so many things. He taught her about winemaking and lovemaking. Before him, she'd had no idea that physical intimacy could transport a person to an alternate state of being, where there was nothing except disembodied bliss.

She was forty-two when he came into her life, fifty when he passed. She sometimes suspected he'd refused to move on to the place the soul was supposed to travel after death because he was waiting for her. The dreams she experienced of him seemed so real. His spirit wasn't a constant companion, but there had been dozens of moments she'd felt him with her. April May had remarked the same thing. So had Lizzie – the daughter he'd made up and who had later come to be.

The memory of yesterday's storm pushed out her reverie of Lionel, and she sat up and swung her legs around. She needed to check on April May

~~~

"Come," April May said at the sound of a soft knock. The door opened to reveal Cessie in her nightclothes. Even clad in flannel and with her hair mussed from sleep, she was pretty. "Have I ever mentioned how irksome it is that you can look that good in the morning?"

Cessie came closer, looking at her arm with concern. "It's swollen," she said worriedly.

"Well, of course, it's swollen. I took a perfectly decent bone and snapped it in two."

Cessie felt April May's forehead for fever.

"I'm fine," April May said. "The arm aches, but I'm taking powder every few hours."

"You need food, then. Biscuits and gravy?"

"I wouldn't say no." April May was glad when Cessie gave a quick smile and hurried from the room, because she suddenly felt a pull of strong emotion, and Cessie would read more into it than there was. She just felt a bit fragile, was all, which wasn't something she was used to. She felt old and fragile.

~~~

Cessie knew Garrett was up and about because of the blazing fires in the hearths. He'd also started coffee and had the oven heated.

"Figured you'd make biscuits and gravy," he said as she walked into the kitchen. He was seated at the table, still in his coat, his face red from the cold.

"You're right. Thank you," she said, going for her apron. "You've been out then, I see."

"Yes, ma'am. To milk the cow. It's so bright, it about blinds you."

She looked out the window at the bright blue sky and diamond encrusted frozen snow. "Glorious winter splendor."

"It's still a sheet of ice, though. I kept low to the ground, ready to break a fall, just in case. How's April May?"

"Her arm is swollen."

"I thought about that. I got some towels damp and put them outside to freeze. We'll keep switching them out until the swelling comes down."

"Good thinking. How's your head?"

"It's hard. I'm fine."

She grinned as she began making dough.

"It was quite a day, wasn't it?" he commented.

"Oh, Lord," she said with a shake of her head. "May we never know another like it."

"It kinda feels like it changed everything."

She turned to him with the bowl in her arm and a long wooden spoon in hand. "What did it change?"

"Guess I should have said it feels like a day where everything changed. Dang blizzard could have gotten us all."

She nodded thoughtfully. "I want to know how everyone fared, but I dread learning, too. I just don't think everyone could have survived it. Do you?"

He shook his head, a regretful look on his face. "Not as sudden and fierce as it was."

146

She turned back, finished stirring the dough and then turned it out to knead it.

"Cessie?"

"Yes, honey?"

"Do you believe you can fall in love with someone in one day?"

A smile sprang to her lips, but she kept her back to him. "I think that love is ... magic. It's in the world, but not exactly *of* this world. It doesn't go by our rules about what's proper and what's not." She paused. "Yes, I do believe you can fall in love in a day. In an hour. Some swear it can happen at first glance."

"Tell me if I can help you," he offered.

"Come fry some sausage for me."

He got up and took off his coat, placing it on the back of the chair.

Standing next to one another, concentrating on their tasks, she said, "She is special."

"I know," he agreed. "I've never met anyone like her."

"She's been through a lot," Cessie said. "I don't think she ever thought it could or would be any different for her, either. The adjustment—" she paused and released a breath.

"It's been hard?"

She shook her head fretfully. "I know what I mean, but I'm not sure how to say it. I think she is learning herself in a new way because of her changed circumstances. It might seem like that should be easy since her life is better now, but ... any time you have an eye-opening, everything looks different."

"I think I get what you're saying. Sometimes, she seems like she's trying to figure out what's right and what's real. Usually, she's so dead-set sure of everything." He broke off and laughed. "Listen to me. I just met her, didn't I?"

Cessie laughed, too. She pressed the cutter into the dough, her favorite part of biscuit making.

Garrett reached over and kissed her cheek. "Thank you," he said.

It hadn't been so long ago that he'd become part of their lives, but he was there now. Part of their lives, part of their hearts. She gave him a smile of great affection.

~~~

Susanna woke from such a deep sleep that she didn't recall where she was for several moments. She rose, stretched, and went to the window. The day was shockingly bright, the sky blue. Sunlight glinted blindingly off frozen snow.

By the time she dressed and presented herself downstairs, Garrett was in the parlor involved in what appeared to be a serious conversation with the mayor. The sight of it stopped her in her tracks, but she hurried on, glad they hadn't noticed her.

Cessie was having coffee with T. Emmett Rice in the kitchen. Susanna knew him from waiting on him at Wiley's. "Mornin," Susanna said. She was embarrassed by being there, not to mention having slept in as if she was a fancy lady guest. "Can't believe how well I slept."

"Well," Cessie said with a smile. "We had quite the day."

"I am awful glad to see you, young lady," Emmett said. "Poor Mrs. Simpson is beside herself with worry. So are your friends."

Susanna felt a crushing guilt. It hadn't even occurred to her that others might be worried about her. "I'm sorry, I—"

"No," Emmett exclaimed. "Every time we get a happy turnout, we need to thank the Lord above and do a little jig."

"Sit," Cessie urged Susanna. "I'll get you some breakfast," she said as she rose. "I made biscuits and gravy."

Uncertain as to protocol, Susanna sat.

"Dad-blame storm took everyone by surprise," Emmett continued. "Never seen anything blow up so quick."

"Did everyone come through it alright?" Susanna asked.

Emmett shook his head. "So far, we know of seven souls that perished in the storm."

She had no idea what to say. "I'm sorry."

"It's a good thing you were here to help," he said tenderly. "We're beholden. How'd you learn to set a broken arm?"

148

"Here you go, honey," Cessie said, placing a shallow bowl of split open biscuits covered in hot sausage gravy and a glass of milk in front of Susanna.

It smelled delicious and it was a welcome diversion, because Susanna didn't want to offer the details of how she knew what she knew. "Saw it done once," she hedged. "It's just a matter of putting the bones back together and then binding it to stay. Leastwise, I hope it is. I hope I did it right." She picked up her fork, but looked at Cessie, unable to restrain her curiosity any longer. "Isn't that the mayor in there?"

"It is," Cessie replied.

"We drove here together," Emmett said.

"What's the mayor want with Garrett?" she asked, even though it was none of her business.

"To offer him a position in his company," Emmett replied.

Her jaw dropped momentarily; it was such a startling notion.

"He's sending Lonnie away," Emmett confided quietly.

"Shouldn't Lonnie go to jail?" Susanna asked bitterly, keeping her voice down. "If everyone knows he did it—"

"Lonnie denies it."

"That's because he's a big liar!"

Cessie patted Susanna's arm to calm her down. It made Susanna feel foolish. After all, who was she to get upset about what had happened to Garrett? "Sorry," she muttered.

"More coffee?" Cessie asked Emmett.

"No, I'm fine. Thank you." He looked back at Susanna. "We all want to protect Garrett," Emmett said in a kindly tone. "But he should have choices."

T. Emmett Rice was a good man, and not just because he had good manners and tipped better than most.

"He can accept the mayor's offer or not," Emmett continued, "but it's good that he gets choices to make."

Susanna cut into a biscuit. Glancing back up at Emmett, she asked, "Do you know if they had school yesterday?"

"They did, but half the children didn't show up. I can report that teachers and students are all fine. The schoolhouse has good stoves and it was well stocked."

149

"Do you know if Lily was there?"

"She wasn't. I was going to take her and Caty and Rebecca and Jake home this morning if they were."

Susanna laughed breathily as a geyser of joy was released so forcefully that tears sprang to her eyes. She ducked her head, embarrassed by the strong reaction, and put her attention on pushing around her food until the lump in her throat subsided.

She'd eaten all the breakfast she wanted when Lonnie and the mayor came into the kitchen. She looked up and met Garrett's gaze, although she couldn't read what he was thinking or feeling.

"Lawrence, do you know Miss Jones?" Emmett asked.

"How do you do, Miss Jones," the mayor said.

"How do you do," she repeated, feeling incredibly foolish. Never before had those words come out of her mouth, and it sounded like it, too.

"Perhaps I could look at April May's arm?" Lawrence Hastings said to Cessie. "I've set my fair share of broken bones."

"Oh?" Cessie asked curiously.

"As a young man … in the war, I worked in the surgery. I thought I'd be a doctor until that experience."

"Well," Cessie replied. "Isn't that something? Let me just make sure she's awake and presentable," she said, rising gracefully. "We'd very much appreciate that."

"Could I—" Garrett said.

Susanna saw he was speaking to her.

"Talk to you a minute?" Garrett finished.

She nodded, rose, and started from the room.

"Susanna, will you be coming back with us?" Emmett asked. "We've got plenty of room in the sleigh."

"Yes, sir. I should. Thank you."

Emmett gave a nod and a smile, and she walked on, stepping over in the hallway so that Garrett could take the lead. He did, and she followed him to a cozy room at the end of the hallway that featured curved fan-back chairs of blue.

The curtains were floral, there was an ornate card table and chairs and packed shelves of books. There was a fire in the hearth, although it was nearly out of life. Garrett went to stoke it. He added more coal from the bin.

"This is a nice room," she said.

"They call it Mama's drawing room," he said. He put the shovel up and turned to her.

She realized she was wringing her hands and stopped. She put them by her side, determined to keep them still.

"The mayor," Garrett said. "Offered me a position. To learn the mercantile business. For good pay."

She waited.

"What do you think?" he asked.

"What do *you* think?" she asked carefully.

He shrugged. "It took me by surprise, that's for sure."

"I bet."

"I always thought I'd work with my hands," he said, stepping closer to her. "The thing is, I learned recently that I could still do that. Maybe not as well as before, but better than most. I discovered it when I stopped in the smithy and got to helping one of the apprentices. Wayman said the same thing. It surprised us both."

She watched him carefully. It was evident he felt something deeply.

"Of course, by then, I was here and helping out and I've liked that, too. I've liked it a lot. They really do need help around here. Not to say they can't manage, but some things just don't get done and there is so much here that could be done. It's really good land." He paused. "I don't know anything about the mercantile. I never expected something like that to come up."

"What exactly would you do if you went to work for him?"

"He called it a management position and said there's a bright future to be had."

His face was flushed and his eyes were bright. So he liked the idea?

"What are you thinking?" he asked warily.

"I'm thinking he's the father of—"

"That's why he's doing it," he interrupted.

"Guilt," she stated.

"Maybe. In part. Or responsibility, which isn't exactly the same thing. Lonnie won't be around for much longer anyway. The mayor is sending him away."

"Just seems strange is all," she said.

"But a man's got to look at all his choices, right?"

She was quiet a moment. "Emmett said the same thing."

"He said it to me, too. What do you figure other people would think?"

She drew back, bothered by the notion. "Who cares what people think? It's your life. You're the one that's gotta live it and be happy with it."

"Yeah, well, I can't help wondering," he said with a shrug.

"Wondering what?" she snapped. She didn't know why she was so bothered by the thought of him working for the mayor, other than it seemed like a big ole' payoff for the guilt the man felt. Not that it wasn't better than not feeling any guilt, she supposed.

It was also irritating that Garrett was worried about what other people thought. What if he knew the real truth about her and where she'd come from? What if he'd had one glance at her in her old life? If she'd stumbled into Green Valley looking like the no-count, poor-as-dirt slave she'd been, what would people have thought then? Was that what he cared about?

"If I make a good living, maybe I'd be looked on more favorably."

Now she was really thrown. What was he talking about?

"In terms of marriage someday. Maybe this," he said, holding up his fingerless hand, "—wouldn't count as much."

She gawked because he was wanting to know her opinion on how much a girl might want him if he made good money, given his damn stump? He'd brought her in there to ask her that? Could he not see how insulting that was? "No one worth their salt is gonna let your hand make a lick of difference," she stated, trying to keep all emotion out of her voice.

"Really?"

"Well, of course, really," she replied testily. She was blushing hotly because of all the nonsense she'd thought in the night. She'd thought he'd might actually like her. "I gotta go." She turned toward the door.

Naturally, he did the gentlemanly thing and got to the door first, opening it wider. "I think you're the most special girl I ever met," he said.

She froze, and then she looked at him, completely baffled about where he was coming from. Was she truly special to his way of thinking or was she special because she'd just told him what other girls might think of him? She felt the warning and pressure of tears again.

"That's kind of you to say," she uttered in a thick voice before she raised her chin and marched out the door, heading back to the safe ground of the princess room.

~~~

"Susanna," Cessie called as she knocked.

"Yes, ma'am," Susanna called back as she started toward the door. She'd straightened the room and was ready to go.

The door opened and Cessie stepped in with a blue coat draped over her arm. She had a smile on her face until she saw that Susanna had been crying. "What's wrong?"

Another damned lump was in Susanna's throat and her eyes tingled warningly. She hadn't cried since she was eight – until she'd stepped foot into this place. She shook her head, not trusting her voice.

"Sit down and talk to me," Cessie said, setting the coat on a chair. "Honey, we can get you back to town tomorrow or the next day. Emmett will go straight back to Wiley's and let them know you're alright."

Susanna shook her head. "I need to go," she said in a whisper.

Cessie led Susanna to the edge of the bed, and they sat. "You and Garrett didn't have words, did you?" It was asked sadly and without blame.

Susanna shook her head. She was trying to hold in the emotion she felt, but it was like trying to hold back a flood. "He's v-very special," she managed in a shaky whisper.

"Yes, he is. And so are you."

Susanna looked away from her with a sigh. Someone like Cessie, who had always been beautiful and loved wouldn't understand. Some girls weren't the princess. Cessie was and Lily could be and should be, but not her. A charmed life just wasn't for her.

"What's upset you so?"

"I can't," Susanna whispered.

"Alright," she said, patting Susanna's leg. "Then let me tell you a few things. First, you set sister's arm perfectly. Lawrence says it will heal just fine."

That was a relief to hear.

"Second, in case you were wondering, April May behaved herself admirably. She was perfectly polite to the mayor. Whom she doesn't care a great deal for."

The levity helped. Susanna wiped her eyes and sniffed, then managed to take in a decent breath.

"I want you to promise me not to be offended by something," Cessie said, rising.

Susanna nodded, although she couldn't imagine being offended at anything Cessie had to say.

Cessie picked up the coat she'd carried in. It looked lush and thick, a mesmerizing cobalt blue. "Sister and I want you to have this."

Susanna's jaw dropped.

"I bought it as a Christmas gift for April May a few years ago. You want to guess how many times she's worn it?"

"Five?"

"That would be five too many. She tried it on once but then she never wore it. She claimed it was too rich for her blood. So we want you to have it. It's our way of saying thank you."

Susanna didn't know what to say.

"April May once said I should give it away if it bothered me that it wasn't getting used. Now it feels like I was just waiting for you to give it to. You're not offended?"

"No! But I ...I don't know what the right thing is to do."

"Do you like it?"

154

"It's the prettiest thing I ever saw."

"Try it on," Cessie said with a pleased smile. Susanna stood and Cessie helped her into the coat and then stepped back to look. "I knew it," Cessie said jubilantly. "Go look."

No coat could have felt warmer or more luxurious, but when Susanna stood in front of the mirror, she blinked in surprise. Her face showed traces of crying, but she wasn't ugly. She looked more fragile than she'd ever imagined possible. The coat was magnificent. It was too good for her. "It's too much," she uttered in a thick voice, running her hands over the front of it.

"It certainly is not too much. With the hat, which I left downstairs, it's just right. You look wonderful."

How could she accept such a gift? But how could she refuse? She put her hands in the deep pockets, felt something and pulled out gloves made of soft leather.

"Those aren't a perfect match," Cessie said with a mischievous smile. "But I hope they'll do."

"Thank you," Susanna said thickly, meeting Cessie's eyes in the mirror.

Cessie, standing half in back, half to the side of her, wrapped her arms around Susannah and squeezed gently. "Shall I ask Emmett to wait for you or do you want to stay?"

She shook her head. "I have to go."

"This room is yours anytime."

Susanna had never hugged anyone of her own volition, but now she turned and hugged. When she pulled away, Cessie said the sweetest words anyone had ever uttered to her. "You're one of ours now."

Chapter Sixteen

L evi struggled to wake as someone knocked lightly. Before he could rouse himself, he heard the door open, followed by the sound of footsteps. His head hurt and his body hurt. In fact, he felt so sluggish and heavy; he couldn't have stopped someone coming at him slowly with murder in their eyes and a knife raised in both hands.

Fortunately, the person entering was the same woman who'd helped him earlier. She bent to feel his forehead. "Fever's gone down," she commented. "By a lot. You want a drink of water?"

He nodded. "Please," he whispered. His mouth was painfully dry. She picked up a filled glass from the table beside his bed and brought it to his lips as he lifted up onto an elbow. When he was satiated, he lay back down.

She walked over, sat in a chair and picked up some mending from a basket next to her. *Gretchen.* She'd told him her name was Gretchen. She wasn't particularly attractive, but he liked her face. It was the face of a woman who'd lived and lost and saw the lessons and even the humor in it.

The memory was coming back to him now. When he came to on the kitchen floor, she'd been tending him with the help of Jim, an unusually big man with an unusually pungent body odor. He was Gretchen's brother and a simpleton.

Jim helped him to sit up so that he could drink water, and Gretchen could tend to his back. As she did, she affirmed what he'd already recalled, that two men had come into the inn close behind him, almost as if they'd followed him. She hadn't thought anything about it at first, not until they began encouraging him to seek another inn.

"Better and cheaper, they said." She gave an insulted huff. "There is no such place. There's better, far better, and a few others are cheaper, but no place is both better and cheaper."

Eventually, Levi had been helped into a chair and managed to eat a meal of broth and bread before Jim half carried him upstairs and then left to fetch a particular doctor. Gretchen confided something while they were waiting. "If Jim stays quiet, the look of him will usually keep a man in line."

Now, Levi managed to sit, but his back felt strange and tight with each move. He was still trying to put the whole story together in his head. It was morning, mid-morning, but time had passed since he'd been discovered. Which had also been in the morning. It must have been yesterday morning. "The doctor—"

"He was here," she said, looking up from her mending. "You don't remember?"

He shook his head.

"Well, he aided the sewing up process with a good, strong whiff of the smelly stuff. You took fifteen stitches, but it'll heal fine. Of course, it will leave a scar to remind you to think twice before drinking with cagey strangers," she added wryly.

Levi sighed. It was an awful feeling to be broke and in debt. Broke, he was used to. Hell, it was all he'd ever known, but not while owing others. And he'd actually had money. That was what was so sickening. "I'll have to find work to pay you and the doctor," he admitted. "But I'll do it. You got my word."

She smirked. "Oh, I was smart enough to get paid."

His eyes widened.

She nodded. "Yes, siree. I didn't like the look of those two, not one bit. Didn't know if they'd lure you off or not, but I had you pay for your room and board. Two days' worth."

The surprise and relief that washed over him was so sweet, he felt lightheaded. "Truly?"

"Of course, truly. And I might have bloated the cost just a bit. You didn't seem to mind." She chuckled. "There's no worry on the doctor's account either. We have a sort of arrangement. He helps when I need, and I keep my mouth shut when he takes a room for … certain company."

"What company?" he asked curiously.

"That's for me to know," she stated flatly. "You'll need to keep still and rest for a day or two, but after that, you can help

157

around the place while you get your strength back if you want to. I can't pay you anything except for room and board, but you should take it."

"I'll take it! Thank you. I'm grateful."

One side of her mouth turned up in a lopsided smile as she went back to her mending. "You slept through a blizzard yesterday."

"A blizzard?"

She nodded. "Bad one. There's probably three feet out there, but it was the comin' down that was like nothin' you've seen. No telling how many are dead from it."

He'd slept through a day and a blizzard? It was hard to wrap his mind around it. "The last few weeks is all mixed up in my head."

"It'll all come back," she said.

He closed his eyes and leaned his head back, drowsy, but not wanting to sleep any more. "Does your husband work the inn with you?"

"Never had one, never wanted one."

He looked at her. She hadn't looked up from her mending or changed her expression. She seemed to mean what she said.

"I was the second oldest girl in a family of fifteen. I wasn't about to let that same lot be my life. Childbearing, child rearin', housekeeping. Never ending." She paused. "There was one man that got close, but he didn't cotton to having Jim around."

"You own this place by yourself then?"

"I don't own it, at all. I work for the cheap buzzard who does. He pays me a pittance but he allows me to keep Jim here. Jim works, too, but doesn't get a thing for it except room and board. I've managed to put a bit by, but it's no thanks to him."

Levi looked out at the brightness from the window. "Those men," he murmured. "They stabbed me?"

"No. Bashed you in the head with the butt of a pistol, by the looks of it. Then tossed you down the cellar steps. And wouldn't you know it happened when I'd gone to get Jim to get rid of them? Jim and me came back and the three of you were gone. Wish now I'd paid more mind to Surry barking."

158

"But my back. How—"

She shook her head. "You took a bad tumble down the steps and landed on broken bottles. Bad luck, that was. See, a couple of bottles got away from Jim when he fetched a case for me, only I didn't know it. He's afraid of the cellar, so he didn't want to tell me, knowing I'd make him go back and clean it up."

"Why's he afraid of it?"

"The dark, the smell, the rats. Rats the size of—" she held her hands a foot apart to show the size. "Nose to tail. Vile things. Well, not anymore, thank goodness. We got rid of them. Tell you this much, if you'd have been done like you was done a month ago, the rats would have had you for a hardy meal, bleeding and unconscious as you were."

It was a revolting thought. A shiver seized hold of him and he tugged the blankets closer.

"Luckily, the rat catcher brought his dogs and killed the lot of them. Carried the nasty things away in a big bag. He left Surry behind for a time to make sure there were no more in hiding since poor little Surry is mostly worthless to him."

Levi felt a tug of resentment at the words. "Why's he worthless?"

She shrugged one shoulder. "Getting up in age and one eyed, to boot. When he was a young thing, a nest of rats got the better of him. The dogs won in the long run, but poor Surry paid with his eye. His nose is still as good as ever and he barks and chases them. And they smell him, too, and hide."

"Surry," Levi murmured.

She chuckled. "That's a story. Turns out, the pup's first master was an Englishman or Irishman or some such thing. He sold the dog to Sam, the rat catcher, telling him the dog's name was Surry. Months later, Sam sees the man again and the man asks after the dog, except by a different name.

"He says something like, So how are you and Rover getting along? Sam says, who? The dog, the man says. The little ratter I sold you. You mean Surry, Sam says, looking at the man like he's gone 'round the bend. Only the man busts out laughing and says, I

159

warned you he was surry," she said, emulating an exaggerated Irish accent. "You know, a surry thing, with only the one eye."

Levi grinned.

She put her mending aside. "I'll get you some breakfast," she said. "Oats, I think. You must be famished."

He wasn't famished, but he felt empty and weak. "I appreciate it, Miz Gretchen."

She rose. "You're a good lad, Levi." She started for the door. "You surely are." She opened the door and stepped through, but then turned back looking stern. "But you should have better sense when it comes to cagey strangers."

~~~

Standing in the middle of the kitchen, Mrs. Simpson's eyes bulged at the sight of Susanna having entered through the back door of the restaurant. She strode to her looking furious, grabbed her close and hugged her fiercely. It was as opposite as could be from the embrace Susanna had shared with Cessie, but no less momentous.

When Simpson released her, the older woman stepped back stiffly and walked to her office without uttering a single word, but Susanna saw the tears in her eyes.

"We've been so worried about you," Callie Jo said, rushing forward to hug her.

"I'm sorry," Susanna said, as Callie Jo rocked her back and forth in her enthusiasm.

"Someone get word to Beth," Peg said.

"She's worried herself sick," Callie Jo said to Susanna, pulling back. "I'll go," she said to Peg. "My shift's done."

"Go," Peg said. "Susanna, take off that fancy coat and hat and get to work, girl."

The words were barked, but Susanna recognized the pleased gleam in Peg's eye. *I'm glad to be alive, too,* she thought. "Yes, ma'am," she said.

~~~

Tommy and Em sat on the sofa with Julianne between them, the three of them watching Lily, Caty and Ben play on the rug in front of them. Tommy's arm was on the back of the sofa and Julianne's head rested against his side.

Lily and Caty were stacking blocks and Ben was taking great delight in knocking them over. His laughter was infectious, even to Julianne, who'd barely made a peep since the incident. She'd clung to one or the other of her parents all the day and evening before and wanted to sleep with them.

They'd soothed and reassured her, and she'd been tucked into her own bed next to her sister, but she'd woken with nightmares twice and had to be talked back to sleep.

They all looked up at the sound of a knock on the back door, followed by it opening. "Hello," Doll called. "Came to check on y'all."

Lily beamed and popped up to meet them.

"We're here," Em said, just before Doll and Wood walking into the room.

"Hello," Wood greeted, which was followed by a chorus of returned greetings.

"Wasn't it something?" Doll asked, giving Lily a hug as she reached her. "I don't ever want to see one of them dern storms again."

"You alright?" Wood asked Lily, brushing her cheek with the backs of his finger.

She nodded, still smiling.

"I'm headed out to check the herd," Wood said to Tommy.

"I'll go, too," Tommy said.

"No," Julianne cried, throwing herself against him.

Tommy and Em exchanged a glance and then Tommy rose with Jules still hanging on tight. As he carried her off, gently patting her back, Doll and Wood moved in closer to find out what had happened.

Tommy went into his office, set Julianne on his desk, then sat in his chair in front of her. He wiped her tears away with the pads of his thumbs. "I have to go do some work now."

She shook her head.

"Yes, I do. I have to take care of this place, and you have to be my big girl." She shook her head again and fell forward into his arms. He held her tight, loving her so fiercely that it hurt. However scared she had been in the storm, he'd been moreso, and so had Em. "You know how afraid your mama was yesterday?"

Jules didn't respond.

Her face was pressed to his neck, and he could feel her lashes tickling when she blinked. "She needs you to stay close by her today. Maybe you can be her special helper." He pressed a kiss to her head. "Can you do that for me?"

She hesitated and then nodded.

He set her back up on the desk and gave her a tender smile. "Who did you get your blue eyes from?"

"You."

"That's right. And you got your spirit from your mama. Did you know that?"

She shook her head.

"It's true. She is so strong—"

She shook her head. "You're strong."

"So is she. In here," he said, tapping his chest. "And here," he said, tapping his temple. "She has more spirit and courage than anyone else I know. You get that from her."

She blinked in confusion.

He rose, kissed her again and then set on the floor. "Scoot," he said playfully. She started off, walking slowly, and he followed, grabbing his coat and hat on the way.

~~~

Matthew Morley, owner and editor of the Green Valley News and Record, finished setting the type on the story of the human toll of the blizzard. He straightened, removed his spectacles, and rubbed his eyes.

162

The death count from the storm was twenty-three, which sounded like a small number in relation to the devastation it represented in this town. He'd titled the piece 'The Blizzard: The Tally and the Toll', but he didn't feel quite satisfied with it.

For the most part, as best they knew, death had come to those who had tried to make it back home after a chore or a simple excursion. The storm had hit with such suddenness and ferocity, there was no making it to shelter before the body shut down. Some had made it a stone's throw to their destination, their frozen bodies discovered only after the storm had abated.

For the father coming upon his son halfway between barn and house, it was a sight permanently and horrifically frozen in his mind. That man was Phillip Booker and his son was twelve-year-old Billy.

It felt important to name and acknowledge every victim because twenty-three was not just a number. It was that many vital lives extinguished, most with families who would never be the same. Young mother, Rachel Cobb, for example, who had left her two-month-old son with her mother while she went to the store. Or 82-year-old Ira Wilson, found outside his home. No one knew or would ever know why he stepped out.

Bertram Early, a miner and father of six.

Janet Douglas, her sister Felicia Redmond, and Felicia's nine-year-old daughter, Meredith, found in their wagon halfway between town and the Redmond farm.

Matthew opened his eyes again, put his spectacles back on and bent forward, elbows to worktable, to reread the piece. It needed to be good. It needed to be right.

~~~

Down the street, Doc Simmons took a much-needed break, adding a nip of brandy and heaping spoonfuls of sugar in the inky-black, hours-old coffee left in the pot. For as bad as the death count was, there were many more injuries to deal with.

Frost bite, whether it be a nose or toes or feet or fingers or hands, had kept him and the other doctors of Green Valley busy.

Already today, he'd seen four patients and amputated a dozen toes. He took a sip of the coffee and cringed; it was so bitter. Then again, so was losing toes.

Chapter Seventeen

A week later, Emmett drove Susanna to the Martin-Medlin farm to see Lily. It just so happened to be the same day Garrett stopped by Wiley House to pay her a visit. For Susanna, the cold day had been highly enjoyable, and the farm was as wonderful as Lily had described, but it was sorely disappointing to have missed Garrett.

He hadn't left a note either, so she didn't know what his decision was about the mayor's offer or how April May was faring. Emmett said she was doing well, but she would have liked to have heard it from Garrett.

It was strange how many different kinds of lives there were that most folks just took for granted. The Medlin farm was full of people and busyness and good feelings. It made a body perk up and be glad to be amongst them. They'd had lunch in the long house, and it had been a unique experience.

Between the several farmhands, Tommy, Em and their little ones, plus Doll, Wood, Lily, Emmett and herself, there must have been twenty of them. There was constant talking, laughing and jesting all through the meal, as if they were all family.

It was hard not to stare at dark-haired, blue-eyed Tommy Medlin because he was devastatingly handsome. Em was lovely in a soft, natural way, and it was obvious her husband thought there had never been a more beautiful woman to ever walk the earth, but it was difficult not to keep sneaking glances at him.

Watching their little ones, she wondered if they would ever have any notion of how lucky they were. They'd grow up good-looking, loved, well taken care of, and happy. How could they not?

But the best part of the day was seeing how Lily had blossomed. Not only had she put on much needed weight, but she was dressed well, she had color in her face, and her hair was shiny. She was proud of their house and her room, for good reason, and

Wood and Doll weren't just the couple she lived with, they'd become her adoptive parents.

"We landed in a good place, didn't we?" Susanna said lightly when they were parting.

Lily nodded. "Like it was chosen for us, don't you think?"

It was an interesting thought because she hadn't chosen the place. She and Levi had decided to risk everything and run away. It was Mr. Dennis who had selected the location. Had it been happenstance or something else? She'd never believed in that *something else*, but she wasn't so sure anymore.

In fact, looking back on it, that he'd even given her the opportunity was bewildering. Looking as she did? Being as surly as she was? But he had taken a chance on her and sent her here. Then she'd been caught with Lily straight away. They could have been in a real mess, but Mrs. Simpson, known for running a tight ship, had not only given her a second chance, but arranged for Lily to live here.

Susanna had hoped the Martin-Medlin Farm would be a place where Lily was fed enough and kept warm and not overworked, but she couldn't have dreamed up a better place than this one.

Emmett was ready to leave and so Lily hugged her tightly. "I love you," the girl said.

"I love you, too," Susanna returned.

Lily pulled back, surprised and moved to hear the words, and then she smiled the prettiest smile known to all mankind. It made Susanna wish she'd admitted her feelings a long time ago.

~~~

Bella sat against her pillow strewn headboard clutching a monogrammed pink satin pillow while listening to some of the girls going on and on about Susanna Jones. How she'd transitioned into a butterfly. It was ridiculous. Some of the townspeople had obviously taken to her for some reason. They probably just felt sorry for her.

The far more interesting thing she'd learned was that Garrett Trentwell was being taken under the mayor's proverbial wing, while Lonnie, the man she'd chosen to be her intended, had been shunned and cast off. The irony was sickening. Garrett had wanted her, and she'd spurned him for Lonnie, as any right-minded girl would have. But Lonnie was now the outcast to be replaced by Garrett? She rose, tossed her pillow down and walked toward the door.

"Where are you going?" Margaret asked.

"I need some air," she replied, hoping they would get the hint and vacate her room. She had invited them in, encouraged the chatter and steered it where she'd wanted it to go, but now she knew. What she needed now was confirmation of what she'd heard and, if it was true, a plan to turn things around to her advantage.

Her one-year anniversary with Wiley's was in a matter of a few weeks and she had no intention of remaining a waitress beyond it. She needed to know by then if she was staying in town as a newly betrothed lady or returning home. She'd been enamored with the idea of being first lady of burgeoning Green Valley, and it was still a vision worth seeing through. But how? Or maybe with whom was the better question.

~~~

"Barbados?" Lonnie practically spat. "What are you talking about?"

"We have interests there that we can possibly expand," Lawrence stated calmly. He'd come to the shop to have this conversation, and upon inspection of Lonnie's office, it was clear he should have had it some time ago.

What his eldest had been doing with his time was not clear, but it hadn't been spent working. Lonnie's office, the largest in the building, had once been his own office. He knew how it had looked. Now it was a dusty mess without organization or indication of a project of any sort. His other employees could all account for their time, but not Lonnie.

167

He had avoided this meeting for far too long, but a change was very clearly in order. He had allowed the situation to go entirely too far.

"What interests? I'm not going to sodding Barbados. It's halfway around the world!"

Lawrence bit his tongue in an effort to remain calm. The truth was, he was as angry at himself as with Lonnie, and justifiably so. For as slack as Lonnie had been, he had been equally so. More so. He was the parent and he'd been negligent at what was right under his nose.

"What interest?" Lawrence repeated. "We own a large share of a sugar plantation, and it may be wise to expand it. There is a market for sugar. There will remain a market for sugar. You will go see the state of things there, report your findings back to me, and we'll decide how to proceed."

"Why me? I know nothing of it."

"Then learn! Don't you think it's about time you learn something? Look at this place! What useful work is being done here?" When Lonnie didn't answer, his anger nearly boiled over. "Do you know anything about what we do?"

"Buy and sell?" Lonnie retorted. "No, let me expound. Buy low and sell high. Do I have the hang of it?"

"You have made life difficult for all of us," Lawrence stated in a low voice. "With your irresponsible, drunken behavior. The brawls. The attack on the blacksmith."

He paused a moment to see if Lonnie would defend himself or deny it again, but he did not. In fact, there was sheer defiance in his son's gaze. "So you will go," he continued coldly. "Either to Barbados or somewhere else of your choosing. I will support you should you decide to stay with the company, although I will expect both effort and a code of behavior you have not demonstrated thus far. If you choose to leave us, I'll do what I feel is fair and reasonable."

Lonnie sat back in his chair. "And if I don't *choose* to leave at all?"

This isn't how Lawrence had hoped the conversation would go, although that had probably been naïve on his part. "That is not an option any longer."

Lonnie stared in disbelief. "So what if I refuse to leave? This is my home, after all."

"If you refuse to leave this town, find another place to live and another means of support."

"You cannot be serious! You would cast your own son aside?"

Lawrence's throat ached and his heart was breaking, but it was past time for him to face his failure as a father. He had failed both his sons. If he hadn't, they would be happier and they would be leading more productive and balanced lives. "I am ashamed of your behavior. I'm ashamed of myself for ignoring it and possibly cultivating it. But I have to cut the aprons strings or you will doom us all."

Lonnie glowered. "There were never any apron strings. You'd like there to be puppet strings, but I won't be a puppet. You say 'jump' and I say 'how high?' No!"

Enough had been said. Maybe too much. "Think it over, son."

"That's rich! You threaten to cast me aside and then call me son? How dare you!"

"Be careful," Lawrence warned. "Be very careful." After another few moments of staring at one another in strained silence, Lawrence started from the room. At the door, he turned back and fixed his eldest with a look of utter resolve. "Remove your things from this office today. One way or the other, it is no longer yours. I will be moving back in here."

Lonnie had the good sense not to reply, so he turned and left, going down the long staircase at a brisk clip. In the lobby, he nodded to Mr. Todd, the clerk, and continued out the door, anxious to get back to his small office in town hall six blocks away, near the center of town and pack it up. He'd never needed it. It had been for show, and the show was closing.

From the cracked doorway of his second-floor office, Timothy watched his father leave. Given the grim expression on his face, it was possible he was staying true to the decision of sending Lonnie away. Moments later, a crash was heard from his brother's office. Lonnie throwing something, no doubt. Timothy shut the door, crossed back to his desk and sat.

His job involved the general management of most accounts. The oldest accounts were still managed by his father. Mr. Todd, their head clerk, kept the books. Theirs was a flourishing business that did close to a hundred thousand dollars of revenue per year, so there was plenty of work to go around, but Lonnie's job had never been made clear, at least not to him. Lonnie fancied it as a general running of things which was preposterous.

Timothy suddenly found himself wondering how alike his brother and father might be. Each of them loud and brash in order to get their father's attention. Was that what it was? He'd never thought of himself as lucky, but he'd always understood where he stood and so he'd never endeavored to achieve his father's esteem.

That's so not true.

He reached for his pen, but then set it back down again. Why did he do that? Why did he fool himself? He had always wanted his father's approval. For that matter, he'd wanted his brother's, as well. For the whole of his existence. At least, until recently.

If he ever had a child, especially a son, he would do it differently. He would promote their self-esteem, listen to their stories, let them know how special they were. He would let them know they were loved.

He heard a slamming of the door and knew it was Lonnie, making a statement, albeit a childish one. If things remained true to form, either Lonnie would leave and go on a drinking binge or he'd barge in here and demand to know what he knew. Or both.

There was plenty of time for him to do his usual disappearing act. Lonnie didn't know of the sliding panel in his office that he could so easily slip behind. Bertram Todd knew, but he would cover for him as he always did.

Lonnie would demand to know where he was and Mr. Todd would look nonplussed and say, "I don't know. Shall I look for him?" Poor Lonnie. He was a despised buffoon, and he had no idea of it. Timothy did not move and, moments later, his door was thrown open by his livid elder brother.

"What has gotten into our father?" Lonnie demanded as he barged in.

"What do you mean?" Timothy asked dispassionately, not looking up from the ledger he'd just bent over.

"He's making me go to Barbados!"

Timothy looked up in surprise. He hadn't known the plan. "Oh?"

"That's all you can say?"

"I didn't know," Timothy said casually.

"What *do* you know?" Lonnie asked suspiciously, coming closer.

Timothy leaned back in his chair, suddenly rather enjoying the exchange. He'd never had the upper hand with his brother, but maybe things had changed. "I know father has seemed different lately."

"Different how?"

Timothy shrugged. "He's concerned about the town's opinion of us, but it's more than that. I think he's begun examining his own choices in life." He paused before adding, "He asked about Garrett Trentwell recently."

Lonnie's eyes narrowed. "What did you tell him?"

"The truth. That I didn't touch him. As you well know, I went home … after trying to get you to come with me. I can't speak to anything else that happened. I think I know what happened, but I cannot say for certain." Lonnie's fists were clenched by his sides and he looked ready to pounce and punch. Timothy didn't care. "Father's offered him a job here. To make up for … his misfortune."

Lonnie's face had reddened. "My job? He offered *my* job to a blacksmith who doesn't know a goddamn thing about trade?"

Timothy shrugged again. "You'll have to ask him. He wasn't specific."

"You're in this," Lonnie accused. "Up to your eyeballs. I know you're in this."

171

"I have work to do," Timothy said in a bored tone, going back to his ledger. "Shut the door behind you, will you?"

Lonnie didn't shut it; he slammed it hard enough to shake the building, which Timothy found curiously amusing.

Chapter Eighteen

B reathing hard, Garrett took a break from chopping wood and looked around at the fine morning. The sky was cloudless and bluer than he'd seen in ages. The snow was shimmering, melting fast, the sound of dripping was everywhere. Only days ago, the world had been frozen, and today – this. He'd had to take off his coat, he'd gotten so warm chopping.

He saw April May walking toward him from the barn, where she'd been one-handedly raking out stalls. She refused to be kept down. Strength don't come looking for you, she'd said. You got to force it back. She had the same attitude with herself that she'd had with him, one of the many reasons he adored her. She had a self-proclaimed tougher hide than Cessie, but no less of a soft heart.

"What a day, huh?" she called as she approached.

"Yes, ma'am. Couldn't be nicer if it tried."

She reached him and sat on an upended stump, looking appreciatively at the pile he'd created. "You gettin' us ready for the next one?"

"Hopefully, we'll never see one of those again." He put down the ax and righted another stump for him to sit on.

"You were awful quiet when you came back yesterday," she commented, shielding her eyes from the sun's glare so she could see him better. "Was everything alright?"

"I'd hoped to see Susanna, but she'd gone to the farm to see Lily."

"Ah."

"I went to the smithy instead and had a nice visit."

"How's Wayman making out?"

"Good. They're getting more done now."

"Did you see Lawrence?"

Garrett shook his head. "No, ma'am. I don't know what to tell him yet."

"What do you want to tell him?"

Garrett leaned forward, elbows to knees, watching a small mouse peeking out from the woodpile. "I don't know," he admitted. "I really don't. I was making fifteen dollars a week and never thought that much about it. I liked the work."

She nodded.

He looked at her. "He's offering fifteen hundred dollars a year."

Double the salary he'd been making. "You been by to see the place? See what the work would be?"

She was asking, despite knowing the answer. He shook his head.

"Why not? What's holding you back?"

"For one thing, I can't imagine being inside all day. Not working with my hands."

The window to the kitchen opened with a dull scraping sound. "April May," Cessie called. "You want to walk over to the cottage? I want them to join us for supper on Saturday."

"Sure thing," April May called. "Give me a few minutes."

"And Garrett," Cessie said, "I'd like to include Susanna. Can you see to that?"

He grinned because having a good excuse to go back this soon was thrilling. "Yes, ma'am."

"Oh, and Emmett, too," Cessie added. "Will you stop by and ask him?"

"Will do," he called back.

April May chuckled. "Nothing makes her happier," she commented after Cessie had closed the window again. She stood. "You want my advice?"

"I'd be glad of it," he replied, meaning it.

"Go see Lawrence and find out what's what. Where you'd work and what you'd do and who you'd be around. You don't need to give him an answer right then, but once you've seen the place and heard him out, I bet you'll know if you want the opportunity or not."

That made sense.

174

"And, if you still don't know, sit down and put a measuring stick to it. On a scale of one to ten, how content would you be working at the mercantile?" She paused. "How content would you be if you returned to the smithy?"

Garrett blinked in surprise.

"Of course, I know about Wayman's offer," she said with a smirk. "You enjoyed that life and you already know what the future would look like there, so that'll be easy to measure."

He nodded.

"You know, you mentioned the salary, but money don't mean diddly if you don't like what you do. How much do any of us really need anyway?"

"Money doesn't buy happiness," he murmured.

"It sure as shootin' don't, honey. Who said that, anyway? Ben Franklin?"

"I have no idea."

"Well, anyway, the last thing to measure is staying on here."

He drew back in surprise. "Here?"

"Why not? You can clearly see we got more to do than one old woman can handle, even when I'm fully armed again. We can't pay what Lawrence can in cold, hard cash, but maybe we can pay more in other ways. I feel confident we can come up with an arrangement that would suit all." She turned and started off. "It's all about that measuring stick."

He looked out at the mules grazing in the field. Another choice. Another interesting choice.

~~~

At not quite three in the afternoon, Lonnie paced the floor at Jackals attempting to explain his plan. He was three sheets to the wind, ranting about being forced out, and talking in circles. First saying he would go, but he wouldn't really go. He would pretend to go. After he was gone, he wanted the business set on fire.

Once the mercantile went up in flames, who would be blamed except Trentwell? The cripple with an ax to grind. That would get Trentwell for thinking he could take his place.

175

His father would get a lesson, too. He would learn who he should have cared about. As for himself, he'd not only be free of suspicion, he'd be exonerated. Everything would be set to rights.

"But it's your legacy, eh?" Andre asked. "Your business. It will be all yours one day. Why would you give that up?"

"One word," Lonnie said scathingly. "*Insurance*. We'll get paid on the building and the stock that's lost. See? I won't be out anything. Just the opposite. I'll get back what's due me."

"What's in it for us?" Sal asked coldly.

Lonnie sat. "Before you set it ablaze, take what you want," he replied flippantly.

Sal looked pointedly at Andre, wanting nothing more than to reach over and slit the throat of the arrogant little prick. Andre read the look clearly but held up a hand for patience. "How would we go about it?"

"My key. Except it can't possibly be *my* key when I'm miles away on the open sea," Lonnie replied, slurring his words. "If you get my meaning."

"So, you say goodbye to the folks," Andre said. "You leave. Except you don't really leave. What will you do? Come stay with us? Shack up in Honey Creek?"

Lonnie shrugged because he hadn't figured it all out yet. Not down to the small details, anyway.

"You tell us the best time to go," Andre mused. "Exactly where to go. All the details. We take what we want and then burn it down. Is that it?"

"Yes."

"How do we know this isn't just drunk talk?"

Lonnie felt a rush of resentment. "I've been thinking of nothing else for days."

"Alright," Andre said pleasantly. "I agree. You do this for us, we do this for you," he said easily. He looked at Sal.

Sal nodded slowly, looking hard at Lonnie. "None of us ever to talk on penalty of having his tongue cut from his head," he said, leaning forward for emphasis. "Agreed?"

Lonnie hesitated a moment because of the malevolence in Sal's eyes. He was having second thoughts, loud ones, but he'd gone too far not to agree. At least, for the moment. He nodded.

Andre spit in his hand and stuck it out.

There was no choice, so Lonnie did the same. The hand he shook was cool and Sal's eyes were colder than Andre's grasp. Suddenly, there was not enough air in the place. "I'll tell you when," he said.

"You do that," Sal said.

Lonnie made himself walk more slowly than he wanted to, especially as he noticed the looks of loathing on the faces he passed. The fear and trepidation he felt was enough to make his bowels feel loose.

Chapter Nineteen

astings' Mercantile was impressive. After speaking to April May, Garrett went to the mayor's office without knowing if he'd be seen or not, but the mayor gave him a warm reception and then walked him over to the mercantile.

Mayor Hastings, who told him to call him Lawrence, called it the shop. It was not like any shop Garrett had ever seen. The foyer, with its polished wood and lush carpets, was elegant, and the offices were spacious with fancy desks, armchairs for guests, and built-in shelves stocked with books and decorative items.

The warehouse had more than fifteen hundred square feet of well-organized goods stacked on floor to twelve-foot ceiling shelving. There were bottles, barrels, crates and casks, all of it carefully inventoried and accounted for. They documented when items were received and where it was going. They kept careful track of what it cost them and what it was being sold for. They were middlemen because they didn't make the products, nor did they sell to the public. They sold to entities who sold to the public.

Timothy Hastings showed Garrett around and explained the business. He even showed him the office that would be his if he chose to join the firm.

The idea was strangely thrilling. Garrett had not expected to be impressed or to feel the possibility of fitting in, but he was and he did. He hadn't known Timothy before that afternoon. The youngest Hastings seemed thoughtful, intelligent, compassionate, and yet he had a head for business. He'd expressed regret and empathy for the attack.

"I'll train you, should you choose to join us," he'd pledged. "We'll find your niche. There will be some part of the business that you'll enjoy and be good at, and that will contribute to the bottom line."

"I don't have the right clothing," Garrett admitted, glancing at the tie and paisley silk vest Timothy wore beneath a faintly pinstriped jacket.

"We'll take care of that," Timothy replied. "Parker can have you set up with new clothes in a flash."

Lonnie had not been seen during the tour and Garrett wasn't looking forward to that encounter. It had to occur sometime, though. What he *was* looking forward to was seeing Susanna.

When he left the mercantile, he went to Wiley House. He rang the bell and waited to be admitted. When the door opened, it was by an attractive woman of perhaps thirty with a book tucked under her arm.

"May I help you?" she inquired.

"I'm here to see Susanna if I may. I'm Garrett Trentwell."

"Of course," she said with a friendly smile. "Come in."

He stepped inside.

"The parlor is just through there," she said gesturing to it. "If you'll wait there, I'll get Susanna."

"Thank you." He started to the parlor while she walked in another direction. He was glad to find the room empty. He thought about where he should sit. He tried an upholstered chair first but sank down too far. He got up and went to the edge of a settee, where Susanna could sit next to him, if she chose.

"Garrett," a voice said.

He stood and turned to face Bella standing in the doorway. The welcoming smile on her face was a surprise. "Hello," he returned.

"How are you?" she asked, coming closer.

How odd that she was speaking to him. And like an old friend, no less. "Fine, thank you," he replied coolly. "Yourself?"

"I'm well," she returned. She stopped an arm's length from him, a concerned expression on her face. "I've thought about you so much over the last weeks. And prayed for you."

What was this? She'd never given him the time of day and she'd prayed for him?

"I'm so horribly sorry for what happened," she added tenderly.

He nodded. He never knew what to say when someone expressed sympathy. "I've learned to cope. Thank you for the kind words, though."

"Did I hear right? You're here for Susanna?" she asked with a doubtful expression on her face.

"Yes."

"The two of you are friends?" she asked, as if the notion was somehow distasteful.

Now *that* was the expression he recognized. Was the notion distasteful because he wasn't good enough for a Wiley's girl? "Yes," he replied defensively.

"Then I guess you know about her beau?" she asked reluctantly, as if hating what she had to share.

The words were like a punch to his gut. "I beg your pardon?"

"She's practically engaged."

Susanna …engaged? As in engaged to be married?

"I don't want to see you hurt again," she continued. "His name is Levi."

It couldn't be true. Susanna would have said so. He didn't believe it, wouldn't believe it, but a sense of confusion and hurt feelings began surfacing despite the denial. After all, he'd made it clear to Susanna that he fancied her, and she'd had plenty of opportunity to mention a beau much less an engagement.

She could have mentioned it while they spent a whole day and night trapped by the blizzard. Or she could have told him the next morning. Or she could have sent a note. "What makes you think," he began

"Oh, she talks about him all the time. She expects him to come here for her. That's the plan."

He swallowed. "She hasn't said anything to me."

"She has had a hard life," Bella said sadly. "It's possible she wants to make sure—"

"Make sure?" he asked when her voice trailed off.

She shrugged delicately. "That he shows up as he promised to do. Better to keep two men on the string then end up with none."

So he was a prize fish on her line? Or maybe he wasn't the prize. Maybe Levi was the prize. Levi probably had two hands.

Bella touched his arm. "I want you to know something. As soon as I learned about what happened to you, I couldn't have anything more to do with Lonnie. He begged and begged, but I couldn't have anything to do with someone who would do such a thing."

Garrett shifted on his feet, antsy and a bit queasy. He didn't know what to say to her and he didn't particularly want to be having this conversation. Where was Susanna, anyway?

"I should go," Bella said, taking a step backwards.

She was as beautiful as ever, so why wasn't it affecting him like before? Was it due to the shock of what he'd just learned?

"Bye," she said. Hesitantly, she turned and walked to the door, glancing back at him briefly before disappearing.

When she was gone, he sat, reeling at the fact that Susanna had a fiancé. It might not be true, though. It might not be true at all. But then why would she have been talking about him to the other girls?

Susanna stepped into the room, walking quickly, and he stood again. "Hello," she greeted perfunctorily. She seemed surprised to see him. And a little disturbed maybe? "I ain't ... I mean I don't have long. Because I got to get to my shift."

"Well, I won't keep you," he replied testily. "It's just that I was supposed to ask if you wanted to come to supper on Saturday."

Confusion flickered on her face. "You were supposed to ask? What does that mean?"

"Just what I said. Cessie wanted me to ask you."

She looked aggravated. "Well, so sorry you had to go to the trouble. Or maybe you would have come, anyway. Let me guess; is there someone you'd rather ask?"

He crossed his arms in frustration. "Maybe I'll answer you when you answer me. Is there someone you'd rather go with?"

She huffed.

"It's not a complicated question, is it?" he demanded.

Her jaw dropped. "Oh! Like I'm not smart enough to answer a complicated question?"

"I didn't say that. I really don't know how smart you are."

181

"Smart enough to know when you'd rather have someone else on your arm!"

"Yeah? Well, maybe I'm smart enough to know you'd rather have Levi be with you." She drew back as if slapped, but she said nothing. So it was true! She just hadn't expected him to know.

"Yeah," she said quietly. "So?"

It was true. She'd played him for a damn fool. "Look, I was just sent to—"

"I heard you," she interrupted. "Cessie wants me to come to supper."

He just stood there, too angry and hurt to offer any reply.

She took a few deep breaths as if to control the temper that wanted to unleash itself. "Will you tell her I have other plans?" she said in a shaky voice. "But please thank her anyway."

"Yeah, I will," he said, already stepping around her. In fact, he couldn't walk fast enough.

Tears rolled down Susanna's face and, for once, she didn't try and stop them. So Bella had told her the truth last night. Garrett wanted her. Bella. Well, of course he would. What man with eyes wouldn't?

She wiped her face and walked to a back corner of the room, determined she would collect herself before she went back upstairs and was seen by anyone. What was wrong with her? It hadn't been long ago that she'd told Jean she wasn't looking for a man.

And she hadn't been!

And she wasn't!

She'd come here to work and make money and to get Lily far away from Cheever, and she'd accomplished all of that. So what did she care if Garrett Trentwell got all googley-eyed around Bella Byrd? What a stupid name anyway.

Except who was she to talk, when she didn't even have a surname? Not one that meant anything, anyway. They'd given the name Jones to every nameless child at the home. Children who hadn't been loved enough to even get a name from those they'd come from.

Her chest ached. When Bella sought her out to tell her Garrett had been in love with her and probably still was, she thought Bella was saying it just to be cruel. It seemed like sugar coated poison. But when Bella passed her on the steps mere minutes ago, she had an apologetic look as she whispered, "I tried to warn you."

Damn her! And damn Garrett, too, for telling her she was the most special girl he'd ever met. They'd just been words. Empty, damned words. *And damn me, too, for being so stupid.*

Stupid, nameless, ugly girl!

~~~

Lonnie lay on his side in a sweaty, tangled heap, half on the bed half off. A basin was on the floor, one that had been repeatedly used to vomit in. Hopefully, there was nothing left on his stomach to come up.

He was beyond miserable in every way. He looked around, but he had no idea what time it was. All he knew was that he'd had terrible nightmares about swimming in blood and getting it in his mouth. He'd been unable to escape. It was a virtual river of blood, and he'd woken up retching.

He closed his eyes and groaned. Everything in his life had turned to shit. His father had turned his back on him, and his own brother didn't care. No one cared. If it had been Timothy sick in bed, Marian would have been caring for him. Bringing him food and drink and drawing him a bath.

He suddenly recalled going to Jackals yesterday and his heart began pounding. What had he done? As the memory began returning, he pulled himself up against the headboard, reached for a dampened pillow and hugged it to himself.

God almighty, he'd asked them to burn the business down once he was gone. He'd offered them his key. Told them they could take what they wanted and then to burn it to the ground. "Oh, God," he whispered.

He hadn't meant it! Why did he do these things when he was drunk? He had to make it right somehow. He felt the pull of nausea again and quickly went over the side of the bed, heaving. He threw up until there was nothing more, but still the dry heaves racked his body.

"Marian," he called when it was finally over. He needed water to drink and a bath drawn and for her to take away the damned basin. "Marian!"

~~~

Marian, seated at the kitchen table, glanced up from the grocery list she was making at the sound of Lonnie calling for her. She reached for her cup, drank the last of her tea and then stood. She picked up the list and walked out the back door to see to her shopping, grabbing her shawl on the way out.

<u>Chapter Twenty</u>

O n Saturday evening, Reverend Stephen Thompson entered the sanctuary after a long stroll around town. It was his habit while seeking inspiration.

First, he prayed and then he opened the bible and blindly pointed to a passage. Whichever chapter and verse it fell on he pondered, hoping he'd been guided to it. A sermon did not always come from the scripture, but, more often than not, it started the thought process that led to the message. Today, his finger had landed on a rather dark verse about redemption in the book of Colossians.

It was unusual to see someone sitting in a pew at this time of evening, and even more unusual to see who it was. "Lonnie?"

Lonnie didn't turn to look at him, nor did he reply. He just stared straight ahead.

As the reverend reached the pew where Lonnie sat, he experienced a tremor of awe that the scripture he'd fallen on earlier related to him.

"I've destroyed everything," Lonnie uttered in a flat voice. "That's who I am."

"Why do you say that?"

Lonnie shook his head.

"I'd like to help, if I can," the reverend said.

"No one can."

"God can. You can turn it over to him."

"He'd never listen," Lonnie replied bitterly. "Not to me."

"Worse men than you have received forgiveness and gone on to live fruitful lives. One even became an apostle of Christ."

Lonnie sighed heavily, but whether in disgust or fatigue, the pastor couldn't tell. He went one pew ahead and sat, turning to face the younger man. "I was led to a verse this afternoon, a verse that begins, '*And you, who once were alienated and hostile in mind, doing evil deeds—*'"

Lonnie looked at him.

The point of the scripture is that with true repentance and atonement, you can be washed free of sin. You can begin again." Lonnie looked wan and exhausted, as if he hadn't slept in days. "What is it you're sorry for?" the pastor prodded.

"Everything."

"Saying 'everything' means nothing. I don't know what all you've done that needs forgiveness. And you don't have to tell me, but you have to lay it before God. All of it. He'll see into your heart. If you are truly sorry, then ask for forgiveness. Beg for it. On your knees."

Lonnie's chin trembled, and he looked down.

"Acknowledgment and atonement comes next. What can you do to make up for the wrong that you've done? The effort must be made."

Lonnie stood, muttering his thanks.

"You don't have to travel this path alone, Lonnie."

Lonnie turned and walked on.

"We can pray together if you like."

Lonnie stopped but didn't turn back around. "No, thank you. But I heard what you said."

After a beat of silence, the reverend said, "I'll be praying for you."

Lonnie nodded and left.

~~~

Outside the church, Lonnie put his hat on and pulled the brim low. The rain had cleared out, leaving a scent of freshness, but he walked homeward with his hands shoved in his pockets and his head down.

At the sound of distant laughter, he looked up. Lights from various establishments on Main Street shone and gleamed on wet cobblestones. He suddenly and unexpectedly felt an appreciation for the beauty of the town.

He watched people going here and there, all immersed in their own lives. Were most people happy? They seemed happy. Damn it, he had so much to regret! If he could take it all back, he would, but he couldn't. All he could do was get out of town before any more damage was done.

~~~

At the same time, Marian set a platter of sliced roast pork surrounded by baked cinnamon apples in front of Lawrence.

"It smells wonderful," he commented.

"It turned out well," she agreed, glancing over the rest of the dishes on the table. Collard greens and hot rolls.

"Why don't you join us?" Timothy asked her.

Only Lawrence and Timothy were present, which was the only time she might have been tempted, but she gave Timothy a quick smile and shake of her head and left the dining room. Lawrence was already helping himself to the pork.

~~~

Lonnie stepped into the dining room before they'd finished the meal. "So tell me about Barbados," he said in a resigned tone, causing Lawrence and Tim to experience a jolt of surprise. Lonnie helped himself to wine, then began filling his plate.

Lawrence and Timothy exchanged a look. "You've had a change of heart then?" Lawrence asked cautiously.

Lonnie sat. "You made a good point. It's time I be of some use." Lonnie picked up his fork but set it back down again. "I don't like being a disappointment."

Lawrence nodded gravely. "Before you leave, speak with Garrett Trentwell and offer him an apology. Whatever he decides to do with it, you must offer it."

"I'm going to. The truth is … not that I expect anyone to believe me, but I don't remember much of it. But I do know I was the cause of what happened to him."

187

Against what probably should have been his better judgment, Timothy found himself believing his brother's remorse, even given its sudden onset. "Barbados seems interesting to me," he commented.

Lonnie looked at him.

"It's warm. Tropical. A very different society." He looked at his father. "Coffee is something we ought to look into, as well."

Lawrence nodded.

"In fact," Timothy said, "I wouldn't mind going myself. If you could spare us both."

Lawrence didn't react, except to look worried. "That may be a lot to put on Todd," he hedged.

"I'd get everything caught up," Timothy said. "And keep my part of the trip to a few weeks."

Lonnie looked at his father and back to his brother, questioningly.

Lawrence pushed back his plate, finished with the meal, and looked pointedly at Lonnie. "If you were to say who was in on the attack on Trentwell, it might help."

A flicker of fear crossed Lonnie's face. "Help what?"

"Lawrence junior, there is repair that needs doing. If we want forgiveness from this town, we must give them something. Something besides 'I'm sorry.' Not that I doubt you. I'm … I'm glad to hear you say it. More glad and thankful than I can say. But you did not attack that young man by yourself."

Lonnie looked away.

"Did you?" Lawrence insisted.

"You don't know what you're asking. They'd kill me. They'd kill us all."

"Who?" Lawrence demanded, leaning forward. "Those Pettijeans?"

"You said that's where you were going that night," Timothy said to his brother. Part of him was both expecting and dreading a display of temper or a sneering comeback that would belie all he'd said.

Lonnie looked at him and then his father with an expression of pleading. "You have no idea how dangerous they are."

188

"I know how dangerous they would be in a prison cell," Lawrence retorted. "Which is where they belong."

"They tortured a man in Louisiana," Lonnie stated. "Flayed his skin one strip at a time."

Timothy dropped his fork with a clatter and sat back in his chair, sickened by the thought.

"Well, there went everyone's appetite," Lawrence said dryly.

"They tell that story with details about the technique and the sounds it makes when—"

"Stop it," Lawrence ordered crossly.

"How the man screamed," Lonnie added hauntingly. "It's not just the revolting facts they share. It's the enjoyment they took from it. They still take from it."

Lawrence considered his son a long moment and then took a drink. Putting the glass down, he watched the dark red liquid as he slowly twirled it by the rim. "You believe it to be a true story?"

"Of course, I do."

"Where did it take place?"

"I don't know. The Bayou."

"Bayou means water," Timothy said. "It's not a specific place."

"I don't know where. They once said north, I think. The north shore. The man's name was Cormier and his brother was sheriff of the parish. That's why they had to clear out of town and they ended up here. They just picked up and cleared out and started over again. And they'd do it again," he warned.

Lawrence didn't comment, but he wondered if the knowledge he'd just acquired might be enough. If the Pettijeans had, indeed, killed a man, and they knew the man's name, and it happened to be the same name as a sheriff, they ought to be able to find out and pass on their current whereabouts.

Best case scenario, the Pettijeans could go back to where they came from to face justice *after* it was made known they were the actual attackers of Trentwell. That would solve a few problems.

~~~

Garrett had little appetite. He felt despondent being at the dinner table with so much love and affection abounding. Jeremy and Lizzie Sheffield had four children, ranging in age from two to thirteen, and the couple was still in love. He would have given anything to be like that, but it didn't feel like that choice was going to be his to make.

Lily was there with Rebecca, the eldest Sheffield child. He'd caught Lily clandestinely studying him throughout the meal, and it made him wonder what Susanna had said about him. Although, why would she have said anything? It was likely he'd imagined any feeling she harbored for him.

When the ladies, Rebecca and Lily got up to clear the table and serve dessert, Cessie handed two-year-old Luke to him. "Hold on to him, will you, honey?"

Lizzie started to object, but April May flitted her away.

Emmett rose, "Gentlemen, lady," he said to Jenny, the four-year-old Sheffield child, causing her to giggle. "Excuse me." He stepped out of the room to visit the facilities.

Garrett had never held a little one, but the child seemed fine with it. He was a cute thing; all the children were. Luke grabbed hold of his spoon and waved it around as if mesmerized by it.

~~~

Rebecca scraped the food left on plates into a pail and put the plates in a basin of warm, soapy water as her mama, April May and Cessie conversed while getting dessert ready to serve. Lily had been helping, but she'd slipped away.

Cessie sliced the cake, Mama ladled on the strawberries and April May added whipped cream. Rebecca loved being part of kitchen duties, whether a meal was being prepared or they were cleaning up from one. There was more visiting and sometimes secret telling than work. It felt special, a place for ladies.

"Where's Susanna?" Mama asked quietly.

April May shrugged and shook her head.

"We think they had words," Cessie confided.

"He's had a long face ever since," April May added.

190

Rebecca walked over to the table drying her hands. "Lily wanted to see her."

April May handed Rebecca a plate of dessert. "Take that one to Jake," she said, handing her one with extra strawberries.

She pulled a pout. "You're not going to tell any secrets while I'm gone?"

April May gave her a look. "Since when do I leave you out of secrets?"

Rebecca grinned as she took the plate.

"Give this one to Jenny," Mama said, handing her a plate with a child-sized portion.

~~~

Luke banged the spoon on the table.

"No, Luke," Jeremy said to his son.

"Want me to take him?" Jake, the eight-year-old, offered. He was a quiet, polite boy that Garrett liked a lot.

"I think we're okay," Garrett replied, patting Luke's back.

As if to dispute the fact, Luke grinned and responded with a series of bangs on the table, so Jeremy snatched the child while maintaining his humor. "They call these the terrible twos," he said to Garrett.

"Terrible twos," Jenny repeated laughingly.

Jeremy stroked her hair as he passed her. He seemed an excellent father. The sort of father that Garrett wanted to be one day if he ever got the chance.

"What was Susanna doing?" Lily asked him shyly. She'd quietly come back into the room.

"I'm not really sure," he replied uncomfortably. "It might be that she ... just didn't want to."

Lily looked confused.

"She strikes me as pretty loyal," he commented.

She nodded. "She is."

"Probably wants to be true to Levi and all."

Lily looked even more confused, but then the ladies were coming back in with strawberry shortbread.

191

"We love Levi," Lily said. Worriedly.

He nodded, knowing that he shouldn't have brought it up. It served him right to have salt rubbed in the wound.

"He's our brother."

Garrett jerked his head to her.

"So is Nate. We don't care what color skin he has."

Garrett swallowed. Levi wasn't white? And he was like a brother? His heart had begun to hammer. "They're not sweethearts? Levi and Susanna?"

Lily look scandalized. "No!"

"You're sure?"

She nodded resolutely. "We're brothers and sisters. Only none of us have the same folks. But we're still brothers and sisters."

A piece of cake was put in front of him by Rebecca while Cessie came from the other side with coffee. "Thank you," he murmured, looking down at it. He felt guilty, but also relieved enough to be giddy. And suddenly ravenous. "This looks good."

Chapter Twenty-One

It was a chilly Sunday morning, but the sun was shining and birds were chirping and calling as Susanna stepped outside Wiley House and started toward the restaurant. She didn't notice Garrett standing at the corner of the building until she was nearly even with him, and then she stopped abruptly, her eyes wide.

"Who is Levi to you?" he asked. "I need to hear it from you."

She drew back slightly. "What?"

"Is he your beau? Are you practically engaged?"

"Are we— *what*? No! Are you out of your mind?"

"Then who is he?"

Her face flushed with anger. "He was one of us. At Cheever's. Taken from the damned orphanage to be worked as a damn slave. I've known him since I was eight years old. What do you mean who is he? He's my brother. There were others through the years, but they didn't all become like blood. The four of us there at the end, each one of us would have given our lives for the others."

"Bella said the two of you were practically engaged."

Her jaw dropped momentarily, but then she seemed angrier than ever. "What would Bella know about anything? Nothing, that's what! I'll tell you what I know. I know people and she is a piece of—" she broke off and lifted her chin. "I would say what she is, except I am refraining from cursing. Especially on Sunday. But," she practically shouted. "You want to know what she said about you? She said you were in love with her. That you'd been after her and she'd turned you down flat."

"The first part of that isn't true," he replied. "But the second part is."

She felt a profound let down.

"What I mean is, I got an invitation to Mr. Howerton's Christmas gala last year. Well, I didn't get it exactly. It was given to Wayman, but he couldn't go, so he gave it to me." He shrugged. "I thought she was pretty, so I asked her." He paused. "She turned me down. Looked at me like I was dirt."

"You ain't the one that's dirt," she said, and then started walking again.

"I'm sorry," he called.

She stopped and then turned back to face him. "What for?"

"Being jealous."

Being jealous? The words sunk in and her heart started to beat harder. Being jealous … of Levi? Being jealous because Bella had claimed they were practically engaged? "Jealous?"

"I've been going crazy," he admitted.

She took a few steps back toward him. "Because Bella said—"

"Yeah, because Bella said! And then I thought you admitted you wanted to be with him."

"See him!" She came closer and stopped in front of him. "I want to see him. Of course, I do. You said something about coming to dinner with him."

"Instead of me."

"Why would it have to be instead of you? He's a brother to me!"

"Aw, damn it, Susanna. Why are we always fighting?"

"Well, if you didn't say such—"

He grabbed her shoulders and kissed her, ending her statement. When he pulled back, they were both silent until he said, "I was only trying to help you not cuss just then."

"Guess I can use all the help I can get," she said weakly.

"Forgive me?"

She nodded.

"Can I walk you to work?"

She shrugged and turned from him but was glad when he fell into step beside her.

"I want to court you," he said.

She felt the pricks of tears on the back of her eyes, so she kept her face away from him in case it was obvious. "You do?"

"More than anything."

The words were precious, but she gave a casual shrug. "Alright." She could see him smile out of the corner of her eye and it was hard to keep from smiling herself. She stopped and looked at him. "On one condition."

"What's that?"

"Never mention Bella's name to me again. She's nothing but trouble."

"I agree. And I agree."

She grinned and they started walking again. "Pretty morning, isn't it?"

He reached over and took hold of her hand. "It's a lot prettier, now."

~~~

As the sun began setting, Garrett played fetch with the dogs on the Blue's front lawn. April May rocked on the front porch as she shelled peas, and Cessie had gone in to check on the ham that was baking and perfuming the home with its savory scent.

April May noticed a man on horseback on the road and started to call out a hello, thinking it was Jeremy, but it wasn't. "Well, I'll be," she commented.

Garrett looked but didn't recognize who it was, at first.

"It's Lonnie," April May said.

Wags took advantage of Garrett's distraction and jumped up and got the stick from his hand. Sure enough, it was Lonnie Hastings coming up the driveway. What the hell?

April May set her bowl aside and stood. "Pretty sure, he's not here to see me." She started inside as Garrett started back toward the porch, disturbed. "Call if you need anything. Come on, Wags. Sheeba, come! Dinner time."

The dogs followed her in. Lonnie dismounted and walked slowly toward him. He didn't speak until he stopped some four feet away. Garrett was standing in front of the porch but hadn't walked up the steps.

Lonnie took off his hat. "I came to apologize."

Garrett felt a wave of resentment that prevented him from replying.

"I," Lonnie began. He cleared his throat and shifted his weight from foot to foot. "I have a problem with, uh, drinking. I don't even remember most of what I do afterwards." He paused. "I'm trying to stop."

Garrett shook his head. He wanted to say something – but all he really felt was resentment. It was practically choking him.

"I know I don't deserve forgiveness. Not for you or Alford or a lot of other stuff I did. I am sorry, though. I wish I could take it all back."

"Do you remember it?" Lonnie asked coldly.

"I remember being in DeWitt's. Getting mad. Then I remember walking … I guess it after I was kicked out."

"Walking where?"

"Jackals."

Garrett knew of the place, but he'd never been or wanted to go. It was known as a place where hard men went to drink and either fight or watch one. Wayman had called it a place for killers and cutthroats to let off steam. It was no place for a decent man, he'd declared.

"Later, I remember walking home. I know I … helped jump you because there was blood on me. I remember that." Seconds of silence lapsed before he added, "My brother wasn't involved."

"I know. He told me and I believe him. He feels responsibility, but that's not the same as being the one who did it. The one who caused it," he said bitterly.

"I don't expect your forgiveness."

"Good," Garrett retorted. "Because I don't give it."

Lonnie nodded slowly. He cleared his throat. "Would it help if my fingers were cut off, too?"

Garrett gawked, but Lonnie appeared to be in earnest. "How would that help? What do you think that would do for me? Nothing, that's what! And it wouldn't make anyone feel sorry for you, either, if that's what you're thinking."

"I don't want anyone feeling sorry for me. I want to be forgiven. I want to deserve to be forgiven. I know I don't, but I want to change."

"Maybe you do and maybe they're just words. Either way, it doesn't do a thing for me."

Lonnie inhaled, exhaled and put his hat back on. "I had to ask. I am sorry." He hesitated a moment more and then turned to leave. Garrett just watched because he had nothing more to say to him.

Chapter Twenty-Two

L ily got up from the floor of the family room in Tommy and Em's home to get a dampened rag for Ben. He had a runny nose and had wiped snot over half his face. It didn't seem to bother him as he played with wood blocks, and Caty and Julianne were oblivious to it as they played with their dolls. Lily started to the kitchen, but stopped before she reached the door, captivated by the sight in front of her.

Tommy was sitting in a chair and Em was rubbing his shoulders. His eyes were closed, enjoying the massage, but it was Em's expression – the contented smile on her face that was arresting. The two of them were talking softly, although Lily didn't hear what they were saying.

Em laughed at something, and Tommy grabbed hold of her and plunked her down on his lap. He lowered her in his arms and kissed her, and she didn't resist.

The kiss was promptly interrupted by Caty and Jules who ran past Lily and into the kitchen, having heard their mother's laughter, and so Lily followed, since Em had already gotten up. "Ben needs a rag," she said, avoiding looking at them.

She knew her face was warm and she didn't want them to know that she'd seen them. The moment she'd just witnessed was the most sensual she'd encountered. One day, she hoped someone would love her like that and she'd love him back, just like Em and Tommy.

She wasn't sure if she was heard, since Caty and Julianne were pestering to know what was so funny until Em handed over a damp rag. "Here you go."

"I'll do it," Caty said. She took it and went back into the family room.

"I guess I'll go on home," Lily said with a shy smile. Em pressed a kiss to her forehead and thanked her. As Lily strolled back home, she wondered why some people were so lucky and others so unlucky? She saw Doll step out their front door with a big wooden bowl in hand.

"Hey, sweetie," Doll called cheerfully. "You want to help me make cobbler?"

Lily smiled and hurried on. She didn't know the answer to the question about good and bad fortune but, without question, she was one of the lucky ones. She could only hope and pray that Levi and Nate were doing as well as her and Susanna.

~~~

"Help," Levi shouted again. Feeling sick from pain, he lay back and stared upwards at the sky thinking that he couldn't win for losing. His foot was caught in a damned trap. He'd tried to pry the iron jaws apart, but he lacked the strength.

After a few weeks spent recovering at the iInn, he'd started off again for Green Valley. He couldn't afford train passage, but he had two good feet and determination. He also had all the time it was going to take because he wasn't going to stop until he got there. Unfortunately, after only a couple of days into the journey, he felt himself wearing down fast.

Surry had been his companion, a gift from Gretchen, but the dog scampered away when Levi's foot was caught. If someone didn't come help him, he'd lay there and bleed to death. "Help," he bellowed up at the sky. "Please, help," he said weakly.

Gretchen had declared he was rushing it, but he was tired of being somewhere he didn't want to be with more journeying ahead of him. He wanted to make it to Green Valley. He wanted it now more than ever, but maybe he wasn't supposed to make it. Maybe the journey was cursed. Maybe he was cursed. But he wasn't supposed to lay here and die like this.

He heard Surry barking as he ran back, and Levi struggled to raise himself onto his elbows. Two men crashed through the woods with Surry in the lead.

"What we got here?" one of them said.

They were rough looking, one with a shotgun resting on his shoulder. Their hats cast their faces half in shadow, but they seemed menacing.

"Looks like you done went and sprung a perfectly good trap," the man with the shotgun said, lowering it to his side.

Levi knew there was no way he could fight them. He'd come a long way, but what would be would be, because he didn't have the strength to fight them and win. "The trap messed up a decent foot, too," he replied.

"Your little mutt brung us," the man with the shotgun said as he stepped closer. "Came barkin' and snappin', tryin' to lead us off." He knelt, setting his gun aside. "We got some bears roaming here about," the man said as he took hold and pried the iron jaws apart.

Levi drew on the last of his strength and pulled his foot free, but now blood flowed fast from the wound. Surry was whining and shaking. "It's all right, boy," Levi said.

"Go back for the wagon," the first man said to the second. "And tell ma to get a poultice ready."

"Alright," the other man said. He turned and started off.

The man kneeling beside him, shoved the hat back on his head and looked at Levi. "Rough road, huh, fella?"

"You could say that."

"Well, we got to get the bleeding stopped." he said, removing his bandana from around his neck. "Name's Connor. Carl Lee Conner."

"Levi."

Carl Lee put the bandana just above Levi's wounds and tied it tight. "Levi what?"

"Jones, but the name doesn't mean nothin.' It came from the orphanage I was left at."

The man sat back on his bent leg, looking at Levi curiously. "Left in a basket, so to speak, huh?"

Up close, Carl Lee didn't seem menacing. "This here is Surry," Levi said. "His name means more than mine."

Carl Lee grinned. "What's that thing that the fella' Shakespeard says? What's in a name? Not a hill of beans."

Levi shrugged. He didn't know any fella' named Shakespeard.

"How long you been on the road?" Carl Lee asked. "Or have you always been a skinny fella'?"

"I've been traveling awhile," Levi said weakly as he laid back. "That made me feel sick," he muttered.

"Yeah. An inch and a half of iron spikes driven in your ankle will do that. Decent boots would have helped some."

Levi closed his eyes and tried to concentrate on not vomiting.

"My brother'll be here soon and we'll take you back and get you fixed up. Bet you got a hellava story to tell, huh? Didn't escape prison or nothin', did you?"

"No, sir."

"Then again," Carl Lee mused. "If I was in prison, I'd do every damn thing I could to break out."

Levi could tell by the sound of his voice that he was looking for his brother's return. "It was a kind of prison," Levi admitted.

"Well. Like I said, I'da broke out, too. Don't hold it against you none. Unless you did something terrible bad to get there."

"I was left in a basket, so to speak. Only crime I know of."

"Yeah," Carl Lee said conversationally, "I bet you got one hellava story. Once we get your foot tended, we'll trade you for it, over some pork and beans and cornbread with molasses."

Levi smiled weakly. "Deal."

~~~

Susanna and Garrett were seated close together on a cushioned, two-seater swing that overlooked the large pond on the Blue property. It was one of their favorite spots and it was particularly beautiful on this May evening. The weather had been warm for days, but late evenings were still cool, so they cuddled under a blanket as they looked out on a starry night and the dark shimmering pond as they talked.

Susanna loved these evenings. She cherished their alone time and the nights she spent at the Blue house in the princess room. Whenever she had an evening off followed by a morning off, she spent it there.

Moonlight gleamed off the softly rippling surface, crickets and tree frogs chirped, and there was an occasional splash of water as a fish jumped or a turtle entered the pond. Their topic of discussion had been supper the night before when Garrett had dined at the Hastings home. So far, he'd described the house, the meal, and the housekeeper, whose invalid husband also lived there.

"What was it like to be around Lonnie?" she asked when he didn't volunteer it.

"It wasn't too bad. He seems different. Quiet." He shrugged. "Sad."

She grunted.

"I didn't know him before," Garrett said. "But he seems different than the mean drunk we saw that day in the restaurant. His father and brother say he's different. I can tell you he hardly drank, and then he left to go upstairs early." He paused. "Speaking of upstairs," he said slowly.

She looked at him.

"They invited me to stay there, to live there, when I start work."

Her eyes widened. "Did you tell them you would work there, for sure?"

He nodded. "I did."

She looked back out at the water. The news wasn't exactly a surprise, because he'd been leaning that way, but she still had mixed feelings about it.

"I told you Lonnie was leaving for Barbados."

"Yeah."

"Timothy is going, too. They leave in ten days."

She knew more was coming.

"I'm going to start training day after tomorrow, so I'll know what I'm doing when Timothy is gone. And, about living there, I'm thinking I wouldn't want to stay for a long time, but it could help me save up some money."

"You're saying living there wouldn't cost you? At all?"

"That's right. I'd get room and board for free, and I'll be earning a good wage. So, I was thinking, in less than a year, I could probably get a house. Lawrence said he'd help."

"You call him Lawrence?" she asked, looking at him with a doleful expression.

"He said to," he replied defensively. "It feels a little strange, I admit, but that's not really the point."

"What is the point?"

"The house. Getting a house. For us. I hope."

She stopped breathing for a moment.

"Why do you look so surprised?" he asked, stopping the motion of the swing.

"It's dark out here. You can't really see how I look," she hedged.

"I can see you fine. You don't like the idea? You think it's too soon?"

Damn it, she couldn't breathe right. "The idea?"

"Of us getting married and settling down. Buying a little house and—"

Her face ached because of the tears and emotions that sprang to the surface. She laughed and hugged herself to him.

"Aw, sweetheart," he said tenderly, stroking her hair. "You know how I adore you."

She clung to him, putting her hand on the spot over his heart. She could feel it beating almost as hard as hers was. "I love you, too."

"We'll do everything proper-like," he said soothingly. "When the time is right. But it's what I want."

She nodded. "It's what I want, too," she said in a strained voice.

He kissed the top of her head and then lifted her chin up to give her a kiss on the lips. She wrapped her hand around the back of his neck, desirous not only of a deeper kiss, but of showing him how much he meant to her. How much he'd changed her.

Their kisses had always been sweet and shy, but, as a gulf of need inside her surged, she arched upward, needing the caress of his lips, and still wanting more. His grip tightened around her and then they were standing. Or had he lifted her? She was slightly off balance, her eyes closed, floating, and she hadn't had a drop of wine.

The kiss grew more searching and all she could do was cling to him as she swam in new, heady, wonderful sensations. Her heart pounded and her nipples tingled. She pressed herself to him and felt his hardened manhood bulge against her leg.

"Whoa," he said as he pulled away. "I'm suddenly feeling very ungentlemanly."

"Me, too," she said breathlessly, stepping back in to kiss him again.

He laughed but held her back. "I think it's time I take you home, before we get ourselves in trouble."

She smiled wickedly. "I've always been trouble."

He took hold of her hand and began walking her back to the house, but she didn't mind. She was walking and floating at the same time. It had been the happiest night of her life so far, but a lot more of them were coming. Days and nights. "I love you, Garrett Trentwell."

He put his arm around her and squeezed. "I love you, future Mrs. Garrett Trentwell."

Happiness suffused her entire being.

~~~

Louis Swanson followed his deputy, Bill Talbert, to the jail after the younger man had fetched him, saying that two men were there and wanted to see him.

"They talk funny and have a look about them," Bill reported.

"What sort of look?"

"Hard. Like bounty hunters. They sound sort of French or something."

Swan figured he knew who they were. As he walked into the jail and saw them standing there, he was almost certain of it. One man was lean and dark and about his own age, the other was younger, thirty or thirty-five, a large man with leathery skin and two different colored eyes, one blue and one brown. They had removed their hats but had pistols in their holsters.

Swan took his hat off and put it on the rack. "I'm Sheriff Swanson."

"Remy Cormier," the lean one said, coming closer to extend his hand. "Sherriff of St. Tammany Parish. You sent word about the Pettijeans."

"I did. To learn the truth of a tale I heard," Swan said, shaking the man's hand.

"The story is true," Cormier stated in a pronounced Cajun accent. "It's no tale."

Swan glanced over at the other man, who was eyeing him guardedly.

"This is Paul Meche, one of my men," Cormier introduced.

Meche nodded but didn't move or offer a handshake. Swan returned the nod. "You've come a long way," he said to Cormier.

"Sal and Andre Pettijean killed my brother," Cormier said. "I would have gone much further. They tortured him and then left him to die over a debt in dispute. We came upon him just in time."

"To save him?"

"There was no saving him. They'd skinned him alive."

Swan cringed. He'd heard as much from the mayor, but it was still sickening to hear it stated aloud.

"The wounds had festered. Insects had gotten to him. I meant that we were in time to learn what happened. I think he stayed alive so that we'd know and he'd be avenged. He died right after. We went after the scum, but they'd cleared out after learning we'd found Etienne alive."

"I'm sorry for your loss. It's a terrible thing, but I don't know what you're expecting here."

Cormier shrugged. "To exchange good deeds. You tell me where they are, and I will remove them from your nice, clean town. They don't belong here."

"Can't disagree with you on that point, but they'll have to stand trial and our judge is poorly. Last few trials, we've had to get the traveling judge here. That can take a few days or three weeks."

"They were tried. *In absentia.*"

"Guilty," Meche said.

Swan looked from man to man. "Gentlemen, I'm going to need you to hole up for a day or two while I confirm what you say.

It's not that I don't believe you, but I need to know I'm on solid ground."

Cormier considered him for several moments. "Can you assure us they won't be warned that we're here?" he finally asked.

"They won't learn it from us," Swan replied. "I can assure you of that."

Cormier nodded. He put his hat on and touched the brim. "See you soon." They started out.

"Sheriff Cormier," Swan said before they reached the door. "Is the plan to take them back for sentencing?"

Cormier turned back, Meche didn't. "Sentence done been passed," Cormier replied. "We're here to see it carried out."

"Is it just the two of you?" Swan asked warily.

Cormier shook his head. The merest smile touched his lips. "No, sir. Like I said, we came to get this done." He tipped his hat again, opened the door and they left, closing the door behind them.

"Geez, Louise," one of his deputies said under their breath from the back of the room. Swan turned to see all three of his men agog.

"Yeah," Swan agreed.

Chapter Twenty-Three

Sitting in the library of the Hastings home, Garrett finished reading *The Prince and The Pauper,* by Mark Twain. It was children's fiction, but he'd enjoyed it. It had been a good diversion. He rose from the comfortable leather chair and put it back on the shelf.

It was the second night he'd spent in the Hastings' home. Except for some awkward moments between himself and Lonnie, everything was going well. Meals were good, his room was comfortable. This evening, there had been games of backgammon.

Lonnie hadn't joined in. Instead, he had gone between attempting to read and frequent trips to the window to peer outside. He'd been five days without a drop of liquor, but he seemed edgy and rather lost without it. Timothy had quietly made that observation on one of Lonnie's many, restless trips from the room. Between Lawrence, Timothy, and Garrett, however, there was a surprising ease and camaraderie.

One of the nice things about being in town was how frequently he could see Susanna, if only for minutes at a time. Tomorrow, they would have dinner at an inn, and she'd been invited to dinner here in the Hastings' home on Friday. She was already fretting over what to wear and what they might ask her.

Garrett left the library, startling Lonnie who was on his way in. Both muttered beg-your-pardons and attempted to step around the other. Lonnie stepped back, gesturing Garrett onward, and Garrett went by. On impulse, Garrett turned back. "Sorry if I've made it uncomfortable for you."

Lonnie shook his head. "I'm the one who made it uncomfortable. I truly do hope you'll like the business."

"I do, so far."

"I'm just learning it myself, as ridiculous as that is."

"Your brother is a good teacher."

"I know. I was too proud at first to admit it, but … I know he is. He has good ideas, and they are not all as revolutionary as my father makes them out to be. He's probably just envious he didn't think of them first." It was said without rancor, almost with good humor.

Garrett nearly grinned. "Well, goodnight."

"Night."

As Garrett walked on, it felt like an important bridge had just been crossed, and he was glad to be on the other side. He hadn't completely forgiven Lonnie yet, but the process had started.

~~~

"I get the feeling he's trying to avoid us," Sal said the next evening as they watched Lonnie walking home after playing billiards at a place on Second. Lonnie boy had reformed of late. It was rare when he went outside the confines of work and home.

But a deal was a deal, and they were out of patience, especially since Lonnie was planning to leave town within a few days. He thought they didn't know, but they'd kept tabs. Johnny started to giggle with excitement until Sal warned him to shut it.

~~~

Lonnie was whirled around and slammed into a wall, face first, breaking his nose and smashing his cheekbone.

"Hello, Lonnie," Sal breathed into his ear.

It took a few seconds for recognition to register, and then panic filled Lonnie. He'd been so close to getting away. So close.

"Where have you been?" Sal asked.

Lonnie's arm was twisted behind his back so hard it felt wrenched from its socket. "Sick. I've been sick."

"Oh," Sal replied. "We didn't know." Sarcasm was thick in his voice. "Anything we can do to help?"

"Let go of me," Lonnie grunted. "Would be good."

Sal abruptly let go and stepped back and Lonnie slowly turned to face him. Andre and the moron cousin were also standing there.

Lonnie swiped at his bloodied nose, breathing hard. "Why did you do that?"

"Word is, you're leaving town."

"I'm being sent away! I told you that."

"So you're not skipping out on us? The plan is still on?"

Lonnie swallowed. "It was," he lied. "Until you broke my face."

Sal shook his head, his expression hard. "That's not broke. I can show you broke."

"We never got arrangements straight," Andre said. "When were you bringing us the key?"

Lonnie swallowed again. They knew he was lying.

"Let's go see the place," Andre said calmly. "Like I said, we got to make arrangements. We need to know what's worth taking."

"Look," Lonnie protested.

"No, *you* look," Sal said, stepping close. He slammed his fist into Lonnie's midsection, doubling him over and then brought down his powerful forearms onto Lonnie's back, knocking him to the ground. He bent down and rifled through Lonnie's pockets until he had his keys in hand. Standing back up, he reared back and repeatedly kicked him, landing blows to the head and body, despite Lonnie curling up.

"Let's go," Andre said coldly.

Lonnie groaned. The world seemed skewed and quickly growing too dark. He watched his assailants' feet go by and fought to hang on to consciousness.

~~~

The Pettijeans entered the front door of Hastings' Mercantile without having been seen on the way. Inside a few gas lamps burned low.

"Nice place," Sal muttered.

Johnny's eyes were huge, and his mouth hung open. Sal and Andre wasted no time finding their way to the warehouse, and Johnny followed, touching things as he passed. The warehouse was a massive space to be as orderly as it was. There was a tall ceiling and rows of stacked shelves with well-marked boxes, crates and barrels, each with a neatly written label full of information. Dates, cost, weight, intended destinations and more.

The organization and neatness of it appealed to Andre. Seeing it made him loathe Lonnie all the more, pissing on something like this. But all the better for them. He walked aisles discovering the wealth of goods. Bundles of silk. Brass spittoons. Tea, sugar, and pocket watches. Women's petticoats. Tobacco. There seemed to be huge quantities of tobacco.

"Madeira," Sal exclaimed. "Crates of it!" He whooped. "We'll need a wagon."

"We'll need a wagon," Johnny repeated.

"We'll need a fleet of them," Sal laughed, opening a bottle.

"A fleet of them," Johnny repeated gleefully before hurrying on to find something Sal had not yet seen.

Sal tipped back the bottle and drank. Wiping his mouth with the back of his hand, he burped loudly. "I just decided I don't hate Lonnie anymore. I think he and I are going to be good friends, after all."

~~~

Timothy sniffed as he woke. He'd fallen asleep at his desk trying to get caught up and now his neck was stiff. He rubbed the back of it and bent his head from side to side. He heard a man's whoop from downstairs and sighed heavily that Lonnie was drunk again. What he was up to was anyone's guess.

He rose with a moan of fatigue and left his office. Whatever Lonnie was up to, he didn't care. He was going home to bed. The muscles on one side of his neck ached, but at least he'd caught up his work. Todd could easily handle whatever had not been done. He felt sluggish as he walked down the stairs. He crossed the floor and opened the door but turned back at the sound of something in the warehouse. Laughter?

He crossed to the warehouse, disgusted that Lonnie had relapsed to his old behavior. And right before they were to have set sail! Timothy took a few steps in, ready to have it out with his brother, but stopped abruptly at the sight of a strange young man. So, not only had Lonnie gone and gotten drunk, but he'd invited others back to raid their stock? It was too much.

The man in front of him made a sudden lurching move, there was a flash of shine in the air and Timothy felt a burning pain in the center of his throat. He tried to gasp but couldn't. He dropped to his knees, knowing that it was over. It was all over. There was an inexplicable rush of movement because he was falling.

~~~

Lonnie used the wall to get up. He felt blood trickling down his face from a cut on his forehead. He wiped his face with the back of his sleeve and stumbled forward, limping badly, one hand holding onto his ribs. He didn't know if they were broken or just badly bruised, but that wasn't important at the moment. He had to get to the sheriff's office where at least one deputy would still be on duty.

~~~

"Damn it, Johnny," Andre snapped furiously.

Johnny rocked side to side. "He scared me. He scared me."

Sal came up behind them, saying, "Shit! Lonnie followed us? Is he dead?"

"It's not Lonnie. Look at the clothes."

Sal squatted to turn over the body. It wasn't Lonnie, but there was a strong resemblance. His brother, then. Johnny's eight-inch blade had hit the center of the man's throat severing the artery and windpipe in one fell swoop.

"You're a hellava shot, Johnny," he said under his breath. He looked up at Andre with a shrug. "Done now." He looked back to the body and withdrew the blade. There was a trickle of blood from the wound, but no gushing, because his heart no longer beat.

"He s-scared me," Johnny repeated.

Sal stood and looked to Andre. "What now?"

"We send Johnny back for the wagon and load what's most valuable. We take the body and dump it."

"Then burn the place?"

Andre sighed with disgust. It was infuriating to have been given an opportunity to make a great haul, only to have Johnny destroy it. They'd been fools to let him come.

"On second thought, why bother?" Sal asked. "I say we leave it and lock the door behind us. It's not like we have a key."

"Why bother?" Andre repeated with disgust. "Because Lonnie will sing!" He turned back to access the inventory. "We take the wine, the rum, the watches—" he listed as he walked, looking up at the many stacked crates.

"There's furs over here," Sal said as he followed. "Maybe we can get three or four wagons."

"Can I have what's in his pockets?" Johnny asked.

"It's your kill," Sal replied, without looking back at him. "Take it."

~~~

Bill Talbert, one of the three deputies on duty, was hunched over the desk working on a crossword puzzle when the door opened. He looked up at a badly worked over Lonnie Hastings. "What in blazes happened to you?" Bill said as he stood.

"The Pettijeans jumped me." He made his way to the closest chair and collapsed in it. He was shaking all over.

"Darren," Talbert yelled to the cells in back, where fellow deputy Darren Olsen was sleeping. "Wake up!"

"They took my key to the shop," Lonnie said. "They're going to rob it."

"How many of them?" Talbert asked urgently.

"Three that I saw."

The front door opened again and Art Wilson, the other deputy on duty stepped in, blinking in surprise at the sight of Lonnie. He'd been on his rounds and about to report that all was calm but, clearly, he'd missed something.

"The Pettijeans jumped him," Talbert explained, stepping around the desk. "They're probably robbing the mercantile right now. Three of them, maybe more. I'm going for Swan. See if you can rouse lazy bones, even if you have to pour a pitcher of water on him." He stopped even with Lonnie and handed over his handkerchief. "Try and stop the bleeding," he said. "Keep pressure on it."

Lonnie took the handkerchief and pressed it to his head, but he felt a pressing need to leave.

"You should lay on the floor before you pass out," Art suggested before he headed back to wake Darren. He wouldn't need any water to wake him either. Darren only had to hear that Swan was headed back. That would get him up.

~~~

Lonnie got back to his feet and left again, not bothering to shut the door. He couldn't wait. He had to make it to the shop. An inner warning was making him quake from something other than pain. *Fear.* There was a cold, gut-wrenching fear filling him.

When he was a block away, he saw that the front door of the mercantile was open. It made no sense. They should have been taking care not to be noticed. Unless they had come and gone and assumed he would follow to see the damage and conceal their invasion. Was that it? He walked on, holding his ribs.

He slowly pushed the front door further open, his breath held. It was quiet, but then he thought he heard voices from within. Stepping in sideways, he crept closer to the warehouse, but stopped when he saw blood and, beyond it, a prone body. Recognition hit. The clothing. The hand.

Oh, God. No!

Lonnie rushed forward, terrified, even as he told himself it couldn't be. Ignoring the Pettijean's voices only yards away, he pushed the warehouse door further open and looked down at his brother's body, staring uncomprehendingly at the open and yet unseeing eyes and gashed throat.

213

Tears flowed down his face, and he was shaking hard enough that he barely had control of his movement. He knelt and touched Timothy. He was as warm as ever. He was dead, but still warm. But dead. Beyond life. Beyond help. His little brother. He heard Andre's voice again and looked up, hating them more than anything else he'd ever felt. Hating them more than he loved anything.

He stood and pulled Timothy's body from the room and silently closed the doors to the warehouse. He would burn the place down with them in it, and himself, too, but he had to trap them first.

He went for the broom and stuck it through the handles of the double doors, then went and found a length of chain from a supply closet. He returned and began snaking it through and around, no longer caring about the noise it made. They had killed his brother and he would kill them. He would kill them all, himself along with them. Because it was his fault. His brother was dead, and it was his fault.

The voices got louder because they realized they'd been caught. He was about to get a lock in place when Sherriff Swanson called to him from the door. He turned to see a group of incredulous men watching him. "They killed my brother!"

Swan walked further in, staring down at Timothy's body. "We'll do this," Swan said.

"They should die," Lonnie begged.

The warehouse doors shook violently as the men inside attempted to open them from within. Swan stepped to the side of the door, moving Lonnie back and hollered that they were surrounded and to put their weapons down. "When the doors are opened, you'll kick all weapons out. It's the only way you'll make it through this."

"We didn't do anything but come in," Andre called. "We didn't kill that man!"

"We'll sort all that out," Swan returned. "But do what I say." In the silence that followed, he turned to Lonnie. "Go get the doctor," he said quietly, but sternly.

"Why?" Lonnie asked hopelessly.

"Cause we need proof of what happened. Then go and get your father. He has a right to know."

Lonnie left, crying anew.

Swan looked down at Timothy feeling disheartened because he'd never given the young man a fair shot. He'd tarred him with the same brush as Lonnie while, by all accounts, he was a very different person. Now he was deceased. It was such a waste, and for what reason? He banged his fist on the door. "What were you doing here?"

"Lonnie gave us the key. This was his plan. He wanted us to burn it down. He said we could take what we wanted, as long as we burned it to the ground."

Swan exchanged incredulous looks with his men.

"Bullshit," one of them said.

"It's true," came the exclamation from inside. "He brought the proposition to us. In front of other people," he added. "He hates his father. Hated his brother, too. It's why he killed him."

Except Timothy had not suffered a beating and Lonnie had. They were of similar build, so it wasn't logical that one of them could have beaten the other without some sort of reprisal. "It's odd that Lonnie's beat up, then."

"That was part of it. We had to do that, so it would look real. It was supposed to look like he'd been attacked like his brother, only he'd escaped. But he killed his brother, ambushed him."

"It's not making any sense," Swan said with a shake of his head.

"That's only because Lonnie went to get you too soon. He must have gotten confused or something. Or maybe he thought he could blame us. I don't know. But this was his plan, except we were supposed to burn the place down before you got here. I can prove he came to us with this. Others heard him."

Swan walked away, because he needed a moment of fresh air. Two of his men followed. "Go tell the mayor," Swan said to Art. "He needs to know, and I'm not sure how keen Lonnie will be to tell him."

Art nodded and started off without comment.

"Darren—"

"Sir?"

"Go fetch Cormier and his men." He took a few steps away, wondering if he was making the right call. "I think we're going to handle this situation by what they call extradition."

"Yes, sir," Darren said as he hurried off.

"I have a feeling they can deliver a more suitable day of judgment than we can," Swan murmured to himself when Darren was walking away.

~~~

"Lawrence," Marian said from the doorway of the parlor, her voice full of tension.

Both Lawrence and Garrett looked up from their game of chess to see Marian looking strangely alarmed and incredibly pale. Garrett had never heard her use the mayor's first name before. She usually just said Sir if she had to call him something.

"A deputy is here to see you," she uttered.

Lawrence looked puzzled as he rose. "Town business, I'm sure, although it is odd for them to calling at this hour." He was already in motion, heading for the door. He reached Marian and stopped. "Are you unwell?"

She shook her head rapidly but looked away and stepped back.

He looked confused but walked on.

Marian looked at Garrett and shook her head slowly.

He rose and came toward her. There were tears in her eyes. "What is it?"

She brought her hands to her mouth in a prayer pose and ducked her head, her face a mask of pain – as if she couldn't bear to say.

He touched her shoulder in a show of support and walked on. A deputy stood in the front hall, hat in hand, looking mournful and saying he was sorry.

"I don't understand," Lawrence said in a small voice.

Garrett stepped up behind him. "What's happened?"

216

"You should come, sir," the deputy said, addressing it to Lawrence. He then flicked his gaze to Garrett, including him in the invitation.

Lawrence stood utterly still, looking bewildered.

"What is it?" Garrett asked the deputy. "What's happened?"

"It's his son," he said apologetically, glancing at the mayor. "Timothy. He's—"

"He's what?" Garrett asked sharply.

"Dead, sir. He was ... I'm sorry, but he was killed earlier. You should go to the mercantile."

Garrett, too, shook his head because the words made no sense. Timothy had only gone back to the shop to finish up a few things. He was young and smart and had a wonderful future in front of him. He was a good person who wrote interesting stories and had a good heart and had a future of his own making in front of him.

He had ideas about the business. Ideas about getting warehouses at docks and shipping directly from supplier to buyer, without using themselves as a stopping point. Faster return on profit, he'd said.

"You need to come, sir," the deputy repeated, looking at Lawrence.

Garrett placed his hand on the mayor's shoulder, and it seemed to spur him forward. Garrett followed.

None of them spoke. It was five blocks to the shop and none of them said a word. They focused on the path before them, lit by a cloud covered moon and the occasional streetlamp.

Men were standing or milling in front of the mercantile. Garrett recognized Sheriff Swanson and a few other men. His heart beat hard as they neared the place. The tension was high, and Swan looked grave. He walked up to Lawrence, stopping him. Lawrence was deathly pale and walking unsteadily.

"I'm sorry," Swan said. "It was too late when we got here. The doctor said he was ...killed instantly. There was little or no pain."

Lawrence made a strange sound, a sort of internal whimpering, and brushed by the sheriff. Swan followed close behind and Garrett fell in step behind him, feeling strangely disembodied. A new group of men, strangers, were converging, and there was muffled shouting coming from inside the shop. It all seemed bizarre and incongruous. Why were they all there? Why was this happening?

The moment he stepped inside, he saw Timothy on the ground, although someone had covered him up with a jacket. Lawrence had reached him and dropped beside him. Steeling his courage, he pulled the jacket away and, only then, did he begin to accept what he'd been told. Lawrence seemed to crumble. He cowered over his son and cried pitifully.

Garrett shook his head. How was it possible? They'd all had dinner together and talked of Barbados only hours ago. Garrett could still recall Timothy laughing. He'd been looking forward to Barbados

Behind him, the strangers talked with a curious accent.

Garrett felt ill. He took a few steps back until he reached a wall. He saw Marian in the doorway, staring at Timothy. She'd draped a shawl over her head and clutched it tightly to her. Tears ran down her face.

Where was Lonnie? The question seemed to be floating around, along with a story of how men had attacked Lonnie, beaten him, and gotten his keys.

Someone had covered Timothy back up, and men were assisting Lawrence from the building. He appeared to have shrunk, although surely that wasn't possible.

Swan walked up to Garrett. "You'll go with them?" Swan asked, jerking his head toward the retreating party.

Garrett felt himself nodding, but his legs felt like stumps. "What happened?"

"Some men jumped Lonnie and got his key to the place, then came here and surprised Timothy."

"What men?"

"Sal and Andre Pettijean. You know them?"

Garrett shook his head.

"They run Jackals."

Jackals. Garrett sighed and lowered his head.

"It's a bad night for the mayor," Swan said. "As bad as they come. I won't say you owe it to him because you don't. It would be a mercy though. You seem to have been able to put the past behind you."

The strangers with accents were pushing in, and the sheriff's men were stepping back. "Who are they?"

"Timothy Hastings wasn't the first victim of the Pettijeans. They killed a man back where they came from in a brutal way. These men are taking them to pay for that. It'll pay for Timothy, too."

The doors to the warehouse were opened and pandemonium set in when the men who'd been trapped inside, stepped out. Then they realized who was waiting for them. Then there was yelling and cursing and panic, and the Pettijeans were tackled and clapped in chains.

They were shouting accusations about Lonnie giving them a key and wanting them to burn the place down, about Timothy already being dead when they arrived, but it didn't faze or detour anyone.

Garrett left the mercantile. He started back to the mayor's house, but, after several yards, he stopped. He made his way to a lamppost, squatted, and listened to the shouting and resistance from the mercantile.

Timothy was dead. How could someone that alive suddenly be dead for no good reason? In a blink of an eye. Alive one hour, dead the next. Alive and then dead. Garrett got back to his feet and started in a different direction because there was something he needed to do.

~~~

Garrett raised his fist, hesitated, and then knocked. Not loudly, because it was past visiting hours. Past lights out, even, but it was possible someone was up. When there was no response, he knocked a bit louder. And then louder still. He eyed the bell and then looked up at the door and then further up the upstairs windows. He reached the bell cord and tugged.

It was the astonished housemother who opened the door a few minutes later. In her housecoat and with her hair down, she looked pretty and as young as those in her care. He felt a heave of sadness that she'd had her brief, marital happiness swept away, but it also strengthened his resolve.

Because fate was sometimes monstrously unjust and unkind. Things happened that weren't fair or right, and all anyone had was the time right now. You had to claim the moment in front of you as if it were one of the last. Then the last moment could never take you by surprise. There would be no 'I'm sorry,' unsaid. No 'I love you,' unstated. "I'm sorry for the late hour," he apologized to the housemother.

She opened the door wider. "What is it?"

He started to say, only his throat closed. He cleared it. "Timothy Hastings was murdered tonight," he said in a low voice that carried past Deena Beard and to the stairway, which was packed with almost every resident of Wiley House.

It was their collective gasp, that made the housemother turn to see the wide eyes and horrified expressions. "Come in," she said, turning back to Garrett.

"I'm sorry," he said again as he stepped in. "But I need to speak to Susanna."

The girls began coming down the stairs, Susanna amongst them. She had eyes for no one other than him.

"What happened?" Mrs. Beard asked. Her hands were clutched in front of her, her eyes full of compassion and sorrow.

"I'm not sure exactly," he admitted.

"But you know for a fact—"

He nodded. "I was … there. Afterwards, I mean. I saw his body."

"How?" she asked disbelievingly. "Was it a fight?"

"No. He was attacked. With a knife," he said reluctantly. The words were hard to get out.

She covered her mouth with her hands.

Garrett looked at Susanna knowing that she'd heard. They'd all heard. It hadn't been his place to announce the tragedy, but he had to see her and tell her. "You know when I said we'd do everything right?" he said to her.

She nodded. Her gaze was locked on his.

"Well, I don't want to," he said. "I love you and I want to marry you the very second we can."

She broke free of the others and ran to him.

He swept her up in his arms and held her tightly. "I'm so sorry," she whispered to him.

He nodded. When he could relax enough, he pulled back to lower himself to one knee, still holding her hands "I don't have a ring to offer at this second, but I have my heart, which I give you. I love you."

Smiling and crying, she nodded.

"I know you already said you'd marry me, but I needed to see you and say all this and to get down on one knee before you." He stood and kissed her. It was so right. The two of them were so right. He reluctantly withdrew. "I've got to go back," he whispered to her. She nodded again. He wished he could pick her up and carry her out and never be without her ever again, but he needed to see to the mayor. "I love you."

"I love you," she whispered back.

He pulled away, nodded to Mrs. Beard, and left.

~~~

In the almost deafening silence that followed Garrett's departure, Susanna didn't move. She stood looking at the door and then her gaze shifted to Deena Beard. Mrs. Beard went to her and embraced her, and Susanna clung tightly, needing the connection. A year ago, no one would have been able to convince her she would welcome a woman's embrace, much less need it.

She sensed the rush toward her. She was suddenly being hugged and patted and congratulated. The very air felt electrified with the shock of the bad news. Beth was crying – several girls were crying, and there was no way to know if it was in sorrow over Timothy Hastings or joy over her engagement or both.

The group made their way into the parlor because no one wanted to be alone.

"That was the most romantic thing I ever saw," someone declared.

Bella gave a roll of her eyes and turned to go upstairs. She gave Angela, the closest thing she had to a friend, a sideways bob of the head, urging her to come, but Angela ignored her for once.

Beth squeezed Susanna's hand. "Are you alright?"

Susanna nodded, although she felt strange. Almost lightheaded.

"Your hand's cold," Beth said. "And you're shaking."

How a person could be this happy and sad at once was a mystery, but that's how she felt.

"Poor Timothy," someone murmured.

"Poor Mayor Hastings," someone else replied, to which several girls nodded.

"He was only eighteen or nineteen," Callie Jo grieved. "I liked him."

Jean slipped an arm around her and pulled her over, allowing Callie Jo's head to rest on her shoulder.

"I liked him, too," Margaret commiserated.

"Let's pray for them," Mrs. Beard said. There was general, unspoken agreement, and they all bowed their heads, Susanna included. Had she become someone else entirely? Even if she had, it wasn't a bad thing. It was the very opposite of bad, and yet a part of her refused to accept it.

It was the same part that suspected this existence would all fall apart, because girls like her weren't supposed to be loved and happy. They weren't laughers. They didn't have girlfriends. They weren't pretty. They weren't special.

Even now, she wasn't really praying. She was half hearing Mrs. Beard's softspoken words about Timothy's soul winging straight to heaven, and wishing peace and acceptance for the family left behind.

Susanna did wish those things, but mostly she was thinking about Garrett. He had the best heart, and he loved her. He loved *her*. She couldn't contain her emotions any longer and she began crying. The next thing she knew, she was embraced by everyone around her, and she did need it.

222

Chapter Twenty-Four

Lonnie fetched the doctor, as the sheriff asked. He'd been returning with the man when he saw his father a block away. Lonnie halted in his tracks, unable to go further. Unable to face his father. Fortunately, the doctor didn't notice he'd stopped. Lonnie watched Garrett follow his father into the shop and most the men standing outside closed in behind.

What would he say to his father? What was there to say? Even if no one else ever knew the truth, his father would know that he'd brought this devastation down on them. If he'd never stepped foot in the debauchery of Jackals, none of it would have happened.

Marian walked gracefully and silently toward the shop, her face a mask of grief. She'd cared deeply about Timothy. Why couldn't it have been him killed instead of his younger brother? Lonnie turned and started toward home. He was anxious to get there, but in no condition to run.

Naturally, the house was empty except for poor old man Boyd languishing in the downstairs guest room. The kindest thing would be to put him out of the half-life he'd been condemned to. Lonnie went into the study and to the gun cabinet. He opened it and selected the Colt six shooter he'd always fancied. He then rummaged through the drawers for the right bullets.

At twelve years of age, he'd been able to dazzle his brother with his knowledge of each gun in the cabinet. He'd picked up this very one and stroked the seven-and-a-half-inch barrel saying, "This is a Colt single shooter. Standard cavalry model. Gunslingers generally prefer a five-inch barrel. I'm going to have both when I grow up."

"Me, too," Timothy had agreed, his eyes shining.

Oh, God. Why hadn't he taken better care of his brother? He bowed his head and cried, heedless of the tears and the running of his nose. He gasped and his head jerked toward the door at the sound of the back door shutting. He stepped back, breathing hard.

223

He couldn't do it. He couldn't have the conversation with his father. Clutching the gun tightly, he walked to the door and listened. It was Marian who'd returned. He heard her crying. He wiped his face with his sleeve, went the other way and silently left through the front door.

~~~

Garrett hadn't made it far from Wiley House when something caught the edge of his peripheral vision, like a flash. He turned abruptly, but there was nothing there. However, half a block away and on the other side of the street, Lonnie trudged away from town with his head down. Garrett sensed that he'd been meant to see Lonnie, and the instinct made him shiver.

He followed him, noticing something odd about the way Lonnie moved, both hands to his side, his head down. It was apparent he didn't want to be seen. Nearing the end of Main, Lonnie turned toward the church.

Garrett halted a moment, but then walked on. If Lonnie was in the sanctuary and in prayer when he arrived, he would leave without being seen. He wanted to believe that would be the case, but a queer feeling urged him to quicken his pace.

He reached the church courtyard and looked toward the cemetery wondering if Lonnie had gone to visit his mother's grave. Stepping quietly, he went into the cemetery, but didn't see Lonnie, although it wasn't easy to see anything at this hour. It was an old graveyard with ancient trees and rows of well-manicured bushes standing like proper sentinels.

Moonlight filtered through the budding trees, casting irregular shadows on the ground and gravestones, while the cascading branches of weeping willows kept what looked like an active vigil, swaying as they were in the night breeze.

As Garrett stepped passed tall headstones, benches and statues of angels and lambs, the light of the moon caused the marble to glow. He was no more superstitious than anyone else he knew, but this was not a comfortable place to be alone in the dark.

He didn't see Lonnie, and it didn't feel right to call out, so he turned to go to the church, but froze when he noticed something odd a few yards to the right. It looked like the legs of a man, sitting against the tree.

"Why are you here?" Lonnie asked, causing him to jump.

"I saw you," Garrett replied haltingly.

Lonnie leaned forward enough that moonlight illuminated his tear-streaked face and the pistol he held against his chest, and Garrett felt his blood chill in his veins.

"What are you doing following me?" Lonnie asked accusingly.

"It's because your father needs you."

Lonnie sat back again and was swallowed by darkness. "He doesn't need me."

It must have been a combination of the night's strain and tragedy, the place they were in and the vast open space that made Lonnie's voice sound ethereal. He sounded hopeless. In fact, the very air seemed to resonate with despair. He was planning on taking his own life. Garrett knew it as surely as he knew anything. "Yes, he does."

"My brother is dead … because of me."

"They jumped you."

"Yeah, but they only knew about me … they only knew—" Lonnie's voice broke and he wept. "It's my fault! If I'd never gone there, he'd be alive! Why can't I be dead? Why couldn't it have been me?"

"Lonnie, your father needs you," Garrett repeated, squatting down. "You have to go to him."

"He w-won't forgive me."

"Hello?" a man's voice called. "Who's there?"

Garrett practically jumped out of his skin. He stood and saw the pastor coming through the arched gate. "It's alright, Reverend Thompson. It's Garrett Trentwell. And Lonnie Hastings," he added after a brief pause.

"Tell him to stay away," Lonnie warned.

"Stay back," Garrett called. "Please. We're talking."

The pastor stopped.

"He wants," Garrett said, "—a little privacy."

"His father needs him," the pastor called, tension thick in his voice.

Garrett understood the tension. Lonnie's desolation was such that he might well end his own life any moment. Lonnie might also turn the gun on him.

"Go away," Lonnie bellowed. "Leave me alone!"

Garrett jumped, and the pastor took a step back. "I understand your grief, Lonnie—"

"You don't understand anything!"

Garrett swallowed hard. This wasn't going to end well. Maybe it was time for him to leave with the pastor. Protect his own hide.

"I know your father needs you," the pastor stated. "That needs to be your first consideration." There was no response to this, and the pastor turned and walked away.

"He'd have been better off without me," Lonnie muttered. "Everyone would have. The world would have."

"If that is true," Garrett began.

"You know it's true," Lonnie interrupted heatedly.

"Then you really owe him. You owe everyone." Silence followed, a silence which Garrett almost broke, except for he didn't know what else to say.

"You can't—" Lonnie uttered. "There are things you can't make up for."

"You can try. You can ask." Garrett took a step backwards. "Reverend Thompson is right. You owe him that."

"You didn't forgive me," Lonnie reminded him bitterly.

"I wasn't ready." He took a breath and exhaled. "But I am, now."

Seconds of silence lapsed before Lonnie said, "You're just saying that."

Garrett shook his head. "I'm not," he said quietly, meaning it. He hadn't even realized he had forgiven Lonnie, but he had. The anger and bitterness were gone. Replaced by pity, maybe. Or sympathy. Maybe it mattered, but maybe it didn't.

He'd always considered himself to be the most average person alive, not terribly lucky or unlucky or special, just someone meant to have a normal, laborer's life. Then a winning game of poker had cost the loss of his hand and the life he'd known. But he'd found other places and people, good people who filled his heart and altered his path. It was even possible that he was better off for the misfortune. "Let's go," Garrett urged.

Lonnie didn't move and Garrett wasn't confident enough to make a physical move to offer a hand up.

"I can't," Lonnie said, just above a whisper.

"How do you think your father would survive it, if you—"

There were several seconds of silence before Lonnie got up and stepped into a pool of pale light that washed all color from him. "I'll ask for his forgiveness," he said in a flat voice, still devoid of hope.

"Maybe you should just offer your presence. I doubt anything can really reach him tonight. Other than you just being there."

Lonnie came closer and offered over the pistol. "Will you take it? I don't want him to see it."

Garrett gladly took it, heaving a sigh of relief, and the two of them began the walk home. Once there, Garrett saw Lonnie inside, exchanged a few words with the deputies who were waiting there, and discreetly handed the pistol over to Marian to put away. She seemed to understand what it meant without an explanation. Then again, she lived there and had for some time. She knew a great deal more about all of them than he did. He told her he'd be back tomorrow. It just didn't feel right to stay tonight.

As he walked away, both exhausted and far too keyed up to sleep, he knew he would show up at the mercantile tomorrow. He had no idea what the day would bring or what his future would be now, but no one besides Mr. Todd would be there. He would offer his help until he was asked to go away.

Chapter Twenty-Five

"Mrs. Simpson," a new hire named Cici beckoned on a late Saturday afternoon in late May.

Simpson turned to her with an exasperated sigh, looking up from a new menu she'd been working on. Doll Summers Shaw, that meddlesome know-it-all, had suggested they needed more variety in the menu. While she'd given Doll her infamous stare down followed by the comment that she mind her own menus, a nerve had been struck.

The sigh, however, was because Celia Jaeger grated on her nerves. She was a whiner with a baby voice, two things Simpson loathed. Annabelle Simpson did not believe for one moment that nature had condemned Cici with that voice. No. Cici thought it was darling. She'd probably been told as much. "What is it?"

"Someone's here. I think he's a beggar," she said. "What do we do about that?"

"Is he begging?"

"No. He asked for Susanna."

Frowning, Simpson rose and stepped by the diminutive Cici with her prancy poses and her baby voice, thinking Cici's mother ought to be horsewhipped for such a creation. She went into the dining room where a young man in ragged clothing was standing at the front of the restaurant, hat in hand.

He was thin and there were dark circles under his eyes, but the state of his attire and his physical appearance did not excuse Bella and Lucy looking at him with distaste. If Bella was not on her final few days, she'd send her packing along with Cici. She'd had it to her eyeballs with overprivileged young ladies. While they were a slim minority of her girls, they were a major pain in her hind quarters. "May I help you?" she asked the lad when she reached him.

"I was hoping to see Susanna," he said apologetically.

228

She blinked, suddenly realizing who he must be. "Are you a friend?"

He nodded.

"Who has come a long way to be here?" It was ridiculous, but tears wanted to spring to her eyes. The damn things hurt.

"Yes, ma'am."

"Are you Levi?"

He drew back in surprise. "Yes, ma'am."

She smiled. "I'm Annabelle Simpson, manager of the restaurant. Come sit and have a meal."

"Oh … no, ma'am. I just came to see Susanna."

"And so you will. She's not here at the moment, but I'll see that you get to her right after you eat."

"Ma'am," he said uncomfortably, shaking his head.

"It's on the house," Simpson said quietly. "I am so pleased to see you. Susanna and Lily have told me so much."

"Is Lily alright?" he asked with an incredulous expression, as if barely daring to hope.

She smiled. "She's far better than alright. Come." Simpson led the way, managing to scowl at her cheeky help and order the special in a pleasant voice at the same time. "In fact, bring two." She looked back at Levi. "I hope you don't mind if I join you?"

"No, ma'am," he said, stuttering slightly.

"Today's special is my own version of colcannon," she said. "Braised beef tips in a mound of mashed potatoes and cabbage. Does that sound alright?"

"Oh, yes, ma'am. Sounds better than good."

She led the way to a window booth, and Bella came close behind with a bright smile on her pretty face. Had there ever been a more spurious young woman?

"What can I get for you to drink?" Bella asked.

"Anything you want," Simpson said to Levi.

"Do you have buttermilk?" he asked.

"We do," Simpson said. "And I'll take my usual," she said to Bella.

"Right away," Bella said cheerfully, which did not fool Simpson one iota.

"As I said," Simpson began when Bella was gone, "I'm the manager, so I was the first one in Green Valley to meet Susanna." She had Levi's full attention. Even when a basket containing freshly made biscuits and corn muffins were placed in front of them along with a dish of salted butter, he barely glanced at them. "Please, eat," she urged, before continuing her explanation.

Their food arrived quickly, and he was hungry enough that his fork trembled in his hand as he lifted it to his mouth. The sight of it wrenched her heart, especially seeing him conscious of using his best manners. She told him of the first night and the days since, starting with Lily's story and segueing to Susanna's. She told him of pairing Susanna with Beth, and what occurred the day Garrett Trentwell sat in her station.

He finished his plate, had a second helping, ate most the bread and downed three glasses of buttermilk as he listened. He heard how, after Timothy Hastings funeral and burial, the mayor had gone into seclusion for days before emerging to resign from office. He was a changed man with a weight to bear that seemed to be slowly crushing him. Lonnie was equally changed. Only a week ago, the two of them had left for Barbados. Mr. Todd and Garrett had been left to run the mercantile.

Levi could only shake his head at the story.

"I know," Simpson agreed. "The Pettijeans were taken away, and the rest of their party was run out of town, from what I hear." She didn't share that Jackals had been burned to the ground, since it gave her mixed feelings and painted the town in a questionable light. She'd never thought of Green Valley as a place of vigilantism, but there had been an angry backlash against everything those people had touched.

"So," she said in conclusion, and wanting to bring things back around to a less tragic topic, "Susanna spends much of her time at the Blue farm now. That's where she is. I'll take you after we finish."

"I'm much obliged, ma'am."

"Not at all. Susanna is—" she broke off, wondering how to describe what the girl was to her. "She's a pain," she said laughingly.

230

Levi grinned and nodded. "Always thinks she's right."

"Or justified if she's not right," Simpson added. "Oh, she can be morose. Although not so much anymore."

Levi had picked up his napkin to stifle a belch. Still holding it to his mouth, he said, "She can plumb take your head off, if she's a mind to."

"I can believe that. But she is devoted."

Levi nodded. "Yes, ma'am."

"And a hard worker," Simpson conceded. "I've come to care about her very much, and I will be so delighted to bring you to her. Do you plan to stay in Green Valley?"

"Depends on if I can find work or not. I hope so."

"Well, there is plenty of work to be found. So, welcome."

He smiled. "Thank you, ma'am. I sure do hope so."

~~~

On the brick sidewalk, in front of Wiley's, Levi watched Surry lick her bowl clean aggressively enough that the bowl was scraped along. "That's enough," he said, picking it up. "I know it was good." He glanced back at the restaurant, wondering if he should return the bowl. He hesitated because Mrs. Simpson had gone to the livery to get a wagon hitched, leaving him time to visit the facilities.

When he'd arrived at the restaurant, the waitresses had given him looks of distrust and even disgust. It wasn't a pleasant thing to receive looks like that, but he had the bowl to return.

He went back inside to hand it over, and the reception he received was as opposite as could be from last time. Thanks to Mrs. Simpson, of course. He went back out and walked over to the nearest bench, admiring how pretty everything was. The trees that lined the streets were a vibrant green and the buildings were neatly kept. It was six o'clock in the evening now and Wiley's had gotten busy, as had a few other places.

He sat, and Surry jumped up and got comfortable in his lap. Levi stroked it absentmindedly as he thought about what Mrs.

231

Simpson had shared. He'd been able to picture Susanna's scowl that first night, not to mention Lily's embarrassed revelation of her scar. That thought caused him both pain and regret, and always would. He thought about Garrett Trentwell's situation and how he'd risen above it. The man sounded like someone he could respect and like, but the fact that Susanna supposedly loved him was shocking. She was engaged? They just seemed like words, not like Susanna. He needed to see her for himself to ascertain the truth. Only then would he believe it.

A young woman with dark hair was coming toward him, walking quickly, looking at him with such a look, it left no doubt that she was headed straight for him. He stood. She was beautiful and flushed, wearing a white blouse with puffy sleeves. "Levi?" she said when she'd almost reached him. "Are you Levi?"

He nodded. She smiled and it was such a glorious, joyful smile, he found himself smiling back at her. He hated that he looked as bad as he did. His clothes and shoes had way too many miles on them.

"You're here," she gloried. Tears were actually shining in her eyes.

"I am. Finally."

"I'm Beth. Susanna's friend."

"It's nice to meet you," he said, hoping he hadn't stammered.

"It's wonderful to meet you," she gushed.

Beth. Susanna's friend. She was so beautiful. Simpson had mentioned she was kind and cheery, but she hadn't mentioned how beautiful she was. He couldn't look away from her.

"Susanna and I pray for you and Nate every night."

He drew back, because everyone seemed to be describing a girl he didn't know. "She, uh, doesn't pray."

Beth smiled tenderly. "She does now. I told her how much better it makes you feel. Lily had told her the same thing." She looked around. "Where's Nate?"

"He stayed behind with some folks. He wanted to. It's a really good place for him."

"Oh. Well, that's wonderful."

Mrs. Simpson pulled up in her rig, a fancy two-seater pulled by a deep brown mare of fourteen hands. She and Beth exchanged greetings, and then Beth smiled again at Levi and reiterated how wonderful it was to meet him. "You, too," he returned.

"Bye," she said.

"Bye."

"Levi," Simpson said when he didn't move for several seconds. "Ready?"

He jerked slightly, embarrassed, and came around and got in the rig. Beth waved and he raised his hand as the rig started in motion. His heart was pounding. "So, that's Beth," he said under his breath.

Mrs. Simpson grinned. "That is Beth."

~~~

As the Blues often did in pleasant weather, they arranged a long table in the back yard and dined atop the soft grass and under colorful lanterns that hung from a simple arbor. This evening, they'd enjoyed garlic roasted chicken and new potatoes with green beans, plus Cessie's prize-winning chunky applesauce.

Besides themselves, the company consisted of Emmett, Susanna, Garrett, Lily, and the Sheffield children, since Jeremy and Lizzie had gone to Roanoke on a weekend excursion.

April May had declared it a celebration, given that she'd been relieved of the binding around her arm. Really, it was an impromptu celebration of life since they'd experienced so much death and tragedy in the last few months. If one was wise, one had to up, rejoice and celebrate when and what one could.

Little Luke had refused to nap earlier, and could barely keep his eyes open, so Cessie held him. She'd risen to take him to bed when she saw Mrs. Simpson round the house with a young man beside her. She gasped because it had to be Levi! Cessie knew it instantly by the lurch her heart gave, even before Lily saw him, cried out his name and ran to him. Susanna was only moments behind her, laughing and crying at the same time.

233

April May, Garrett and Emmett all rose and watched the reunion, coming slowly closer to the new arrivals, anxious to meet Levi. Luke jerked awake at the excitement, but then settled back against her shoulder.

"This is him," Susanna said happily as Cessie reached them. "This is Cessie," she said to Levi.

Levi gave a polite nod. "Ma'am."

"Welcome," Cessie said with a warm smile. "I've got to lay this one down, but I'll be back." Cessie gave Simpson a smile and went inside as introductions continued, walking as quickly as she could because she didn't want to miss out on anything.

Luke's diaper had to be changed, and a stuffed rabbit named Bo-Bo found, and a certain song sung before he would settle to sleep. Once it was all done, Cessie pressed a kiss to his head, still humming the song, and walked to the window to look out.

Below was a heartwarming sight. Levi was surrounded, and Wags and Sheeba were frolicking with another little terrier who looked a good deal like Wags. Lily glowed with happiness as she clung to Levi, and Susanna was every bit as joyous. Her hands were clutched together and held to her chest as she listened to whatever Levi was saying.

Garrett stood to her side, as he always would. The two of them were meant to be, plain and simple. For a woman who had never given birth, they all felt like her children.

"Gwannie," Luke murmured.

"*Shh*" Cessie said, coming back to the crib to soothe him. "Go to sleep now," she whispered.

He turned on his side and she stroked his soft hair until his breathing was regular, then she hurried back outside to join the party. It truly was a celebration.

Dear Reader,

I hope you enjoyed Will of the Valley, the third book in the Green Valley series. I love these characters. I've written a lot of books, and Tommy Medlin remains my all-time favorite male protagonist. I also adore April May Blue. If more of us adopted her take on things, it would be a better world. I intend on continuing the series. In fact, Green Valley and its inhabitants are so real to me that I can't stay away for long.

Charity Cases, a book set in Philadelphia in 1888, features Gregory and Charity Howerton who return to her hometown for a wedding and get caught up in the case of a woman who's been wrongly incarcerated in an insane asylum. I hope you'll check it out.

For more information on my books, visit janeshoup.com

Happy Reading,

Jane

www.ingramcontent.com/pod-product-compliance
Lightning Source LLC
Chambersburg PA
CBHW060154180626
46813CB00007B/2752